I REMEMBER YOU

ember you

CATHLEEN DAVITT BELL

Alfred A. Knopf
New York

THIS IS A BORZOI BOOK PUBLISHED BY ALFRED A. KNOPF

Visit us on the Web! randomhouseteens.com

Educators and librarians, for a variety of teaching tools, visit us at RHTeachersLibrarians.com

Library of Congress Cataloging-in-Publication Data
Bell, Cathleen Davitt.
I remember you / Cathleen Davitt Bell. — First edition.
pages cm
Summary: Juliet and Lucas are falling in love, but when Lucas "remembers" things about Juliet he could not possibly know, Juliet begins to wonder if something is wrong.
ISBN 978-0-385-75455-2 (trade) — ISBN 978-0-385-75456-9 (lib. bdg.) —
ISBN 978-0-385-75457-6 (ebook)
[1. Love—Fiction. 2. Visions—Fiction.] I. Title.
PZ7.B38891526Iar 2015
[Fic]—dc23
2014004789

The text of this book is set in 12-point Adobe Caslon.
Book design by Stephanie Moss

Printed in the United States of America
February 2015
10 9 8 7 6 5 4 3 2 1

First Edition

TO MAX AND ELIZA

you, you're not the first to ask

and probably not the last

and i don't expect you to understand

why i stayed upon this rock

after the birds had gone

and all of the waves turned to sand

i am a lighthouse

in a desert and i stand alone

i dream of an ocean that was here a long time ago

and i remember his cool waters and i still glow

—Antje Duvekot, "Lighthouse"

I REMEMBER YOU

prologue

I am writing this down so that I will remember. And because a long time ago, Lucas told me to. Or dared me. He didn't think I *could* remember. Feelings you have when you are sixteen, he said, feelings so strong they could break open your ribs from the inside, they wither as you get older. He said he didn't know how long it would take, but it would happen. He said it would be better that way. Easier. Kinder.

Numbness was what he offered me. And I tried to accept it. On some level, I did accept it. But Lucas, the memory of him, the memory of who I was when I was with him, it was always there. I said I would never forget. And I didn't.

Lucas: I remember you.

chapter one

It was the end of summer. August 1994. My mom and I pulled into the driveway in our beat-up Audi that smelled of her perfume, my mom at the wheel, me slouched down in the passenger seat, pressing SEEK on the radio with my big toe, singing along though I couldn't carry a tune. I was just back from eight weeks at sleepaway camp, and I remember how I felt then: free.

Lucas was mowing my neighbor's lawn. I must have known who he was, because I remember thinking, *There's one of those guys from school.* By "those guys" I meant jocks. I knew Lucas was on the hockey team. I knew he was a year ahead of me too. He'd be a senior when school started.

I remember that Lucas had his shirt off, and I remember that getting out of the car with my duffel bag over my shoulder, I was trying not to look at him. I didn't want to so obviously *not* look either. I liked to think of myself as someone who didn't freak out every time a hockey player took off his shirt.

But I guess I did look. I remember he was wearing dog tags and that they were tossed over his shoulder like a necktie moved out of harm's way. I remember how light the lawn mower seemed in his hands, how deeply tan his skin had become over the summer, how he was scowling at a clump of grass growing right up against my neighbor's fence. I knew that clump; it was impossible to get down on our side of the fence post as well.

Lucas caught me watching him and looked down at the mower, then back at me. Then he let out this ten-gigawatt smile that had a lot of information in it, including 1) we both knew he wasn't going to mow that clump of grass down, 2) he was someone who smiled at people he didn't even technically know, and 3) people always returned his smiles. Which is exactly what I was doing then.

Did he nod? Did I nod back? I don't know.

As soon as I got into the house and passed by a mirror, I thought, *Oh, great.* Greasy hair. Red bandanna. Was that dirt where I'd thought I was tan? At camp, there was a layer of sap and sand and generally nasty woodsiness everywhere. Even the showers were slimy and smelled of mold, and I remember wondering if the veritable force field of scum was obvious, if Lucas had seen.

Now I think back to Lucas with the lawn mower—there was actually a whole crew of landscapers doing the bushes and the edging, laying mulch—and I wish I'd never gone inside. I wish I could freeze time, go back and take a picture, write it all down, the way I'm trying to do now. Had he shaved, or was the line of blond stubble he got at the end of the day already there? Had he bunched up the gray T-shirt he wasn't wearing and tucked it into the back of his shorts? I remember that his chest and back were shining, but like I said, I was trying not to notice. They didn't belong to me then. They would.

I woke up on the first day of school to good first-day-of-school weather. A sky you could bounce a quarter off, my mom would say. A chill in the air to let you know Halloween was one calendar page away. Stepping out the front door to catch the bus, I was thinking, *I approve.*

My fingers flew on my locker combination. I wasn't gushing, "Oh, my God, how *are* you?" to everyone I knew or even half knew. That wasn't my style. But I was glad to be back.

Second-period physics, I was slipping into a seat in the front next to Robin Sipe, who I used to be friends with in middle school and still hung out with at the newspaper, and I turned to scan the room for my best friend, Rosemary. She'd been away at the end of summer and I didn't know her schedule. I didn't even know if we had the same lunch period.

But Rose wasn't sitting in any of the rows behind me. Instead, I found myself face to face with Lucas.

I saw him, felt my cheeks go hot, and turned back around. I thought that would be that. But during class, I kept hearing him drop his pen—he was spinning it across his fingertips like a top and every now and then it would go flying. When it hit the back of my chair, I reached down, picked it up where it had landed, and passed it back to him. Lucas mouthed, "Sorry." I whispered, "That's okay." That was the first time we spoke.

Back then, Lucas had curly hair that he cut so short it didn't look curly, just unbrushed. Our school made all the boys wear button-down shirts. Lucas's was wrinkled and open at the neck. I got a glimpse of a chain and remembered his dog tags.

The year before, I'd written a newspaper article about how all war is wrong and the sign of a truly civilized nation a position of neutrality. A lot of my teachers liked that piece and for a week or two afterward would mention it during class or speak to me about it in the hallway. So I took it as fact: people like Lucas, who glorify the military by wearing dog tags even when they aren't actually soldiers, are perpetuating a problem.

But when I passed his pen back, he held my eyes the way he had when he was mowing the neighbor's lawn, and in that moment, something happened. To me. I felt like Lucas saw me—he saw right through the surface that a hockey-playing jock in dog tags would normally stop at. He saw through debate and the newspaper, the exterior of my high school life. He saw past the fact that I'm pretty enough, I guess, and that kids respect me, and that I'm friends with Rosemary Field. This may sound stupid, but I believed Lucas saw the person I am inside.

By that I mean the person I am when I cry at black-and-white movies with my mom, the person I am when I read the comics in the sun on the front porch after school. When I'm dressed in the UCLA sweats with BRUINS sewn on the legs my dad sends me from California. When I stay up late talking with Rosemary on the phone. When I laugh so hard I snort milk through my nose. The part of me that was there when I was three or ten or fourteen—the inner core that will stay the same forever.

As Lucas's fingers closed around the pen, I held on for just a second too long. I felt weirdly alive, like I'd just inhaled super-cold air.

I let go of the pen and turned back around. Robin Sipe was writing "Homework = 20% of grade" in her notebook, and I dutifully copied her words. I even mimicked her good-girl bubble handwriting.

But then I snuck a peek behind me. Lucas was staring. At me. Still.

The next time I spoke to Lucas was at lunch a few days later. I'd come in late, so there was no line, and I hurried to the counter, only to find him ahead of me, holding a tray. Except for the lady serving the food, we were alone, but I didn't say hi or "How do you like physics?" I was too cool for that then. I probably let my hair hang in front of my face so I wouldn't look like I was hoping he'd notice me. Lucas was drumming his fingers on his tray like he was practicing a keyboard solo, and I assumed he'd do his music, he'd get his food, I'd get my food, and then we'd go our separate ways.

But he turned to me, and the way he spoke, it was like he was picking up a conversation where it had left off. "What are you doing in regular science anyway?" he said. "I thought you were in all the smart-person classes."

How did he know what classes I was in?

"I barely passed chemistry," I admitted, too startled to give up anything but the truth. "My advisor thought I wasn't going to be able to handle honors physics."

"Sheesh," he said. "Why would you want to?"

And because he didn't sound like he was asking that question just to make me feel better—he sounded like he was genuinely contemplating it himself, and maybe for the first time—I laughed. A little too much. "For college," I said. "You've heard of college, right?"

"Yeah," he said. He drummed on his tray some more, and then he looked me in the eyes so hard I thought he was angry. Had I made him mad? Had what I'd said come off as arrogant when I'd meant it to be funny? "I've heard of college." He was still looking at me, as if he were daring me to let go of his gaze. I didn't. I couldn't, even if it was kind of scary.

And then he was gone, whistling, and I was left to decide between hamburger and sloppy joe, not wanting either one.

chapter two

"What is *with* you?" Rosemary said that afternoon. We were driving to McDonald's after her soccer and my debate. She was new enough to driving that she didn't turn her head to look at me as she asked the question, her ponytail pushing straight into the back of the leather headrest.

The car used to belong to her mom and still said MOMS LIMO on the vanity plate. We were pulled up at a red light, and a guy in a black car to our left rolled down his window to shout, "You're pretty hot for a mom!"

Rosemary didn't even turn her head. "Moron," she muttered.

Something that's important to know about Rosemary is that she's gorgeous. She has olive skin and even features, and she moves in a way that's strong and a bit catlike at the same time. Also: she looks older than she is. When she worked for her dad last summer redoing the filing system in his dental practice, no one could believe she wasn't an adult.

Life with Rosemary follows a predictable pattern. She'll ask, "Do you think that guy who works in the jewelry store / who was talking to me while we waited for your mom to pick us up after the movie / who came to do the school assembly about not taking drugs—likes me?" Or: "Was trying to get my number?" Or: "Will call?" Or: "Is going to cry when I break up with him?" The answer is always yes. At school, where she does almost zero to be nice to guys, she always gets told where the party is going to be, so if we wanted to go, we could.

But we almost never do. Instead, we study. I force Rosemary to watch *Doctor Who*, and she calls five minutes before *Melrose Place* comes on. We go shopping and try on business suits and ball gowns we will never buy. We talk on the phone about her love life and my lack of one. I watch Rose play tennis. She watches me debate. When we do go to parties, we mostly stand by as other people pretend to be drunk, which is fun. And then after, we talk and talk and talk. About the future. About where we'll be going after high school is over.

Rosemary had been in the middle of telling me about her new boyfriend, Jason, a surfboarding college student she met on her family vacation in Aruba. She had a picture of him—clean-cut with dark hair and shadows under his eyes that made me wonder if he was worried about something or a little depressed. He'd already written her two letters. He wanted to come see her on weekends. His parents had a second home on a lake, not too far from us.

I guess I'd spaced out, though, and Rosemary had stopped midsentence. She's so even-keeled she's hard to offend, but it was understood between us that when she asked what was wrong with me, I had to tell her. Rosemary used to hang with the über-popular girls—the Torrances, the Melissa Clarks, and the Kathy Kleins—but she doesn't anymore. She says their dishonest, compliment-fishing, boyfriend-swapping ways were a waste of her time on this planet. (Have I mentioned that I love the way Rosemary talks?) What makes us friends, she once told me, is a shared antistupidity policy. You say what's on your mind. No secrets. No evasions.

"Lucas Dunready," I admitted. Saying his name was like diving into very cold water. "He's in my physics class."

"Lucas Dunready?" If it had been anyone but Rosemary, the way she'd said his name would have made me clam up.

Rosemary's always talking about high school guys as if they were barely out of diapers, pointing out in the cafeteria when they make disgusting jokes, or talk with food in their mouths, or smell funky, or get stupid the minute she turns her gaze on them.

"He keeps staring at me. He said hi to me in the lunch line. I don't know."

"So you think he's into you?" she said.

"Maybe he's just friendly?"

"All I know about him is that he's kind of . . . I don't know—" Rosemary was trying to gauge whether she needed to be tactful.

"Oh, just say it."

"Doesn't he live up in the Valley?" Jefferson Valley is a hamlet attached to our town. Kids from there go to our school, but they're not like the rest of us. They put pictures of their car engines in the yearbook. They have different hairstyles. If not for the Valley kids, the rate of college-bound graduates would be higher.

"You think he's a redneck."

Rosemary lifted her hands from the wheel in a gesture of "You said it, not me."

"He plays hockey."

"Do you *like* him?"

That stopped me short. "No!" I said. Because the fact was, I definitely didn't. I just wished I understood why he was acting so strange.

I knew girls the world over are supposed to want nothing more than to have some hulking jock fall in love with them and give them his high school letter jacket or whatever, but that was not me. And not Rose.

I'd always imagined that the kind of boyfriend I'd have would be someone I'd meet in college. Someone who didn't shout out rude comments during assemblies, like all the guys in our school did. Someone who was good at the things I was good at. Someone who respected me. Someone who knew a lot about music, maybe. Or played guitar. Or wore corduroys and rode horses. Wait, not horses. Who drove a Volkswagen. Someone with really great hair.

Definitely not a hockey player.

Hockey players shove the little hockey-players-in-training into trash cans in the middle of hallways. They shave their heads before games so you can see the brutal red skin of their scalps. They have acne from sweating in their helmets.

So I didn't like Lucas. At all. But when I got to physics lab the next day, there Lucas was, looking toward the door, as if he were waiting for me to walk in. He broke into a smile when he saw me, and what I thought then was how nice his smile was. I wasn't thinking about hockey, or the strange way my stomach had turned over when Rosemary asked if I liked him. I was wondering if I would hurt his feelings if I didn't smile back.

"Hey," he said when I sat down. He leaned forward across his desk. He raised his eyebrows and jiggled that same plastic ballpoint pen. He was chewing gum.

"Hey," I said back. Everything about him was moving like the parts in an antique clock, gears winding and rolling to produce a chime.

"You look nice."

Robin Sipe half turned to stare, then swiveled back around in her seat.

"Sorry," he said. "I'm probably not supposed to say that, but you do."

"Um . . . thanks," I said. Was he teasing me?

And then, out of the blue, like this statement would come as no surprise, he added, "I want to take you somewhere."

I didn't answer him. I think I was in shock. Was he asking me out?

"Juliet?" he said.

"Yes?" I hadn't realized he knew my name.

"Yes what?"

But I didn't know what. And Mr. Hannihan was starting the class, deliberately staring at Lucas, so I turned to face the front of the room.

Mr. Hannihan was a new teacher that year. He'd quit his old job three years before so he could sail around the world, but had instead spent the time and money he'd allotted for the adventure making repairs to his boat. All you had to do now to get him off the subject of physics was ask the smallest question about sailing. The boat and the trip he never got to take were the great unrequited loves of his life, and he could not leave them alone.

When the bell finally rang, Lucas was standing at my side. "I'll meet you at your locker after seventh period," he said. I didn't have a chance to reply before he was gone. What was he doing? What did he want? What would I tell Rosemary? Did he even know where my locker was?

chapter three

Lucas did know where my locker was. When the last bell rang, he was waiting there for me. He looked nervous, opening and closing his right hand as if his fingers had fallen asleep. I was nervous too. I kept passing the numbers on my combination lock.

"I—" I started.

He interrupted, "I know."

"You know what?"

"I know you have debate in half an hour." I did. "I just want to take you somewhere before that."

"Close by?"

"It's in the gym." He smiled a cocky, I'm-on-the-hockey-team smile. "You can't say no to the gym, can you?"

He was wrong, though. I could say no. Only I didn't. I didn't even think about it as I headed out of the main school building and toward the gym.

We entered the gym through the trophy room as usual,

but instead of continuing to the locker rooms and the basketball court, Lucas pointed to a door marked EXIT: ALARM
WILL SOUND. I opened the door (no alarm sounded) to find
a set of stairs. As we started to climb in the semidarkness,
Lucas took my hand. I felt a charge pass into my palm. I
didn't know if I liked the feeling of his hand holding mine
or if it terrified me. Maybe both. I was aware of Lucas's
clean, soapy smell and something else too, something musky
underneath that.

The stairs terminated at another mysterious door, which
opened onto . . .

The roof!

Pebble-topped and wide as a beach. So much sky. I felt
like one of those people in an Old West wagon train who
emerge from a mountain pass to find prairie stretching end-
lessly before them.

"I can't believe this," I said, meaning I couldn't believe
that the doors weren't locked, the alarms weren't ringing,
no one had stopped us. And also? The whole open-space
concept was making me feel the urge to do cartwheels.

"I know," Lucas said, his thin lips spreading into something approaching a smile. He knew what? About the cartwheels? About how I was feeling just then? How could he?

He scratched a cheek absentmindedly, and I caught myself thinking that his cheekbone was really lovely, the way it
jutted out in just the right way. Had I ever thought Lucas
was good-looking before, or was it just coming to me?

I moved away from him, walking to the edge of the roof,
which was surrounded by a wall about three feet high. Lucas
tugged on my hand, and I knelt in case someone happened

to look up. It was just after dismissal. There were buses lined up at the main building, and kids were streaming into them. Other kids and the few teachers who weren't staying after were pulling their cars out of the lot. The kids with sports commitments were meandering toward the gym. "There's Rosemary," I said.

Even seen from two stories above, Rosemary was Rosemary. Her stride long and assured, she was checking her nails, and it suddenly occurred to me that if Rosemary had been taken up to the roof by a guy she barely knew, she would find out why. She would ask a direct question.

"So," I said. "What are we doing up here?"

Lucas's smile widened, as if he'd expected me to ask. As if the question were part of a game. "You don't remember?" he said.

"No?" I said. "Am I supposed to?"

"You don't remember being up here with me before?"

"No." I didn't like the question. "Why, should I?"

He didn't say anything, just continued to smile at me, like he was waiting for my brain to work its way around to a different answer. "I just hoped you would," he said at last. "That's all."

I was completely at a loss. "Do *you* remember?"

"Yeah," he said. He took a step toward me. "I do, and it's not a memory I'm likely to soon forget."

I was aware of everything I was starting to like about him. The outline of his shoulders beneath his shirt. The look in his eyes that told me he cared about what I thought.

But I didn't like that step he'd just taken toward me. It made me think about how I was alone up here with him.

How no one knew where we were. How no one could see us.

"Lucas," I said. "You're starting to freak me out."

I'd hoped that admitting it out loud would dispel the feeling. It didn't. I shivered. A wave of fear rolled over me, the kind that makes you run up the stairs at a sprint when you're home alone in case a strange man is out on your lawn. Knowing the fear is irrational does nothing to diminish its intensity.

"You don't remember," Lucas said, confirming now, giving me one more chance to change my mind. Was this a game? Was this some kind of a joke at my expense?

He took another step in my direction.

"I have to go," I said. I did this weird thing where I raised my hands to my sides, as if I couldn't decide between waving goodbye and assuming a defensive position. I think I ended up looking like a flightless bird, flapping ineffectual wings.

I started walking to the bulkhead. Fast. Lucas caught up to me in time to open the door. We went down the stairs together, through the trophy room, and back outside without speaking. He didn't take my hand, and I didn't want him to. But as we moved back into the stream of kids, there was something about the way he lifted his chin that made me wonder if he was sad. Had I done something to hurt him?

He reached out a hand then and patted me on the shoulder. I couldn't tell if it was condescending or an effort to comfort me. "I gotta go," I said, but it was Lucas who turned away first.

. . .

That night, my mom set out the special dishes we used for take-out sushi—ceramic painted to look like bamboo. On sushi nights, we always got the same things—the maki platter, tuna sashimi, and a seaweed salad. We shared all three and split a spicy ginger ale, which we watered down with seltzer.

Sometime recently I'd started to worry that my mom and I were too compatible. I worried I was going to end up living at home forever, watching Lifetime movies and playing cards with her and her best friend, Valerie. Whenever I told Rosemary this, she gave me a look like I was an idiot and said, "You don't do either of those things now."

Which was true. And neither did my mom. But she might as well have. She and Valerie went to plays and concerts and out to dinner. On weeknights, my mom sat on her pretty white couch knitting and watching TV, or drinking a glass of wine and flipping through the *New Yorker* or *Architectural Digest*, while I trundled up to my room to spread out with my homework. We both wore slippers.

But up on the roof with Lucas, there had been no room for cozy slippers and known routines. He'd *scared* me. He wanted something from me, and I didn't know what. I didn't know if he knew either.

"What's the most dangerous thing you've ever done?" I asked Mom.

"Dangerous, my goodness," she said, chuckling as she licked a grain of rice off the end of her chopstick. My mom started dyeing her hair at the first sign of gray, and she has gone increasingly lighter—it's now so blond it's almost white. To keep from looking too washed out, she wears a good amount of mascara and eyeliner, and she looks great, especially when she purses her lips and you can see the light of a joke in her eye.

"Seriously," I said. The demand came out too strong. My mom's tiny, like a bird—I get my height and my thick hair from my dad—and sometimes I felt like a giant, stomping around in a house built for dolls, demanding she be serious and decide things.

"Okay," she said. "Danger." Then she laughed again. "I'm sorry, Juliet. I hope you won't be disappointed that I haven't led a very dangerous life."

"There must have been something." In my head, I was flashing through images of the way Lucas had half smiled at me, the sad slump of his shoulders as we left the roof. "Didn't you ride in a car without a seat belt at least once?" I pushed. "What about when you were traveling?" Right after college, my mom traveled a lot. She was going to get a PhD in art history, but she met my dad and had me, and then they got divorced and he moved to California, so she got a job at a museum doing fund-raising. "There must have been something."

"I was stopped by border patrol going into Pakistan," she said. "If you want to count that."

"Border patrol?" I squawked. "Pakistan?" I knew my mom had traveled in the Middle East with her college boyfriend after graduation, but I hadn't heard about this part of the trip. "I think that counts."

"It sounds more dangerous than it was, I can tell you. Really, it was a formality."

"Were you driving?"

"No!" she said, shocked, as if she'd only have gone on a tour bus with representatives of the US embassy on board. "Jody was driving."

One of the things that might be unique to having a single mom is knowing the names of all her ex-boyfriends. Even though I don't think she'd had a boyfriend since she and my dad split up, her old boyfriends came up with some frequency, just like the dogs she had when she was a kid. (We never had dogs—too messy.) "Were there soldiers?"

"Of course," my mom said, as if I'd asked if there was going to be seaweed salad in our sushi order. "One of the things you see when you travel anywhere outside the US is guns in the hands of soldiers and guards. Even in Italy, it's kind of shocking how you'll be walking into the Vatican and you'll pass some twenty-year-old in a ridiculous uniform carrying an AK-47."

"And in Pakistan? What happened?"

"Well, Juliet, it's hard to remember all the details."

"Come on!"

"Okay, the soldiers had machine guns, and they probably weren't much older than you."

We both paused to digest that information. I thought about Lucas's dog tags.

"They made Jody get out of the car, but I stayed inside. I think they were afraid of me, even though I was dressed very modestly. Women in Pakistan at the time were generally not supposed to show any skin."

"And?"

"And nothing. Jody gave them some money. It was my idea, actually. I leaned out the car window and passed him the cash Grandma Kay had instructed me to carry in my shoe. The soldiers laughed at Jody—I guess a man who lets a woman bail him out is pretty unusual. But they let us go on our way."

"That was it?"

"That was it."

My mom always tells stories about her past the same way—as if there were no hard parts, nothing scary, no danger. Your father and I decided to part ways and now he lives in California and you see him only once a year—tra-la! It's been my dream in life to get a PhD in art history, but because of the timing of your birth and the divorce, I raise money so other people can do the work I always wanted to do—zippee-doo! I got held at gunpoint at a border crossing in Pakistan, where I could easily have been shot—aw, fiddlesticks!

"But what did it *feel* like?" I pressed. I was thinking about the moment when Lucas said *You don't remember being up here with me before?* He'd asked the question like it was a code, our secret password, like we were spies, and it was my turn to reveal the answer. But I hadn't been to the roof with him before. And why did he look at me all the time like he was in on a secret and he half suspected I was in on it too?

"Was the danger—I don't know . . . kind of bonding?" I asked. "Did you feel closer to Jody after?" My mom was looking at me quizzically now. "Wasn't it at least *a little bit* exciting?"

I guess I wanted her to say "Yes, danger is exciting." I wanted her to explain to me why, after nearly running from Lucas on the roof, all I could think about now was going back.

Mom delicately dipped her tuna in soy sauce. "What can I tell you?" she said. "As soon as we had rounded the next bend, Jody got out of the car and threw up on the side of the road. I was okay, but he was really spooked. We cut the trip short."

"He was really that scared?"

"They made him kneel down in the dirt while they went through his papers. He thought he was about to get shot."

"Oh," I said. "Well. That's different."

"Yes," said my mom, neatly popping the tuna into her mouth. "Danger—real danger—isn't all it's cracked up to be."

chapter four

"I'm sorry I freaked you out."

Lucas was leaning across the desk again, smiling in a way that brought back the cartwheel feeling I'd had on the roof and chalked up to wide-open space.

"I'm okay," I said.

"Really?" His clear blue eyes projected a look of such innocence I felt myself wondering how I'd ever thought it possible to be afraid with him. He jiggled his pen, then spun it around a few times for good measure. Then the pen stopped moving. His Adam's apple jogged up and down one time. His eyes, looking at me, were still.

"Why did you say those things?" I asked. "We've never been up on the roof together before."

Robin Sipe, intrepid girl reporter, shifted in her seat, so I knew she was listening. I must have turned in response to her, a gesture Lucas recognized. Without moving his head, he shifted his eyes to Robin's back, then to me again. He held up a finger, jotted down a note, and passed it to me just as Mr. Hannihan was starting the class.

That was the first time I saw Lucas's handwriting. It was horrendous, barely legible—all tiny, sharp angles and letters so squeezed you could barely tell the series of scratches formed words. The note read:

Is your mom out tonight? Can I come talk to you?

My mom was always out on Tuesdays. Tuesday was her take-a-donor-to-dinner night. But how did Lucas know that? Okay, I guess everyone has a mom, and everyone's mom goes out from time to time. But how come he didn't ask if my *parents* were out?

I wrote back to him:

Do you even know where I live?

And he wrote:

Lawn mowing. Do you remember?

It took me a second, and then I did.

After school, I got home early to work on an article for the paper. I set myself up the way I liked to for writing—at the desk by the window in my room—and pretended I was actually able to concentrate enough to get anything done.

I hadn't been able to decide whether I should tell my mom Lucas was coming over. I hadn't told anyone about going up to the roof with him. Rosemary had shrugged when I'd asked her opinion about letting my mom know he was coming to the house. "It's up to you," she'd said. "But I wouldn't mention it to my parents."

I'd decided I wouldn't mention it either, but then, five minutes after getting home, I found myself dialing Mom's work number.

My mom trusted me. She had every reason to. I wasn't into the whole high-school-rebel scene. But still . . . a boy. Alone. In the house. She didn't exactly freak, but the upshot was that I could see him, just not alone in the house. I wasn't even mad at her for laying down the law. I was kind of relieved.

So when Lucas pulled his car into the driveway, I was waiting for him on the front porch. The hockey team didn't have skate practice in the fall, but they had workouts, so Lucas stepped out of his hulking, rusting red car, his hair dark where it was still wet from the shower, the tips drying to blond.

"Hey," he said, holding up a hand halfway as if he wasn't sure I would return the wave. There was something about his hesitation—I felt a lightening of my whole body, the way you feel after you hold your breath.

"My mom doesn't want me to have you in the house," I blurted out before he even got all the way up the path across the front lawn. "Sorry."

Lucas shrugged and squeezed in next to me on the stoop.

His leg was pressed up against mine. It was close quarters, but I was pretty sure he'd sat even closer to me than he needed to.

"It would be okay to take a walk," I said. "She said we could get food or something in the Center." I pointed toward our tiny downtown—besides the library, the town hall, and the post office, there were a few fancy stores that no one I knew shopped at, a café that served lunch, and another for upscale Chinese.

"Great," Lucas said, putting his hands on his knees and standing. I ran inside and got some money out of my desk drawer.

I'd left the front door open, and coming down from upstairs, I could see Lucas through the window in the storm door. He was waiting right where I'd left him, but his smile had been replaced by a look of intense concentration, as if the two pillars that tried to make our stoop into a bona fide porch might be holding a secret.

When he saw me, the look disappeared. "You ready?" he said.

I wondered what would happen if I just said no. My mom always said to trust my instincts, but my instincts were firing in multiple directions. Something about the way he looked at me was frightening. But I skipped out the door and down the step anyway.

The houses in my neighborhood were small and almost a hundred years old, the trees huge and towering, the sidewalks narrow and uneven. Walking shoulder to shoulder, Lucas and I bumped into each other a few times, and each time we waited just a second longer than we had to before separating.

I had worried that we wouldn't have anything to talk about, but Lucas made it really easy. He wanted to know how long I'd lived in the neighborhood, whether I had any brothers and sisters. When I mentioned that my parents were divorced, he asked all about my dad, about what kind of a doctor he was (oncologist—he's a researcher who also sees patients) and how often I saw him (once a year, for two weeks in the summer). His questions seemed so straightforward and normal I started to wonder if I'd just imagined that he already seemed to know too much about me. When he'd written "Is your mom out tonight?" on the note, maybe he'd meant it to be shorthand for "mom and dad." Maybe he assumed dads come home from work late. Maybe it was common knowledge around school that I lived with just my mom, in the same way Rosemary and I knew that Lucas lived in Jefferson Valley.

"How about you?" I said. "Do you have—you know—an intact nuclear family, parent-wise?" He'd already mentioned he was the oldest of three boys. He had a brother who was nine and another who was seven.

"Yeah," he said. "For now."

"For now?"

"My parents fight some."

"In front of you?" It was a nosy question, but something about the way Lucas had been acting with me, like he wanted to skip the getting-to-know-you part and move straight to the let's-go-up-on-the-roof-and-talk-crazy part, made it feel okay.

"Sometimes," Lucas said. "Now that I have the car, I just take off. I bring Tommy and Wendell with me. In a year I'll be gone."

"So you *are* going to college?"

"Hell no," Lucas laughed. "I'm joining the marines. They'll pay for college after a few years of active service."

"You're kidding, right?"

"Why would I be kidding?"

"It's just—I don't know. I've never actually known anyone who wanted to join the military."

"Half my relatives are marines."

Oops, I thought. *Time to backtrack.* "Your dad?"

"And my grandpa. My dad's grandpa. Uncles. There's been a Dunready mucking up the marines since there were marines, probably. We've been in every overseas conflict since World War II."

I tried to keep the look of horror off my face, but I guess I didn't try hard enough. Lucas burst out laughing. "Not everyone goes to law school," he said. "We're not all you."

I stopped walking. "How do you know I want to go to law school?"

He smiled a slow, lazy smile that spread across his face like a cat stretching its limbs after a nap in the sun. He shrugged. "You're saying you're *not* going to be graduating from law school in, let's see . . ." He counted on his fingers. "Two years left of high school, four of college. How many at law school?"

"Three."

He checked his watch as if he could tell time on it in years. "About ten years?"

I laughed at the watch thing. And okay, I did want to go to law school. I loved the image of me in a suit like Valerie's, poring over important documents on a computer, the way my mom and I would find Val when we picked her up for a play or a concert. To me, Val's big desk, her secretary, and her expensive suits signified power, security, intelligence, independence—everything I wanted for myself.

"Okay," I said. "You win. But how did you know?"

"Lucky guess?" He stepped onto a tree root that was pushing up through the sidewalk, balancing for a second with one hand on the tree's trunk, and then spun around in the air to face me, steadying himself by laying his hands on my shoulders.

"I used to think you were too serious," he said, as if now that his face was close to mine, he could tell me something that was just between the two of us. His dog tags were tucked under his T-shirt, but I could see the chain around his neck. "But something changed. I don't know. It's like I can see what you're thinking. All the time."

I felt like my belly button had been pressed up against my spine. But I tried to keep it casual. "Want me to think of a number and you'll take a guess?"

"Yeah," he laughed. "Think of six. Got it? Okay, I'm gonna guess." He put a finger on my nose. "Six!" Belly button. Again. "Am I right?"

I am pretty sure I was blushing as red as the barn-red house we were standing in front of just then. He let go of my shoulders and we started walking again side by side.

"So where do you want to go?" he said. "Do you want to get something to eat?"

"Eat?" I asked, as if I no longer understood the meaning of the word.

"Friendly's?" he prompted.

For no reason that I can name, I laughed.

And then he laughed. I knew he couldn't possibly have understood what I was laughing at, since I didn't even know, but there was something so good in our laughing together. He took my hand and it felt like the most natural thing in the world. He squeezed. He swung his arm forward.

I looked down. Looking at him and holding hands with him at the same time was almost too much to take. *Was* I an open book? Did he really see right into what I was thinking? I'd always thought of myself as decisive, quick to judge, a get-it-done fighter, the kind of person who doesn't wear her heart on her sleeve.

Lucas pointed at something. A kid had built a crazy skateboard jump with a ramp, a two-by-four, and a bicycle wheel. He was getting ready to attempt his first run through it—no helmet.

"You could write the word 'stupid' in three-foot-high letters, and this kid still does a better job of getting the idea across," Lucas said.

I snorted, and Lucas laughed again too.

chapter five

At Friendly's, we ordered grilled cheese sandwiches, french fries, and sundaes, but sitting in a booth with Lucas across from me, his forearms resting on the table as if he didn't want to miss a single thing I thought or said, I lost the ability to eat. Instead, I laughed.

I laughed when the waitress came over and Lucas confessed breathlessly that he was hoping she'd let him order off the kiddie menu because he wanted the toy and—blushing—she said okay.

I laughed when he told me a story about how last year the chemistry teacher left the room and this hockey player named Nunchuck had started mixing chemicals until something exploded.

We talked about TV. *Seinfeld. Friends. The Simpsons.* We talked about kids we knew at school. About Rosemary. He shook his head. "She scares me."

I laughed. Outraged, but enjoying it.

"No offense," Lucas said.

"No *offense?*" We were both laughing now. "She's my *best friend*!"

"I'm sure she's a good person." He could barely get the words out, he was laughing so hard.

After eating his grilled cheese and both our fries, Lucas polished off his sundae, then mine, then pulled a handful of grubby, wrinkled fives and ones from his pocket to pay the check. I pulled out my wallet too, but he said, "No way are you paying. I ate all the food."

"You didn't eat my grilled cheese." We looked at the desultory sandwich with one bite taken out, congealed and lonely on the tan plastic plate, its only friend a single crinkle-cut bread-and-butter pickle. And we laughed some more, as if we both understood at the same exact minute how pathetic it would be to fight over paying for something so forlorn and nasty.

Then Lucas stopped laughing. "Juliet," he said, his voice suddenly husky, cracking on the third syllable of my name in a way that worried me. I smoothed a lock of hair down across my forehead and pulled my wallet back toward me. I knew what he wanted to talk about.

"I don't understand the things you've been saying," I said, hoping to be preemptive.

Lucas looked straight into my eyes and sighed in a comforting, aw-shucks kind of way. "I don't get them either," he started to explain. "But here's the thing. I guess—" He stopped, thought, started again. "I remember—" Another stop. He laid his hands palms down on the tabletop as if to signal he meant business, but he continued to say nothing at all.

"You . . . remember?" I prompted. He smiled a crooked smile. I couldn't help but smile back. He turned his hands over, cupped, as if waiting for them to fill with rain.

"That first day in physics, when you walked into the room and caught me looking at you?" I nodded. "The moment I saw you, I remembered. I'd seen you before." He took a deep breath. "And I probably shouldn't even be telling you about it, but part of what I remembered makes me think I can trust you." He was looking straight at me still, those big blue eyes. If I were our waitress, I would have let him order off the kiddie menu too.

"You can trust me," I said.

"Well, seeing you, I just knew I'd seen you in that exact spot, in that exact room. I knew you were going to sit at that desk. I knew you would turn around to see who else was in the room. I knew you were going to end up looking at me."

I swallowed. I felt like I was standing on a dark stage and suddenly someone had turned on a spotlight. "You *remembered* this?"

"I thought it might just be déjà vu. But it wasn't. Déjà vu fades. An hour later, the memory is gone. But this one stayed strong."

I laughed, as if laughing might turn this whole idea into a joke. He laughed a little too, but it was a running-out-of-gas-on-your-way-to-get-your-flat-tire-fixed kind of laugh.

I looked down at the white Formica tabletop sprinkled with flecks of gold. I didn't know if I thought he was crazy or if I felt flattered that he trusted me. What Lucas was saying didn't feel real. But Lucas did.

"I remembered being with you on the roof," he went on. "I remembered it so clearly I thought bringing you there, maybe, I don't know—I thought maybe you'd remember it too. But you didn't, right?"

I shook my head.

"And now I'm freaking you out?" he said.

I wanted to let him know it was all right, that I was okay, but I couldn't. I was embarrassed, as if *I* were the one who had said something ridiculous. The lights in the restaurant felt brighter. The sounds of plates landing on tables and cutlery being shuffled in bins and soda fizzing when it hit a cup of crushed ice—I couldn't think amid all this noise.

"I need to get out of here," I said. I was already standing when Lucas tilted the grilled cheese plate in my direction.

"You're sure?" He was trying to go back to the part of the dinner when we'd been joking.

I half laughed, half choked.

Once we were on the sidewalk, we started to walk, but it wasn't the meandering kind of walk you might take after ice cream sundaes. I was walking fast, like I was trying to catch a bus, and Lucas was hurrying to keep up. He didn't ask me what was going on. He just followed.

"Juliet?" he ventured after a while. We'd reached a

wooded park near my house where people let their dogs chase squirrels. No one was around. "Can we slow down?"

I couldn't. "Have you thought about seeing a doctor?" I asked.

"I don't think it's something a doctor's going to be able to help me with."

"Could you have hit your head, maybe? Playing hockey? You're sure you don't have headaches or anything like that?"

He stopped walking, and as if he was getting a headache right then, he pushed his hair off his forehead with his fingertips and held his temples between his palms.

"Does it hurt right now?"

"No," he said. "Yes. A little. Stop." He stopped walking. "Can we please stop walking?"

I noticed it was getting dark when Lucas stepped off the sidewalk and headed a dozen yards into the shade of the trees, his eyes fixed on the patchy grass as if he was looking for something he had dropped there. I followed.

"My mom's a nurse," he said, glancing up at me when I put a hand on his shoulder. "She happens to work in a neurology ward. I know all about traumatic brain injury, concussions. That's not what this is."

"Are you sure—" I began.

He interrupted me with a groan. "I've done a terrible job of explaining this to you." He walked even deeper into the trees, and I followed. "But then again, how can I explain something I don't even understand myself?" He took my hand and pulled me behind a tree. We couldn't see the road now. "Juliet," he said, his voice husky.

He smiled, and I felt myself wanting to smile at him. *Stop it,* I instructed myself. *Be rational.* I willed the muscles in my face to play dead. But my mouth was twitching. I knew that.

The moment my smile finally emerged, his exploded. We stood there for I don't know how long, looking into each other's eyes and grinning. All my embarrassment was gone. It was like that time on the front lawn of my house when he'd caught me watching him not being able to mow down that clump of grass near the fence.

He lifted my hand and looked at it, playing with my fingers.

"In physics, the second I realized I'd been in that room before, watching you come in, having you turn in your seat and look right at me, I also remembered being on the roof with you. It was like the two memories were attached to each other."

"You *really* remember being with me on the gym roof?" I said. "You remember it like it happened?"

Letting go of my hand, he pressed his fingers into his temples. I was thinking, *Brain tumor.* A little giddy from all that smiling, I thought, *It's a shame his whole head is going to swell up, because, well, those cheekbones . . .*

He started speaking again, slowly, as if he wanted to give me just the facts without any more interruptions.

"I was kind of hoping that when we went up on the roof, the memory would fade, that once I was up there with you for real, the difference between what I was imagining I remembered and what was real would become clear."

"Did it?"

"Not at all, actually," he said, like he was just realizing it. "It made me remember more. I remembered that the time before, it was dark out. We were up there at night. And I think you were wearing a dress."

"What kind of dress?"

Lucas shrugged. "A dress dress?" He pointed to the space next to his thighs where a dress would hang if he were wearing one. "You looked nice."

"You could have imagined it."

Lucas's eyes grew big with frustration. He looked like someone trying to come up with the answer to a math problem they don't have the first idea how to solve.

"On the roof . . . ," he said. "Okay, fine, I'll just tell you. What I remembered about being up there was that I was kissing you." He stopped, as if waiting for me to yell at him. When I didn't, he went on. "And I couldn't have made up what it felt like. I couldn't have imagined."

I felt like suddenly all the oxygen had been removed from the atmosphere. I couldn't breathe. I didn't want to.

"Look, Juliet," Lucas said. He took my hand and pulled me toward him, wrapping an arm around my back. Despite the craziness of what he was saying, his arm was strong and steady. He was looking at me like he was going to find the answers in my eyes, and I let him look. I looked back. His eyelashes were a darker shade of blond than his hair. His skin was smooth below the stubble on his jaw.

He kissed me gently, and I felt my hands rising to touch

his face. I closed my eyes, but when I opened them again, he was still looking at me the same way, as if he were searching for answers.

"What do you want from me?" I said.

"I don't know. But I want something."

chapter six

The next morning, my attention was riveted by tasks I generally managed on autopilot. They seemed filled with new significance when I imagined seeing them through Lucas's eyes. What would Lucas say about the toothpaste clamp my mom and I used, the neat folds on the tube? Would he find it hilarious and beautiful and stare at it as if he'd never seen it before, the way I was staring now?

I brushed my hair in front of the mirror and remembered how he'd touched it in the park and again on the porch when he kissed me goodbye, gently palming the back of my head. I remembered that he'd said kissing on the porch felt familiar to him. He'd asked me, "You don't remember this? This doesn't feel like something you've done before?"

"What are you smiling about?" my mom asked me over her peanut butter toast.

"Nothing," I answered, trying and not being able to swallow my smile. Two more bites into my own toast, I laughed out loud, then stifled it. I couldn't explain that I was wondering what part of the Lucas story would bother her the most—that I'd been kissing a boy who probably had a hallucinatory disorder? That I'd been in the park after dark? That the boy had no plans to go to college? That he scared me and I was kissing him anyway?

That none of what I was doing was reasonable or wise or careful or planned or smart? And that I didn't care?

My mom looked puzzled. She smiled like she was in on the joke, and then her smile faded when she realized she wasn't.

At school, Rosemary had saved me a seat in assembly. She was wearing a tight yellow miniskirt and had to tug it down as she crossed her legs and moved her backpack out of my way. I was late. "Did Lucas come over?" she said. "You never called me."

"I kissed him," I whispered.

Flipping a sheet of hair to one side to put up a wall of privacy, Rosemary treated me to a pantomimed look of surprise.

"You?" she mouthed. "Kissed *him*?"

"He kissed me," I whispered, and then I covered my mouth with my hand. I was sure that ten people around me had heard.

"What kind of kiss?"

Rosemary had told me Jason was a 7.5 as a kisser, which was a disappointment because she'd strongly suspected him to be at least an 8.3, what with being in college and all.

"It was amazing," I said.

• • •

Newspaper office. Third period. I was writing about how First Lady Hillary Clinton's failed health care reforms actually would have been great for the country when I looked up to find Lucas's eyes on me. I didn't know how long he had been watching me, but there he was, leaning against the doorframe, waiting for me to notice. I smiled and he swaggered into the room. A bunch of kids working at computer terminals raised their heads. I wondered if they thought he'd come to beat them up. The newspaper room belonged to kids who tunneled from honors classes to debate to newspaper to chess, and I could tell Lucas knew that from the way he lifted and rolled each shoulder as he walked. Hockey players never tunnel.

He laid his hands on the table where I was working and leaned forward onto his arms, his elbows locked. His piney, soapy smell again. "Hey," he said in a low voice befitting a library patron, or maybe he was just expressing his desire to talk only to me and not to anyone else in the room. "So this is where a smart kid like you hangs out."

"Hey," I think I said. He lowered himself into the seat next to me. Where his arm brushed against mine, my skin felt warm.

"Did I freak you out yesterday?" he asked. "Do you think I'm crazy?"

I said nothing.

"I'm a little freaked out," he said.

"You are?"

"I had this dream."

"What was it about?"

41

We were whispering, but still, Lucas looked over his shoulder at the kids sitting at the terminals. "I'll tell you later. What are you doing after school?"

"Debate," I said. I looked at him to gauge his reaction. Would he tease me about debate? All he said was "I'll meet you at the circle afterward, smarty-pants." Then he was gone.

chapter seven

Debate practice. I was pretending to take notes on the topic "Is Global Warming Real?" but really I was staring out the window, watching the hockey players emerge from the gym, freshly showered and back in their school clothes.

Lucas was with a group of guys with backpacks slung casually over their shoulders, feet shuffling heavily in untied shoes, slamming each other sideways into lampposts and walls. One had a tennis ball that he was throwing onto the parking lot pavement ahead of him, letting it ricochet off the bumpers of unsuspecting cars. Sometimes another guy would step out in front of him and catch it.

Dog tags. The marines. I thought of what Lucas had told me about his father and grandfather, his uncles and great-uncles and cousins. Every war. He talked about enlisting as if he'd never thought twice about it. The decision had been made before he was even born.

Watching Lucas now, I wondered if he'd look up at the

windows to where I was. Could he find Mr. Mildred's windows? Was he even thinking about me? Waiting for me? Counting the minutes until we met up the way I was?

No. Lucas was piling into a car with the other guys. Even though he'd said he'd meet me, the car was leaving the parking lot. Lucas was gone.

He was gone, and all that was left for me to notice was a single tree that had turned bright orange in the still-green woods at the edge of the parking lot.

"Juliet?" It was Mr. Mildred. Everyone had been called up and was gathering around his desk. He was pinning our index cards to a bulletin board so we could all see the evidence we'd amassed. "Care to join us?"

"Okay." I was scrambling to assess what I'd written on my cards.

But Mr. Mildred has a way of quickly grabbing a stack of cards off your desk even if you're not done, and he did that now.

I've always loved Mr. Mildred. He was a champion debater in high school and college, and it's amazing how fast he can talk and how quickly his brain works.

I joined the others as he pinned up our cards and talked about what makes a good piece of evidence. Shaking a fistful of pushpins gingerly in his palm, he highlighted some of the cards with star stickers, moved others around, and ended up with a neat, coherent package of evidentiary spin. Until, that is, he got to mine.

He slapped my first card onto the board, nailed it with a pushpin, then slapped on the next before realizing it was blank. He flipped through the pile, looking for any other cards with writing on them. There weren't any.

Everyone on the team had been responsible for a different talking point, and now no one was going to have anything substantial to say when the subject of global warming arose. "Juliet," he said. "Is this all you have?"

"I was . . . ," I began. But there was nothing I could say.

"Perhaps you were so overwhelmed by the enormity of the issue you—like many of our elected leaders—were struck mute?" Everyone laughed as Mr. Mildred cocked his head like a dog listening for a whistle being carried on the wind.

"Next time, more?" I nodded, feeling stupid. He looked at his watch. "Okay, let's wrap up these evidentiary outlines and get to work spinning facts"—he made a knitting motion with his hands—"into gold."

As I packed up, he stopped by my desk. "You okay, Juliet?"

I wasn't, but I wasn't about to tell Mr. Mildred why. I didn't even like admitting to myself how naïve I'd been. How had I let Lucas get under my skin?

Then I stepped out of the classroom, and there he was.

"I—I thought—" I sputtered. "I saw—"

Lucas pushed himself up from a slouching position by the lockers, and his smirk widened into a grin. Slowly, like he was moving underwater, he held out a hand as if to take mine, then, looking from one side to the other, he dropped it.

"You thought what?"

"I thought you'd gone off with your friends. I saw you. In the parking lot."

He shrugged. "Dex was playing 'We Will Rock You.' It's kind of a team thing. I made them drop me off right after."

"It would have been okay if you'd gone with them," I lied.

He took my hand for real this time. "No, it wouldn't."

And I think that's what I would miss most later. Lucas's certainty. Looking into his eyes and seeing all of him there, the way I could then.

chapter eight

"So let me tell you about this dream," Lucas said. We were in the deserted stairwell now and could talk in private. He took my hand again, and this time, he held on to it. "You want a ride?"

"Sure," I said. I was thinking about how naturally his fingers wrapped themselves around mine, how soft his skin felt. I was thinking that I wanted him to kiss me. What if I pulled him into a classroom or behind a door, or pushed him back up against a locker?

"I dreamed I was a soldier in a war," he said.

"A war?"

"I wasn't in combat or anything. But I know there was a war going on."

"Which war?" I don't know why, but I had a sudden flash of the Nazi-tanks-arriving-in-Paris scenes from *Casablanca*, a movie my mom and I watch together every time it comes on TV. "Was it World War II?"

"No, nothing like that. We were in a city," he said. "The Middle East somewhere? Everything was the color of sand. The buildings had flat roofs, where people had hung laundry on lines. That laundry worried me. Somehow I knew there could be a sniper behind every bedsheet."

"It sounds like the Gulf War," I said.

"It wasn't," Lucas said. "That was an in-and-out invasion, a war fought door to door. One of the things I knew without really knowing was that this war had been going on a long time. Years."

"So what happened? *Was* there a sniper?" We were out behind the main school building now, heading for the parking lot, and when I was looking at Lucas, I had to squint against the low sun. Lucas was squinting too, but he wasn't looking at me. He was staring straight ahead, like he could see something I couldn't.

"I don't know," he said. "That's where the dream ended. Or sort of ended. When I woke up, I didn't feel the way you usually feel after a dream, when you're like, *Well, that was weird.* I felt like it was *still* real. I felt like I'd really been there. And my body—" He looked down as if seeing himself for the first time. "My body felt heavier."

"What do you mean?"

"I felt . . . older. I felt like I knew what it would be like to have a thirty-year-old body. Like, my knees hurt when I had my pack on. And I was taller. Bigger."

"Dreams are weird like that. You can be six years old one minute and eighty the next."

"But you know how you can't feel temperature in your

dreams?" he went on. "In this dream, I did. I was hot. It was hot out, much hotter than it ever gets here."

We were walking past the gym now, down the hill toward the mostly empty parking lot. I could see the tree I'd been looking at from Mr. Mildred's classroom window, the one that had already turned fall colors.

"Juliet," Lucas said when we got to his car. He was unlocking my door. "I'm telling you, it didn't feel like a dream." Holding on to the handle, he raised his eyes to mine like he was asking for help. "It felt *real*." He stopped, swallowed. I wanted to help him. I could see he was in some kind of pain, admitting this. "I think that dream . . . the way it feels so real . . . I think it might be connected to the things I've been remembering about you."

"Lucas," I said firmly. "It's just a dream. It might feel real, but it isn't." I didn't look him in the eye as I spoke. At the time, I told myself it was to save him from being embarrassed.

Lucas stood for a second with the door cracked. Then he closed it and laid his hand on the roof, bracing himself. "I feel like I'm going crazy. I can't believe I'm telling you any of this. I thought it might help. To tell you."

"It's okay," I said lamely.

"Let's just forget it." For the first time he sounded angry. He pulled open my door. "Could you just get in the car?" I did.

After dinner, my mom was scrubbing a stain on the counter, her white-blond hair bobbing, the wristwatch she wears on

49

a loose chain striking the counter with a clicking sound I'd been hearing my whole life.

"Are you going to start your homework?" she asked. I was leaning against the doorframe, my hands behind my back as if I was hiding something from her.

"I guess," I answered. I certainly had plenty to do. Any second, I'd make my way upstairs, spread my books out around me on the floor, start reviewing subjunctive verbs for French. I had to finish a physics problem set. I had three chapters of *Moll Flanders* to read for English, vocabulary from the Constitution to memorize for history, a few more paragraphs of my newspaper article to write, and if I ran through all of that, I could start, as Mr. Mildred liked to say, "arming myself with facts" about global warming. But I didn't arm myself with anything.

I just stood there watching my mom clean until the phone rang.

It was Lucas. He started speaking without saying hello. "Friday," he said. "How about we go see a movie? I promise: no more weird memories. No more dreams."

"Cool," I said. I didn't know what to say next. There was a part of me that would have gone with him to the movies or Friendly's again or anywhere else, just for the chance to kiss him one more time. And then there was another part that didn't want to go anywhere with him.

In the end, he said, "See you in school," and hung up before there was a chance for more.

chapter nine

On Friday night, when Lucas picked me up, my mom was home, so he came inside and shook her hand. He was wearing a clean sweatshirt and jeans. His sneakers were tied. And all of a sudden I got nervous.

I hadn't been expecting this to feel so datelike.

My mom craned her neck to look past Lucas out to the curb. "Is that your car?" she said.

"Yes, ma'am," Lucas answered. "A Mustang."

Ma'am?

"How old is it?"

"It's an '80."

"Good Lord," my mom said. "That's almost fifteen years old."

"The engine's solid," he said. "Or at least, that's what the guy who sold it to me said. You only have to hit it a couple of times with a wrench to get it going." It took Mom a minute to realize Lucas was joking.

She looked like she was warming up to lecture him about how the car wasn't safe, so I took Lucas by the arm and pushed him out the door before she could speak. But when we were on the sidewalk, she came running down the front path. "Do me a favor?" she said, putting a quarter into my hand for the pay phone. "Check in around nine o'clock, when the movie's over, just so I know not to worry." I slipped the quarter into my pocket, and my mom jogged back inside.

In the car, Lucas gave me a choice of three movies, all playing at an art house. I was surprised that he wanted to see any of them—I would have pegged him as a special-effects and car-chase kind of guy. Was this what he thought *I* liked?

"Are you hungry?" he said. "I was thinking we could get a pizza after the movie?"

"That's fine," I agreed, and from his list, I picked *Flores de Dolor*, because it was the only one not based on an English novel. Of all the foreign films my mom and Valerie take me to, I know those tend to be the slowest.

But *Flores de Dolor*, which was in Spanish with subtitles, turned out to be a quasi-terrifying story about a little girl trapped in a mountain cabin. There were lots of long, boring shots of her arranging dead flowers around a family of dolls. At the end, she ran through the woods while a crazed maniac with a crowbar followed her.

Lucas paid for my ticket. He sat straight up in his seat next to me. He didn't reach over and hold my hand. He didn't look at me. He didn't laugh at the funny parts—not that there were any.

Afterward, on the way back to the car, when I asked him what he thought of the movie, he said, "It was great." But he didn't sound like he thought it was great. He sounded like someone trying to be brave before he gets a shot.

"Well, I hated it," I said, because someone needed to. "It was boring and stupid and pretentious."

"Wow," Lucas said, really looking at me for the first time all night.

"I don't only like art movies," I said. "And I'm not freaked out by your dreams or your memories or whatever. Maybe you're a psychic. Or maybe you have a concussion. Or maybe you're—"

"Crazy?" he offered.

"Whatever," I said. "I'd rather talk to you about all that than have you take me to movies that you think I'm going to like but are actually really stupid."

"I—" Lucas started. I saw something pass across his eyes, almost like I was seeing a shark swimming in the back of a shadowy aquarium.

"Just tell me," I said. "I can handle it."

But he didn't tell me. We were standing in the parking lot next to his car. It was not quite raining, but a fog was leaving a mist on our skin and clothes. Lucas took me by my wrists and backed me up against the car door, then moved his hands to my jawline, looking at all the different parts of my face.

"I'm so glad you hated that movie," he said, and then he kissed me, hard, and I felt like I was finally addressing the sensation I'd had all week, the feeling of floating, like I couldn't feel the connection between my feet and the ground. All that time I'd just wanted *this*, to be pressed up against him, kissing in the dark parking lot, my hair dampening in the mist, Lucas's hands moving down my back and coming to rest around my waist.

When I remembered to call my mom, it was almost nine-thirty. She was cool, though—and she told me Rosemary had called a few minutes before, sounding upset. She'd left a number.

"He just left me here, the dweeb-breath mouth-farting douche bag!" This was Rosemary screaming into the phone when I called her back. She had picked up on the first ring.

"How did you know it was going to be me?"

She started using language that I can't write down here.

"Where are you?" I said.

"I don't know! Jason's parents' country place, but I don't even know what town it's in. He drives. I don't pay attention. It's in the middle of the woods somewhere, next to a random lake. I'm going to have to call my mom or dad to come get me. I am going to be so screwed."

She was talking loud enough that Lucas could hear everything she was saying through the phone. I looked at him. He smiled. I shrugged.

I put my hand over the mouthpiece to ask him a question, but I didn't even need to. He nodded, knowing right away what I had been about to say.

"I'm with Lucas," I said to Rosemary. "We'll come get you. Just calm down and figure out where you are."

But Rosemary wasn't ready for that. "I thought I was being *respectful*," she was saying, "breaking up with him in person. I knew he was really into me, and I didn't want to hurt his feelings, but you know what? Screw his feelings. He started *screaming* at me."

"Mail," Lucas whispered. "Tell her to look for a piece of mail. A magazine label or something with an address on it."

"He threw a *book* across the room. He started asking me if there was someone else. I was like, 'Yeah, how about *anyone* else? That would be better than you.' Jesus, Juliet, how am I going to get home?"

"Rose?" I said. "Are you aware that Lucas can hear every word you're saying?"

Rosemary found a piece of mail.

It took nearly forty-five minutes to get to the town where Jason's country house was, and then we still made a few wrong turns. We eventually had to stop at a gas station for directions.

Finally, a mile down a side road, we found the house. Rosemary had turned on every light and was standing in the doorway. As soon as she saw our headlights, she started running, the lights blazing behind her. "Shouldn't you shut the front door?" I said. "Is it okay to leave the lights on like that?"

"He's lucky I didn't trash the place," Rosemary said. "Do you realize that I could never have explained to my dad what I was doing out here?"

"We can TP the house if you want," Lucas suggested.

"No." Rosemary tossed her hair and sniffed meaningfully. "I'm better than that."

"Nice," said Lucas. "'Cause I'm starving." He looked at me, then Rose. "You guys want to eat?"

Over pizza, Rosemary asked about the movie. "It was *awesome*," Lucas said. "There was this little girl, right? With big eyes." He looked at me. "Huge, right?"

"Saucers."

"And a doll."

"A creepy doll."

"Like Chucky. Like, 'I'm baaa-aaack.'" Rosemary was laughing too hard to get any Coke up through her straw.

"And Chucky and Big-Saucer-Eyes Girl only spoke Spanish."

"You noticed that?" I said.

"Yeah, like, what the heck? The *whole movie* was in Spanish."

Rosemary was laughing harder. We all were.

Then Lucas asked Rosemary about Jason. "So who is this clown?"

"I thought it was so cool at first," she said. "How he took me to restaurants and knew about all the food and liked to drink wine." She spoke with an air of pity, as if she were describing someone with a terminal illness. "But he's not cool. He's pathetic. He's in college. He should be going to frat parties and drinking *beer*. He should have *friends*. I swear, he would rather spend weekends antiquing with his parents."

"Yeah, that's just sad," said Lucas, kind of snorting. We were all laughing again.

After we were done eating, Rosemary went to the bathroom, and Lucas took her place on my side of the booth. He slid his arm around my waist and looked down at me, half joking, half serious, his eyes narrowed to slits. "I hope I never hear you talking about me like that," he said. "If I don't go away nicely when you break up with me, just keep it to yourself, okay?"

I couldn't help it—I giggled. Having him so close to me, pretending to warn me, feeling his face next to mine . . . The whole time I'd been listening to Rose, laughing with her, I'd been wondering when I'd be able to kiss Lucas again, how long I would have to wait, if it would be tonight or some other time.

"I won't," I said, shaking my head. I was laughing still, almost like I was being tickled, but I was also serious. I wanted him to know the truth. "It's not the same."

Lucas started to say something, but then he stopped. Somewhere in the back of my mind, I'd registered a bell ringing as someone entered the restaurant, and now that I was following Lucas's eyes, I saw it was a soldier wearing fatigues, his tiny-boned wife at his side. The soldier was carrying a toddler, and the wife had a diaper bag. They were beaming.

"Hey!" shouted a voice from behind the counter. A man who worked there came running out to give the soldier a slap on the back, and then he kissed the wife. "You're back!" the man said. "She was in here last week and told me you were coming home. You got in just now?"

"Today." The soldier put the baby down so she could toddle, and he rubbed a hand across the top of his stubbly crew cut.

"That's going to be you, right?" I said quietly to Lucas, pulling my gaze away from the soldier. I was teasing, but when I saw the look in Lucas's eyes, I could feel my smile fade. His description of his dream came back to me in a flash—everything the color of sand. Bedsheets on a clothesline. The heavy feeling in his body, his knees, what he thought was an older body.

Was Lucas thinking about the dream now? He squinted like he was concentrating.

"Yeah," he said. He put his hand on his own head, touching his almost-curling hair, imitating, maybe without even realizing it, the way the soldier had rubbed his head.

And then my brain started to go into overdrive, as it sometimes does when I'm in a debate round.

"Oh my goodness," I said. "Of course! Lucas, I just figured all this out."

Lucas pulled back his head like a turtle retreating into its shell. "Figured what out?" he said.

"It makes perfect sense," I said. "Your remembering thing? You're not remembering. You're scared." He gave me a "Huh?" look, but I plowed on anyway, sure he'd understand soon. "You're afraid to join the marines. But you don't want to admit it, so your brain is resorting to these dreams. It's your subconscious trying to tell you something."

Lucas twisted his mouth in an expression of skepticism, but I just kept going. "Don't you see? Your dream isn't a memory, it's a projection of the future." I was inventing the theory as I described it. "You're so sure this is what it will be like you can't imagine it any other way."

"Juliet—" Lucas began, trying to stop me.

"No," I said. "It's fantastic, because this is so easy to fix. Lucas, you know you don't *have* to go. No one's forcing you to enlist. There are colleges for everyone—"

"Juliet—" Lucas tried again.

But I still wasn't done. "Sometimes a plan seems great when you're a freshman or something, but as you get closer to the time, it looks like less of a good idea. You can wait—"

Lucas cut me off. "This isn't about talking to a guidance counselor and picking a career path," he said, his tone sharp.

"Then what *is* it?" In the cloud of self-congratulation at the brilliance of my own theory, I couldn't imagine that he wouldn't see it just like I did.

Lucas took a breath and shook his head. And then he smiled, a slow-moving smile. "It's because that guy's *army*, you bonehead." Like it was a joke.

Passing the soldier and his family, Rosemary came to the end of our booth. She nodded at the seat that Lucas had vacated to sit next to me. "I'm not disturbing you two, am I?" she said.

"Not at all," said Lucas, standing quickly, like he was happy to move on.

He dropped Rosemary and me at my house without kissing me good night.

Was something wrong? I didn't have a chance to ask

him and didn't really want to anyway. As soon as Lucas had stood up from the table, I'd seen how intrusive I had been. I wished I'd kept quiet. I just wanted to go back to the part of the evening when we were kissing by the car. Or laughing with Rosemary over pizza.

Inside, we found my mom reading on her cozy white couch in the living room, her knitting basket at her feet and the TV, muted, turned to the news.

Valerie was with her, working on a crossword, drinking bourbon—her de-stressing routine.

"Rosemary?" my mom said, her eyes narrowing as she tried to figure out what was going on—I'd left with Lucas and was returning with Rose, a good hour later than I'd said I'd be home.

"We met up after the movie," I explained. When my mom didn't answer immediately with "Oh, sure," it occurred to me that she was deciding whether she believed me.

"So how was the movie?" Val asked. "And more to the point, what kind of self-respecting hockey player takes you to a foreign film?" Val hadn't met Lucas yet, but she'd grown up with brothers and loved the idea of him. I think she was envisioning Sunday afternoons on the sofa, with Lucas her surrogate nephew, watching football.

"*Flores de Dolor*? Wasn't particularly well reviewed," my mom said, yawning.

I laughed, remembering Chucky and *I'm baaa-aaack*. "It shouldn't have been."

My mom was looking at me, a question in her prettily furrowed brow. For a second, I considered telling her what was going on, if only just to get it off my chest. I could sit down on the couch between Mom and Val and let them fold me into their easy, protective arms, making like I was still ten, and we'd talk and talk, them hooting at everything I said like I was the most brilliant child ever born.

What would my mom make of Lucas's dream/memory weirdness? Would lawyerly, practical Val have a theory? *They* would believe my subconscious-fear theory, I was sure. They wouldn't be able to tell if a soldier was army or marines.

Before we went to sleep, Rosemary and I lay silently for a while, and I thought, *This is when you tell your best friend what's been happening.* But I didn't. And then I thought, *Now.* Still, I couldn't start.

And when Rosemary finally said, "I should have seen this thing with Jason coming," I was grateful. "The boring ones are always the angriest," she went on. "They don't *know* they're boring. They just think everyone else is blind to their charms." She yawned and arched her back like a kitten. I knew she'd be asleep in five minutes. "Sad, really."

"That he's so boring?"

"That he's so cute. Such a waste."

"Maybe there has to be something a little bit wrong with anyone in college who would date someone in high school."

"You mean I'm supposed to date high school guys?" Rosemary scoffed, then caught herself. "Oh, Lucas. I forgot. Sorry."

"It's okay," I said.

"It's better than okay." Rosemary yawned again. "I could tell tonight. He's crazy about you." She was two breaths away from losing consciousness. "And he should be."

I could have said something about his memories to her then. But just at that moment, her breathing grew even. Rosemary was asleep.

chapter ten

Lucas called the next morning and came over at noon. We walked into town for sundaes. "You know, Juliet, whatever weirdness—" he said, and then he stopped, like even bringing up the topic was getting too close to talking about it. "Are you mad?"

I put my lips together in a smile that was mostly a grimace. *Me, mad?* I wanted to say. Wasn't he the one who should be mad at me for forcing a theory on him when I obviously didn't understand?

But if I said that, we'd be talking about it again, and I didn't want to go there. So I just shook my head. No, I wasn't mad. We looked down into our ice creams until the moment passed.

From that day on, my memories get choppy, like I'm fishing snapshots out of a box where they were stored in no particular order.

Parent-teacher conference day: no school. Was it October? November? I remember picking apples with Lucas. I remember the leaves had started to turn orange for real. We went to Lucas's house afterward.

I'd been there before. Lucas had the kind of mom who insisted I come over for dinner, and she'd given me green peppers to chop two seconds after we'd been introduced. "At long last," she'd said when Lucas brought me into the kitchen, "Lucas's girlfriend." Like she hadn't thought he had it in him.

And Lucas had the kind of dad who, when dinner was called, trudged in from the garage with grease on his hands and shoveled his food into his mouth like he was being paid to eat and took no pleasure in it. Lucas said his parents fought, but they didn't in front of me, except once, sort of, when Lucas's mom was asking about my college plans and she turned to Lucas and said, "See? At least someone your age isn't going off to get themselves killed in the marines."

Lucas's dad waved a hand in the air dismissively. "Don't waste your breath," he said, addressing Lucas as if Mrs. Dunready weren't even in the room. "Your mother isn't the type to understand."

After apple picking, with no one home, I learned more about his family. Lucas took me out to the tree fort he and his dad had built for his little brothers. He pointed out the trail in the woods that his dad had blazed, leading to the pond where Lucas had learned to skate. "My dad wasn't around a lot when he was still in the service, but the times he was here, he was *here*. Now he's around all the time, but it's like he's a ghost. He's nobody."

Lucas showed me his BB gun range, which raised my debate-rhetoric hackles. "Do you know how dangerous it is to have guns and young boys together under one roof?" I said. "Did you know that most gun deaths of children are accidental and happen even in households where the guns are locked away? Boys, especially, will find them." I'd debated a gun control resolution six times my freshman year.

Lucas stopped me by placing his hands on my shoulders. He looked like he was trying not to laugh. "BB guns, Juliet," he said. "We may be gun people, but we're not stupid."

I felt myself calming down. Lucas had that effect on me. Taking my hand in the hallway at school, he'd made me feel like I had traveled somewhere—to a place I wanted to be.

"Besides," he went on, smirking. "Guns don't kill people. People kill people." I sucked in a huge breath, all ready to tear apart that backward NRA charge so many people accepted as gospel.

Then I realized Lucas was kidding.

He put a hand at the back of my waist, pulled me to him.

Inside, the empty house was filled with dust motes, and it smelled like old breakfast. Before, with Tommy and Wendell to distract me, running around in nothing but Lucas's hockey shirts and their tighty-whities, I hadn't noticed that the tile on the kitchen floor was yellowed and the couch in the living room sagged. But now, in the quiet, the house felt tired, like it had seen too much history.

Lucas made us peanut butter sandwiches and then found

me in the den, where I'd gone to study the pictures on the wall, the way you do only when no one's home.

Most were studio portraits. Some were black and white, some were in color, but all of them were of young Dunready men—marines—scrubbed, shaven, shorn, squeezed into dress blues. All had Lucas's even forehead and his nose, which looked like it might have been broken and promised to get a little beaky with age. There was more too: group photos, plaques, glass-framed boxes displaying ribbons and medals, a line of VA hats on the shelves above what looked like family photo albums, a framed poster of the marines hoisting the US flag on Iwo Jima.

"That's my grandpa," Lucas said, pointing to one of the black-and-white pictures. A man with glasses and a dimple in his chin. "And that's my dad." He looked like Lucas with brown hair. A handsome young man. "That's Uncle Wendell. Uncle Charles. These guys over here were my dad's cousins. This guy—Uncle Florrie—he's the one who died in Vietnam, and this guy, Cousin Sal, he kind of went crazy after this POW thing. For a while, he became a Mormon, and then he went totally AWOL, abandoning his Mormon family and joining this group that was—well, my grandma always tried to make it sound like he was in a club, but basically I think he was robbing liquor stores. I only met him once, when he came back east and my grandma had a big barbecue. Totally crazy."

"For real?"

Lucas nodded slowly, so I was expecting bad news. Convulsive ticcing? Ragged clothing? An unmistakable smell of old pee?

With his index fingers, Lucas traced two lines across his upper lip, pinching air in the neighborhood of his jawline. "Huge 'stache." It took me a minute to get what he was even talking about. "I've seen squirrel tails less bushy than what this guy was growing on his lip."

"Wow," I laughed.

"My dad would have put all this stuff in the living room if my mom had let him."

"Wow," I laughed again, though differently this time.

"So you can see . . ."

And I could. I got it now, why Lucas wasn't going to college. Why, when we went to the mall, he always stopped by the Military Entrance Processing Station—the MEPS— where the recruiters knew him by name and made sure he never left without one of the granola bars they gave out for free, a Xeroxed newspaper article about a former marine who started a small business with a VA loan, a video called *A Vision for the Future*, or a copy of "The Few, the Proud" brochure. In this family, if you weren't a marine, your picture wouldn't show up on this wall. It would be as if, in the context of your family tree, your branch didn't exist.

We moved upstairs. Lucas's room had been off-limits when his mother was around. But now I could take it all in: a bureau painted brown, old-fashioned window shades with fringe trim, hockey trophies, brown-checked wallpaper. And a marines poster, a black-and-white image of a man's face, broken out in sweat and straining in agony. One of the man's hands was visible, grasping a rope he was presumably climbing, while police-tape-yellow type boasted:

WE'D PROMISE YOU SLEEP DEPRIVATION,
MENTAL TORMENT, AND MUSCLES SO SORE YOU'LL PUKE.
BUT WE DON'T LIKE TO SUGARCOAT THINGS.
MARINES: THE FEW. THE PROUD.

Lucas pointed to the window, through which I could see the woods behind the house, the surface of the pond glinting through the trees. "See over there? I almost died there once."

"For real?"

Lucas exhaled through pursed lips. "I'd gotten this pair of skates for Christmas. They were used, but they were real hockey skates. My first. It had been warm for a few days and Mom told me no skating, but I didn't listen to her. No one was going to keep me off the ice."

Which cracked, he went on to explain, and as he described falling in, I felt the heavy cold that must have penetrated his winter jacket and jeans. "What did you do?" I asked, feeling impatient. It didn't matter that I could see him standing before me, obvious proof that he had lived to tell the tale. I was still scared. I wanted him to get to the end of the story quickly.

"I broke my way out."

"You *what?*"

Lucas reset his jaw in the manner of someone who was trying to appear not to care. "Ever seen those icebreaker ships in places where the ocean freezes, like Alaska? They have these huge wheels at the bow that basically eat through the ice, clearing a path for the boat. I turned myself into one

68

of them. I don't know how I'd managed to hold on to my hockey stick when I fell through, but I had, and I used it to break a path."

"But you were really young." When I was that age, I was still afraid of the monkey bars.

"I was as old as Tommy."

I tried to imagine a little-boy version of Lucas. In my mind, I saw a crew cut sticking out of the freezing water; he was alone, fighting for his life by beating at the edge of the ice until it cracked in submission. "Did your mother absolutely freak out?"

"I never told her. As soon as I got on solid ground, I ripped off my new skates and just left them there. I ran to the house, went in the back door, and threw everything I was wearing into the washing machine. I somehow managed to turn it on, and then I climbed into my bed in my underwear. My teeth were chattering really hard. I drew blood when I bit my lip by accident. I was scared. But I knew if my mom found out, she wouldn't let me skate anymore."

"You were *nine*?"

Lucas shrugged off the question. "My dad got home—it was the day after Christmas. My mom was working, probably. And I guess he found the laundry. He must have seen the muddy trail from the back door into the laundry room too. He washed everything. Found my skates. Came and put them on the floor by my bed. Didn't say anything. But he didn't need to. He knew how much I'd wanted them, and how much skating meant to me."

Tears were forming in my eyes. Maybe because my own

dad had never done anything like that for me. But thinking of Lucas as a little boy, naked and shivering in bed, I had to ask, "Shouldn't your dad have been more worried?"

"My mom worries enough for our whole family. That's really what her problem is with the whole marines business." Lucas grabbed my hand, smiling again, and lowered his head to look into my eyes. "Don't feel *sorry* for me." He laughed. "I only told you that story to impress you."

He pulled me onto the bottom bunk. I felt a deep ache forming inside me, a fluttering. That was what it was like to be with Lucas. That was how I felt whenever he touched me.

He pulled a mini photo album from a shelf above the bed. "Want to see pictures of my little brothers back when they were still cute?"

I wanted to do anything Lucas suggested. And Tommy and Wendell *were* really cute. There they were riding bikes in a campground, then eating cereal in matching Ninja Turtles pajamas at a picnic table, a pop-up RV behind them. His mom making pancakes, wearing a Santa hat—she had Lucas's blue eyes. A photo of his dad in his marines uniform, squinting at the little-boy version of Lucas holding his hand.

"Your dad—" I didn't know what to say. He looked happy. Hard to tell just from a photograph, but there was something there. Pride?

"He should have stayed in the service," Lucas said. "But my mom couldn't take it."

"Was he deployed a lot?"

"Yeah, and she stopped going with him after a bit. She hated base life. Which I don't get. I mean, I was born in *Hawaii*—paradise, right? And all my mom remembers is that her sisters were out getting educations while she played solitaire and drank vodka for breakfast."

"Your mom?" I couldn't imagine her drinking.

"At Camp Pendleton, which I actually remember, there were kids everywhere. You could get any toy at the PX. And candy. But my mom couldn't get away from that whole life fast enough. She moved home and gave my dad a choice: re-up as a reservist or live alone. Then, after she went back to school and started working, money wasn't such a factor, and she told him she couldn't stand even the reserves. The minute he was discharged, it was like, boom, he was gone."

"He left you?"

"Not physically. But it's like he can't feel anything. Except anger. I can't remember the last time he laughed. And I get it, he loved being a marine. It's who he was. . . ."

Lucas's voice trailed off, and as he took the album out of my hand, he laughed bitterly. Then he rolled over on top of me, kissed me and tickled me, and we were laughing and kissing at the same time and sort of wrestling too. Then just kissing.

This was the first time we'd ever lain on a bed together. We'd always been in a car, or outside, or with my mom, or with Rosemary, or at a party.

Lucas pushed the hair off my forehead. He propped himself up on an elbow. He ran a finger under my jaw and down my neck. He said, "I don't want to ever stop remembering the way this feels. Just this shape here." He let his finger rest in the hollow beneath my collarbone. I looked straight up at him.

But I can't write too much more about this. Because sometimes, when I think about holding Lucas, or being held by him, when I replay the things he said to me, when I hear his voice inside my head, my hands shake and I can't think straight to write. I feel . . . I don't know. I feel too much.

Lucas and I fell asleep in his bed that afternoon, my head resting on his chest, his arm wrapped around me. We had a blanket pulled up over us, and it was so quiet we could hear the hum of the fridge from downstairs.

What woke me was the sound of Lucas crying in his sleep. He wasn't crying out like he was having a nightmare. He was whimpering, and then I saw that tears were streaming down his cheeks.

I called his name. He stirred and seemed to swallow the noise he was making, then sniffed and the tears stopped also. He didn't wake up, even when I wiped a tear from his cheek.

chapter eleven

I started lying to Rose. Not about anything important, just little things. Almost like I was practicing, like I was teaching myself how to lie.

She asked about a new sweater, and I said it used to be my mom's, when actually Val had bought it for me the week before.

She wanted to tell me about an episode of *ER,* and I said I'd already seen it, because I was trying to get her off the phone in case Lucas called. I said I'd meet her at her locker, but I went to Lucas's locker instead.

I don't know if Rosemary knew I was lying. If she did, she never said anything about it. She might have just been too distracted by her own life. And her own lies.

Jason had started calling her constantly, pretending to be someone from our school, leaving messages with her mom, sending her letters that begged her to change her mind about breaking up with him, telling her she was the only person who made him happy.

She'd had to become a hawk with the mail—if her parents found out she was dating college guys, they'd probably ground her for life. That was why when Jason sent her something in a FedEx box, Rosemary stashed it in her backpack, waiting to open it at my house. Which was smart, because her mom would have heard the gasp Rosemary let out when she saw the will-you-marry-me little blue box from Tiffany inside the FedEx package.

Yes, that's *the* Tiffany: the big jewelry store on Fifth Avenue in New York City where Audrey Hepburn stares in the windows and eats a Danish out of a paper bag.

Holding the box in front of her, Rosemary breathed in horror, "Oh, my God!"

I just stared.

"You don't think he's crazy enough to—" she began, and then answered her own question. "No, he isn't."

She was right. Jason wasn't crazy enough to send a diamond engagement ring to a girl who wasn't returning his calls.

But he *was* crazy enough to send a diamond. Rosemary gasped again when she saw it, then gently lifted the delicate gold chain and let the diamond swing into her palm.

"He *does* know you're sixteen?"

She nodded, though honestly I didn't know if she'd heard me. The diamond was sparkling in the light, and she appeared to be hypnotized.

"Rosemary," I said. "Put the necklace down!"

She startled to attention.

"You can't keep it. You have to give it back."

Rosemary assumed a calculated expression that would have been at home on one of the boyfriend-swapping, back-stabbing golden girls she used to hang out with.

"How?" she said in an I-don't-have-time-for-how-much-you-don't-understand-about-relationships tone. "*Mail* it to him? Give it back to him *in person*? Or return it to the store?" She laughed. "For, like, a credit?"

"Oh, come on," I said. "You know what I mean."

"If I return it, he'll just write me another letter telling me he can see I'm still angry and try again."

"He needs to get the message that you're done," I said. But Rosemary wasn't nodding. "You do want him to get that message, right?"

"Sure," Rosemary answered, meaning, I could tell, no.

Later that night, I was sprawled on the carpet in my room, doing my homework. I barely registered the sound of my mom rolling the trash cans down the driveway to the curb. I barely registered the sudden absence of that sound.

But then there she was, standing in my doorway, her ankles looking especially birdlike sticking out of big black rubber clogs. Her hair was kind of sticking out too, like she'd put in too much mousse and hadn't seen what she looked like in the mirror. She was holding the crumpled Tiffany wrapping paper and white silk ribbon in her hands.

"What," she began in a tone I didn't quite recognize. She sounded like a mom on TV. "What, may I ask, is *Tiffany* wrapping paper doing in our trash?"

And honestly, I didn't know what to say. I was so used to telling my mom the truth that my first instinct was to confess to her about Jason and Rosemary. But if I did, she might feel obliged to tell Rosemary's parents. Which was out of the question.

So I did what people do when they aren't used to lying: I lied badly.

"It's nothing," I said.

Lying badly is never smart. Because now my mom was not just freaked out by the Tiffany wrapping paper, but also aware that I was lying to her.

"Nothing?" she repeated. "This is wrapping paper from Tiffany. I know I didn't put it in there. No one's given me a gift from Tiffany in quite some time."

I forged ahead with my lie. "Rose had it at her house. It was something one of her aunts sent her."

"Juliet, you don't lie to me," my mom said. This was a statement of fact more than a command.

And she was right. I didn't lie to her. Except I just had.

"Did Lucas give you something from Tiffany?"

"Lucas?" I was laughing even as I said his name.

Laughing from shock.

Lucas had bought me a grilled cheese sandwich. An ice cream. He'd paid for a strip of photos from a booth in an arcade. "I don't think Lucas even knows what Tiffany is."

"He didn't give you a piece of jewelry from Tiffany that he got God only knows how—maybe from the money he's supposed to be saving for college?"

"Lucas isn't going to college," I reminded her.

She twisted her mouth into a frown.

And I felt a sudden sadness that I was making my mom into the person she was right then—frail, angry, wrong, alone. I wondered what would happen if I just tossed my books aside and ran over and gave her a big hug.

But I didn't get up and give her a hug. I clicked my retractable pen closed and open and then closed again with my thumb, something I've seen my dad do when he brings me along to the hospital and I watch him take his residents on rounds.

"I just want to make sure you're not getting swept away by his . . . energy," my mom said. "I mean, Lucas is a sweet kid. But, Juliet, you're so smart. And—" She stopped. "It's natural to feel things that are . . . physical. But I just want you to recognize them as that. Not to confuse those feelings with deeper ones."

"What can you possibly mean by that?" Again, I felt like my dad on his rounds, scaring his residents with his condescending tone.

"Do you have anything in common with Lucas? Are you letting his emotions dictate yours? These are mistakes everyone makes. Women make. I have made. At your age—at any age, really—you can get hurt. Way more easily than you would think."

My mom's eyes were actually welling up with tears. I thought I knew why—and it wasn't because of me. Was this why she never dated? Had never met anyone after the divorce? She was afraid to make another mistake?

"He's my boyfriend, okay?" I said. "I have a boyfriend.

And yet the earth continues to spin. The sun rises in the mornings. Night follows day. Here I am, sitting on the floor, doing homework like I always do."

"I know."

"Are my grades slipping? Has school called?"

She shook her head, her eyebrows pinched together. I'd closed a door and she was knocking on it, rattling the doorknob from the other side, but I wouldn't let her in.

Rosemary told me later that what my mom had meant was "Don't have sex."

And I could have told my mom that we hadn't. But I didn't want to. Rosemary discussed sex casually, as if it were just one more activity—tennis, soccer—that she was really good at and got the chance to do a lot. But there was nothing casual about the way I felt about Lucas. About touching him. Kissing him. I felt like if I said out loud what the feeling was, I would jinx it. It would desert me. Sung too often, even your favorite song becomes just a series of random notes.

Besides, my mom was done. We'd had a fight and I'd won. Or at least, that was what I believed.

When the phone rang on a Wednesday afternoon and it was my dad, I nearly had a heart attack. "Dad?" I said. "Are you okay?" Like everything in my dad's life, the timing of phone conversations is regimented and precise. We speak every Sunday at five p.m., and there's not a lot of room for variation.

"Your mom asked me to call." He was using the extranasal California accent he slips into when he's uncomfortable giving a patient bad news. "She says you have a special friend and it's time I knew."

Special friend? Could anyone use that phrase and not sound like they were programmed for English vocabulary by a punch card?

Another kid might have moaned, "Oh, God, Dad, this is the nineties!" But there's something about my dad that always kept me from acting that way with him. I'd always known—since I was really little, probably—that there's a certain way you have to be with my father or you'll scare him away.

So I kept my cringing invisible to him, even as he read out loud—and I am not making this up—the correlation some pathetic social scientist had made between the age at which girls start having sex and the educational degree they eventually go on to obtain. The gist was that if I had sex before my eighteenth birthday, I could pretty much kiss law school goodbye.

At dinner that night—sushi again—I pointed at my mom with my chopsticks and aligned my gaze along them, as if I were sighting her down the barrel of a gun.

"Dad called me today," I said. "And if your strategy to keep me from having sex with Lucas is that I'll hear Dad calling him my 'special friend' every time I think about him, that will definitely do the trick. Thank you for that. And for your information, Lucas and I are not having sex. I have no plans to have sex with him at the present time. If at some date in the future I reverse that opinion, I will be procuring appropriate contraception and engaging in practices guaranteed not to result in pregnancy or the contraction of STDs."

She took a sip of her watered-down ginger soda. "Your father called?" Her eyes—big, blue, framed with her trademark heavy mascara—made her appear the very soul of innocence. She didn't bring up the subject again.

chapter twelve

As the fall moved forward, all I wanted was to be with Lucas. I didn't care when Val got tickets to shows. I didn't want to hang out at Rosemary's after school, eating cheese popcorn and drinking the Pellegrino that was supposed to be for guests. I didn't care if Rose was watching *Doctor Who*. I didn't care what Jake and Amanda were up to on *Melrose Place*. I didn't want to try on dresses I would never wear. I didn't want to spend Saturday mornings wandering the museum's galleries while my mom finished up a few projects in her office overlooking the sculpture court.

I made excuses. I'd tell my mom I had homework, then spend the night on the phone with Lucas, pretending that I'd just called him when she picked up the extension downstairs.

I knew my mom was watching me—over the top of her knitting, her glasses pushed down to the bottom of her cute-as-a-button nose, the questions she wasn't asking swirling in her brain. I could tell what she was thinking. She was thinking that Lucas wasn't enough. That he didn't understand the world—her world. That someone not going to college was going to pull me down.

I could have made a case for him. I could have put her mind at ease, telling her about how in physics Lucas was the one who understood how velocity and momentum affect the universe. About how he beat me in Scrabble.

I could have told my mom how much Lucas knew about the marines. How he'd memorized the complex hierarchy of job classification. How, if you wanted to see any action, you'd need to be an "03," and how you needed to time your enlistment with the annual cycle of job assignments to maximize the available choices. He would say things like "Guys make the mistake of thinking only about basic, but you have to plan for four years. You need a good job going in—you don't want to just be a grunt." He talked about how technology was changing the way the military fought. He mentioned Grenada. The Gulf War.

I could have told my mom how protective Lucas was of his little brothers, how because of whatever weirdness was going on with his dad, he had been the one who helped out their Little League team the year before. I could have told her how once, when he and I got stuck in a traffic jam Mrs. Dunready had warned us about, Lucas pushed his hands against the steering wheel, locked his elbows, and said, "You know what I hate about my mom? I hate how she always ends up being right."

I could have told her how generous Lucas was. Generous in ways most people didn't notice. Like, he didn't interrupt people. When Rosemary was talking, he turned his full gaze on her and let her say what she needed to say. He did the same to me, and also to my mom, to his friends, to Mr. Hannihan, although no one interrupted Mr. Hannihan—God forbid he should get off the subject of his sailboat and start talking about physics.

But I didn't tell my mom any of this. Maybe because, from the beginning, there were things about Lucas that I knew better than to tell anyone. Or maybe it was just because what I really wanted from Lucas was Lucas. Undiluted, uncopied, unphotographed, unprocessed Lucas. I didn't want to share him. I wanted it to be just him and me. Alone.

One Sunday, Val invited Mom and me over for her famous chili and I said I couldn't go because I already had plans with Rose.

My mom let me know with a withering glance that she assumed I was meeting Lucas and just not telling her. But she was wrong. I did have plans with Rose—sort of. We were going to meet up with Lucas and his friend Dexter Fine in the park near my house.

"You lied to your mom?" Rosemary said as we waited for Lucas and Dex to arrive. Rose and I were sitting side by side on a bench facing the drained swimming pool. "*Your* mom?"

Uh-oh, I thought. Rosemary loves my mom. She glamorizes her independence. She thinks of her as that camp counselor you never lie to because she's just that cool.

"You lie to your mother all the time," I said. "It's practically a religion for you."

"But that's *my* mom. She wants me to lie to her."

I pshawed.

"If I tried to tell my mom the truth, she couldn't take it. It would be like when those opera singers hit that note that makes everyone's wineglasses shatter."

"Your mom's nice."

"My mom acts like it's the 1950s. All she did in high school was take flower-arranging classes and ride horses. She was obsessed with horses. Which is how I know she was a virgin, by the way. Horses are proof positive."

Rosemary is full of theories like this. I put them in the same category with her knowing when celebrities get arrested or divorced and which teachers are having affairs and who is gay. She called it "gaydar," a word I didn't even know existed until she tried to convince me that my mom and Val were "obviously" an old married couple who kept their true relationship under wraps for my sake and for the sake of their careers. ("Shut *up!*" I had said. That was crossing a line.)

"But your mom talks to you," Rosemary was saying now. "You could tell her about stuff. Like guys. Like Lucas."

"I don't want to," I confessed. Rosemary shot me a look. Maybe she was connecting what I was saying about my mom to my reluctance to discuss Lucas with her too? I wouldn't have been surprised. Every conversation we'd had lately seemed to end with one of us stopping abruptly because to say one sentence more would mean we were in a fight.

Take Dexter, Lucas's friend who was on his way to meet

us at that very moment. Rosemary had been torturing him for weeks, and as I'd watched her draw him in, I'd found myself thinking, *What is she doing?* I mean, the poor guy. He wasn't in Rosemary's league. He never would be.

Dex was . . . well, he was Dex. Lucas's best friend. A good kid in general, but no rocket scientist. He had shiny black hair that fell into his eyes, and he wore impossibly baggy pants. I'd never heard him speak more than five words in a row. The hockey team—playing, lifting weights with the guys, driving around and partying together—seemed to be his life.

And yet here we were, meeting up in the park and then driving over to Dex's house on a Sunday night because Rosemary said she wanted to see where he lived.

"It's nothing special," Dex said, embarrassed and flattered by her interest at the same time.

Dex's house was the kind half the kids in our town lived in—a picture window in the living room, a minivan in the driveway, a basketball hoop over the garage, a wreath of dried flowers on the front door, one backyard spilling into the next. I was expecting the inside to be all about family, with lots of kids, muddy shoes, and sports equipment, a dad cooking pancakes or hot dogs, a mom running school committees.

But when we got inside, the hall was dark. The wallpaper in the half-lit living room was faded. Dex's white-haired mom was sitting at the kitchen table alone, under a single light, clipping coupons and drinking a cup of tea, a pale blue cardigan draped over her shoulders like she was afraid of drafts. His dad was watching golf in the den, smoking a cigar, which gave the house a rich, foreign smell that reminded me of the incense in Rosemary's church. "Hullo!" Dex's dad said affably, but he looked a bit disoriented, like someone just woken from a nap.

"Sorry my parents are so old," Dex said once we were in the basement.

"They're not *old*." Rosemary slapped Dex gently on the shoulder like he had just said something funny. "They're *nice*."

"They're old," Dex sighed.

"Your mom gave us *snacks*." Rose held up the crinkly package of weird Stella D'oro cookies his mom had foisted on her.

"She gave us grape soda," Dex said, matching her cookies with a plastic liter bottle. "Who drinks that anymore? What are we, twelve?"

"I *love* grape soda," Rosemary countered, but she couldn't keep the laughter out of her voice. She ran a finger through the dust on the bottle's topmost curve and ended up snorting. "I've been craving a nice ancient bottle of flat grape soda for weeks."

Now Dex was laughing too, but a little uncertainly, like he wasn't sure he was in on the joke.

Rose extended an open palm. "Cookie me, please," and Dex fumbled bravely with the bag. After he'd finally managed to get the cookie into her hand, Rose sat down on the couch next to me, crossed her legs, and smiled like a cat settling into a sunny spot on a windowsill.

Her cookie sat untouched on her knee.

Dex walked over to the TV, which was part of this wood-paneled, stereo-television console from the 1970s. He flipped on a Celtics game.

"How old are your parents, anyway?" Rosemary asked.

Dex shrugged.

"You don't know?" Rose narrowed her eyes, as if she were looking at a rare specimen of tree frog flown in from the Amazon rain forest to satisfy our scientific curiosity. "You're kidding, right?"

"My sister, Jessie, is the oldest, and she's thirty-five or something, so mid-fifties? Older?" Dex shrugged again. "I didn't know there was going to be math on the test."

"I'll give you math," Rosemary said. "Your sister's thirty-five—that makes you a love child!"

Dex blushed. "Oh, come on."

"You mean an accident." Lucas was fiddling with the rabbit ears on top of the TV to adjust the reception.

Dex shoved him. A playful shove. They were like this together; all the hockey guys were. "How old is *your* mom?" he said.

"You don't want to go there." Lucas held up his hands in a gesture of "I surrender."

Rosemary cleared her throat dramatically. "Are you two done?"

Dex snapped to attention, brushing his hair out of his face. Grabbing a Ping-Pong paddle, he said, "We could—you know . . ." The rubber was peeling off the paddle on one side. "No one uses it anymore."

Rose popped the cookie in her mouth, uncrossed her

skinny legs, extracted herself from the sofa, and, holding Dex's wrist to keep the paddle steady, ripped off the rubber like she was removing a Band-Aid. "Great idea." She turned to me. "You playing?"

"No, she's not," Lucas answered for me, grabbing my hand and somehow making it look like I was pulling him violently down onto the sofa, even though he was basically diving on top of me. "We'll watch," he announced.

Rosemary rolled her eyes and then turned her attention to the table, running her hands over the surface to determine where it was warped, laying out the ground rules for the game.

Rosemary is an amazing tennis player, and she's also got a mean Ping-Pong game, but what she was demonstrating that night wasn't her control over the ball. It was her control over Dex. She flipped her hair. She giggled. She bumped his hip with hers. When he aced a serve, she said, "Dex, Dex, Dex, what am I going to do with you?" and he actually apologized, somehow forgetting that she'd aced him three times when she had served. She treated him like they were old friends, instead of people who two weeks before would have passed each other in the halls without speaking. Like Dex was someone she thought about. A lot.

But he wasn't. I'd seen her roll her eyes when he called her, pumping him for dirt on who liked who in the senior class and which seniors were in a fight while she drew pictures of octopuses on her math homework.

The only thing that made what she was doing not incredibly cruel—at least, Ping-Pong-wise—was the fact that

Dex played with the same kind of aggressive intensity as Rose did. In fact, he beat her. Then she beat him. Then they played a game where the points lasted so long Dex's old-man dad poked his head down the stairs and informed us that "Mom says it's getting a little late for guests." It was nine.

"Want to rent a movie?" Dex said. "Video Galaxy's open for another hour."

"Nah." Lucas smiled ruefully. "My head is killing me." We all knew why—preseason training had started, and he'd been sprinting at practice all afternoon. He stood up from the couch stiffly, offered me a hand. "Want a ride home?"

I looked at Rose. She put her hands in the front pockets of her jeans, somehow making her legs appear even longer than they were. She was looking at me but talking to Dex. "Ever seen any Audrey Hepburn movies?"

"Who?" said Dex.

"Oh, right," she said. "I guess Juliet and I are the only non-Neanderthals in the room."

"Come on," I said to her. The only reason Rosemary knew about Audrey Hepburn was because my mom had introduced her movies to both of us.

Rosemary shrugged. She wasn't looking at me anymore. I think she was deciding that I had failed her. I think her treatment of Dex was supposed to demonstrate how not to let a guy into your inner sanctum. Guys are to be played with and teased, not trusted. *See?* I interpreted her as saying. *This is how we leave them behind.*

But I didn't want to follow her instructions. I didn't want to leave Lucas behind.

• • •

"Poor Dex!" I said to Lucas when we got in his car.

He didn't answer, just reached across me to open the glove compartment, where he kept an economy-sized bottle of ibuprofen. He shook three pills into his hand and swallowed them without water.

"Aren't you only supposed to take two?"

He shrugged. "Three work better." He kissed me. "And frankly," he said, kissing me longer this time and harder, until we both lost interest in the conversation. "Frankly, those two are starting to get on my nerves."

chapter thirteen

It must have been just after Halloween when Dex wrote Rosemary a note on the back of a history quiz he'd gotten a C on. The note read: "If you want to go to the Fall Ball we can go together.—DEX." The corners where he'd folded it were grimy, as if he'd been carrying it at the bottom of a bag.

Rosemary scrawled "K, sure," corrected all Dex's wrong answers, and passed the quiz back.

"You're going to the dance?" I asked. Back when it was announced, we'd decided we thought the whole Fall Ball concept was lame. And then: "You're going with *Dexter*?"

Rosemary shrugged.

"Do you remember that your last boyfriend was the kind of guy who took you to fancy restaurants where he'd ask to speak with the sommelier?"

Rosemary shrugged again.

In the weeks leading up to the dance, Dexter and Rosemary spent a lot of time together, but always with Lucas and me. We went to the movies, hung out at a deserted elementary school playground, rode the carousel at the mall, played foosball at parties, and ran outside in the first snowfall in hooded sweatshirts and jeans, sticking out our tongues.

During this time, Lucas's headaches were increasing. He got fidgety. He picked stupid fights with Dex. He stopped conversations abruptly.

One time, we were in the library, and I had looked up from some notes I was taking, thinking about the evidence coming together for an argument, when Lucas reached across the table and took my arm.

"Where were you just now?" he asked. "It was like you weren't here."

"I was thinking about Desert Storm and coal miners and the CIA," I explained.

"Okay . . . ," he said in that voice he got when something made him feel dumb. He laughed.

"They're connected!" I insisted. "Look." And I explained what I was learning about global warming. That we burn too much gas. That we're running out of cheap energy sources. That the oil we burn now comes from Russia and the Middle East—dangerous places. "You know those guys last spring, how there was that van with a bomb in the parking garage of the Twin Towers?"

Lucas winced as if in pain. Chewing on the end of a pen he was using to draw mustaches on women in a magazine ad for laundry detergent, he shrugged and shook his head. "Why would you want to even think about that stuff?" he asked, like he was angry. "Why can't you just enjoy the here and now?"

I stared at him. He closed the magazine in a rush and slapped it on the table. I half expected him to get up and leave me there, but he didn't; he just looked at me. "I'm sick of being in the library all the time," he said. "Can we go?" He laughed, but I didn't know what was funny. There was something he wasn't saying. I knew it was there, but I ignored it. I willed it to go away.

"It's kind of amazing," Lucas said another time, at a hockey party, where he'd dragged me away from the guys soaking tennis balls in gasoline and lighting them on fire in the backyard. "To think these guys will grow up, most of them, to have families and houses and jobs."

I laughed. "Who are you, Father Time?" And then he did an imitation of Father Time, if Father Time was a zombie who stalked you with raised arms and then grabbed you and threw you down onto the grass while you screamed and laughed.

"Me. Father. Time," he growled. "Me see back and forward in time. Me know the ending to all stories. Me eat pretty girls."

I look back and wonder how, given what Lucas had told me about dreams and memories, this kind of thing didn't set off alarm bells for me. I guess I was happy. And blind. I didn't want to see. I wanted everything to stay just as it was.

It was Rosemary and Dexter who made our plans for the Fall Ball, deciding that we'd meet at a restaurant Dex had picked, deciding we'd go in separate cars.

Up until the very minute Lucas picked me up, I'd continued to think the Fall Ball was an exercise in stupidity led by Robin Sipe and the student council, kids with nothing better to do than try to make us all feel like we were experiencing high school the way it was in movies.

But then there Lucas was—his hair still damp from a shower, his dad's tie too long, the sleeves of his sports coat too short, like he'd grown three inches since the last time he'd put it on, and I found myself thinking, *This is a moment I never want to forget.*

Suddenly I wished I'd gone shopping for something special to wear, spent hours at the mall fantasizing about how great it was going to be, like someone who'd been waiting for this to happen all her life.

Lucas's hands shook as he handed me a clear plastic box containing three roses, a fern frond, and some baby's breath. He was watching me intently, as if he was worried I wouldn't like it.

Was he nervous? About a corsage?

Then, on second glance, I started to wonder if the intense expression in his eyes went beyond "Will she like the corsage?" to something more serious. On the phone that morning, he'd mentioned that he'd gotten another headache playing hoops with Tommy and Wendell. He'd also woken up at five for practice, so he could have just been tired, but he'd had a headache the night before, and the day before that as well.

I lost track of my concern when he took my hand. "That's a nice dress," he whispered. "You look really pretty." As he slid the corsage onto my wrist, I could smell the damp wool of his jacket mixed with shampoo, toothpaste, and his own musky scent.

"Thanks," I said, feeling myself blush. I liked the roughness of his sleeve against my bare arm, the pressure of his palm on my lower back while we posed for my mom's camera.

It was drizzling and just dark when we got in the car. He leaned over to kiss me once the doors were closed, and the damp of the air mixed with the damp of his jacket, the softness of his lips—I wanted to stay there forever, just kissing him, and I guess he was feeling the same way. He pulled me closer. It was getting to the point now where all Lucas had to do was look at me and I could feel my breath straining against my rib cage. Just the sound of his voice could make me feel like something delicious—something magical—was happening to me.

"My mom's watching," I said against his lips.

"It's dark," he answered. "She can't see in the windows."

"She's waiting for the car to start moving."

"We never have enough time," he said. "I never get enough of you."

I wanted to say that I never got enough of him either, but I didn't. I was aware of my mom, waiting under the porch light. I pulled back. Lucas gripped the wheel to stop his hands from shaking and took a breath before he turned the key.

"Sorry," he said, without saying what he was apologizing for. There was an edge to his voice. Was he . . . angry?

At me? Why were his hands still shaking? Why did his eyes seem to bulge?

"Are you okay?"

"Pass me the ibuprofen, will you?" was all he said in reply.

We met up with Rosemary and Dex at the Golf Club. It wasn't an actual golf club like the one Rosemary's family belonged to. It was more of a restaurant attached to nine holes and a shooting range. There were neon Coors Light signs in the windows.

Rosemary grabbed my arm just above the elbow as we got to the table, faux-whispering, "Look! Crayons on the table!" Then mock-complimenting, "Dex, you really did think of everything!"

She was wearing a navy-blue sheath minidress that showed off her square shoulders and long legs. Her only jewelry was the necklace from Jason. The thin gold chain sparkled against her dark skin. The diamond nestled in the hollow of her throat.

Dexter was wearing chinos that were too big for him, a Boston Bruins necktie, and a shirt that could have used some time under an iron. He jiggled a foot under the table, like a little kid who has to go to the bathroom.

We made fun of stuff as we sat there. We made fun of the oversized menus, the oversized sodas. Lucas pretended the oversized napkin was a blanket and pulled it to his chin like he was snuggling up to go to sleep. I remember laughing a lot. But I also remember that Lucas was laughing more than the rest of us. And that he drank four Cokes. And that at one point he was laughing so hard he started to tear up.

"Sorry," he said, collecting himself.

Dex held the fifth Coke Lucas had ordered up to the light. "What's *in* here, buddy?" At that, we were all laughing again.

I remember the potato skins were good.

Then the dance: I have to say, the gym looked amazing. It was decorated with hay bales and cornstalks and disco lights—a weird combination, but it worked. A kid from the senior class was DJ'ing, and all we heard for the first hour was angry, undanceable punk rock. Which shouldn't have come as much of a surprise, considering his T-shirt said DROP DEAD IF YOU DON'T LIKE THE SEX PISTOLS.

Finally, Robin Sipe begged him to change the music, at which point he put on "Celebration," and to be sure his gesture of disdain registered properly, he proceeded to replay it every three songs, standing behind his turntables with his arms crossed over his chest.

It didn't matter. Each time "Celebration" came on, there'd be all this cheering, which was our school's ironic form of booing. It was awesome.

The hockey team must have had a stash of alcohol somewhere, because they kept leaving, and when they came back, they danced like they were insane, lifting their girlfriends high into the air and spinning them around like the sticks they wave in victory after they win a game. Lucas stayed close to me, but Dexter took off with the team a few times, dragging Rosemary along with him. Lucas asked me if I wanted to dance.

There's no other way for me to say this: Lucas was a terrible dancer. I was of the sway-side-to-side school, but

Lucas—well, Lucas looked like he had entered his own universe. He would nod and play air guitar and then do this thing with his feet that was a little bit spastic, like he was dancing to futuristic techno music no one else could hear.

Then he'd look up from his private hyperdancing movement, take my hand, and stare at me in a way that was sad and scary at the same time. I didn't know whether to kiss him, smile at him, or ask him if I should call 911.

Lucas took both my hands in his and moved them in time with the beat. He lifted my left arm and spun me under it, then wrapped his hand around my back like we were swing dancing. He pushed me out again jitterbug-style, holding my hands, our two different approaches to dancing—his mania, my respectable swaying—united in a movement that felt kind of okay.

By the end of the song, Dexter and Rosemary were out on the dance floor with us again. Dex threw a heavy arm over Lucas's shoulder and looked at me. "You ever been up on the roof of the gym?" he asked, raising his eyebrows suggestively.

And at that one simple question, everything changed.

"What are you talking about?" Lucas shouted over the music. He'd stopped dancing. "What the hell are you trying to pull?"

"The roof, man, you've got to check it out," Dex said, laughing.

And out of nowhere, Lucas pushed him. Hard.

Dex stared. For a second, the two of them looked like they were about to get into a fight. A real fight, not the play punching and shoving I was used to. Lucas half raised an arm. Dex's shoulder twitched.

Then Lucas seemed to shake off the mood. He shuddered, as if he had just remembered something, and took my hand. "I—" he started to say.

He had all our attention. He looked from Dex to me and ended up with his eyes on Rose. "Sorry," he said, although she wasn't the one he needed to apologize to. "Turns out I'm not a big fan of roofs." And then, as if a decision had just been made, he nodded to himself and pulled me away from Dex and Rose. "Come on," he said impatiently.

Maybe he didn't hear me ask, "Where are we going?" He certainly didn't reply. As I followed him toward the door, I turned to see Dex staring after us, his mouth hanging open. Rosemary half waved, a "What the heck?" in her gaze.

"We need to talk," Lucas said tersely.

"About what?" I tried. Again, Lucas acted like he hadn't heard.

He pulled me through the trophy room, out of the building, and a little ways down the asphalt path that led to the main school building.

It was still raining lightly. I was hot from dancing, so the moisture on my bare arms felt good. I noticed a mist gathering on the top of Lucas's hair, creating a halo effect around his face.

He took a step closer to me—a group of freshmen was gathered nearby. "Here's the thing," he said. He wasn't looking at me. He was looking at a point in space about three inches above my hairline. "We can't be together anymore."

He spoke matter-of-factly, as if he were answering a

question we'd been discussing, as if what he was about to say weren't going to take me by surprise. Weren't, in fact, going to destroy me. "I think it would be best for us to try to just be friends."

I made a noise like I'd been punched in the gut hard enough to force up air.

Lucas turned on his heel and began to walk away.

chapter fourteen

As Lucas made his way back toward the gym, the only thought that managed to anchor itself in my consciousness was this: *If I let him leave, I will never recover.* Living with my mom—growing up in the shadow of the divorce she's never bounced back from—must have played a role in my thinking.

But honestly, I wasn't thinking. I was acting on instinct. I was acting in the manner of a person hanging from a cliff by their fingernails. It wasn't a calculation I made as I decided to run after him so much as it was the illustration of a fact. I couldn't let go.

"Get back here!" I shouted, running after him. "What is wrong with you!" I grabbed him by the arm. "What the *hell*?"

He stopped. He turned and gave me a look that said "I am way too bored to answer your question." Like he was a rock star and I was a ten-year-old begging for an autograph.

Later, I realized his head must have been pounding. I don't think I ever fully comprehended how consistently his head was hurting at that time.

He sighed. "We're not good for each other." He sounded like he was reading from a manual. "It's not good for us to be so intense about each other. It's high school. We're too young for this kind of relationship."

Only certain words penetrated my thinking. Had he said "good"? "Intense"? "Young"? I didn't understand how those were bad things. My skin felt dead, the initial pain in my gut transforming into numbness as it spread down to my toes and then made its way up to my face.

Lucas was looking at the sky now, as if he were taking orders from the low clouds, which looked pink in the ambient light from the streetlamps. His jaw was tight, his eyes squinting.

And I was getting dizzy. I was starting to sway. I was going to have to sit down, I knew that, but I also knew I couldn't move. As long as I stayed right where I was, the verdict on this conversation was still out. There was still a chance I could get Lucas to explain himself, to change his mind. To get him to admit this was only an incredibly cruel joke.

"But—" I struggled to remember his words, and when I couldn't, I just said simply, "I like the way I feel with you. I thought you liked it too." My eyes had started to sting. To fill with water. There was a bitter taste in my mouth.

Lucas looked at me, grimaced, and looked away. He mumbled something I couldn't understand.

"What was that?" I asked. I might have been shouting. I guess I was acting angry, though inside I was drowning from feelings it was hard to name. I noticed the freshmen looking over at us. "Is this some kind of joke?"

"It's not a joke," Lucas said.

I tried again to breathe and found I couldn't. "This—Lucas—this hurts. I can't believe you'd hurt me like this."

"You need to believe it. I thought maybe . . ."

"Maybe what?"

"No. Maybe nothing. Maybes are over. I just need to walk away from you." He turned back toward the parking lot. "You need to be alone, to have me not be with you."

"No," I said. I was cold now, and I crossed my arms, my corsage brushing the inside of my right elbow, a reminder of how recently things had been good.

"Trust me," he said, and he laughed a little bit.

"Trust?" I repeated. "You're laughing?" The combination struck me as so absurd I felt a full rush of anger, which this time, thankfully, I knew for what it was. I couldn't believe it, but my mom was right. Rosemary too. How could I possibly have given over so much of myself—my happiness—to someone who didn't even want it?

"Were you thinking about breaking up with me when you picked this out?" I shouted. I ripped the corsage off my wrist, and when Lucas turned, I held it above my head, like a challenge. I cringed to realize that beneath my anger I was still hoping he'd come back to get the flowers, to get me.

But he didn't.

Instead, he held up both hands, like he was surrendering, showing me he wouldn't take the corsage back.

So I threw it. I threw it as hard as I could and I stormed past him, back into the dance.

I was crying by the time I reached the gym. I brushed the tears away and skidded across some loose straw, nearly falling. Through the pulsing lights, I scanned each clump of bad dancers for Rose and found her nowhere. I didn't see Dex either. They weren't by the snack table, or the registration table, or the DJ, or the bleachers.

And then there Rosemary was in the hall, on her way back from the bathroom. "Rose!" I shouted, tears streaming down my cheeks. I was choking. Snotting. Seeing me, she pulled me right back into the girls' room with her.

I never wear makeup, and once I was in a brightly lit space with a mirror, I could see that the mascara my mom had helped me put on had run, leaving raccoon-like half-moons under my eyes. Rose grabbed some tissue from one of the stalls and started wiping my face. Her diamond glistened under the fluorescent lights. "What," she said. "Happened." This was a command.

I only got as far as saying "Lucas" before my eyes began to well up again.

"Lucas what?" she said. "Did you guys get in a fight?"

"No," I said. I sniffled. I blew my nose. "That's just it. It came out of nowhere."

"You're crying like he broke up with you," Rosemary said. "Oh, good Lord, did he?"

I cried harder. Rosemary ducked into a stall to grab more tissue. "That's impossible. He's so into you. He's *annoyingly* into you."

"Not anymore."

"No," Rosemary said. "You misunderstood."

"There's no question," I said. "He couldn't have been more clear. I threw my corsage at him."

"Oh, boy," Rosemary said, sighing deeply in a way that let me know she understood how grave that was and also that, given the circumstances, she would have done the same exact thing. Good old Rose.

Or at least, I thought she was good old Rose until she said, "You've got to go talk to him."

"What?" I said.

"You can't just let him walk out on you at a dance like this. You've got to make sure you understand what's really going on, and not just whatever line he fed you."

"Later," I said. "I can't do it now."

"Later," she countered, "he'll have his story all set. If you want to know the truth, this is your moment."

"You think he's still even here?"

"Maybe he's with Dex."

"Where *is* Dex?" I said.

"He's on the roof. Everyone's up there."

And then suddenly, I understood.

"Oh, wow," I said.

"Wow?" said Rose.

The roof.

With Rosemary a step behind me, I threw open the

door, jogged down the hall from the bathrooms, and careened around the corner into the lobby, where, without even checking to make sure a chaperone wasn't watching, I opened the door to the stairs leading to the roof that Lucas had shown me so long ago and started to climb.

The roof. It was all about the roof. It had been all about the roof all night.

chapter fifteen

The stairwell—a painted railing, cinder-block walls, dim lighting—and then there I was, big sky above and pebbles under my feet, the feeling of open space a surprise, even in the half dark.

The hockey team: I saw a cluster of them off to the left, faces and bodies grouped around something. I couldn't see what it was because the only light came from the orange glow of the parking lot, and anything below the line of the parapet was cast in shadow.

I could guess, though. This was the bar.

As Rosemary and I got closer, I saw what they were drinking: Capri Suns, those juices that came in shiny pouches. The student council was selling them downstairs for a dollar each, and up here this kid Nunchuck was using a syringe to inject shots of vodka into them, collecting a dollar as well, though I guessed the guys on the team drank free, because all the beefy, shaved-head hockey players were sucking down juice pouches like preschoolers in the back of their moms' cars.

Just outside the group, Lucas was perched on the edge of the parapet, a Capri Sun balanced listlessly in his palm, his expression neutral, as if nothing upsetting had just happened. He was looking down toward the parking lot.

"He's looking for you," Rosemary said. "He wants to see if you're leaving."

"Well, I'm not leaving." Seeing the slump to his shoulders, the blank expression on his face, I knew I'd been right in my guess. I knew why Lucas had wanted to run away from me. I knew why I had to catch him. I wasn't angry anymore. I wasn't scared either.

"Juliet?" Rosemary said.

"Yeah?"

"Don't let him hurt you. If he starts to say things that are going to eat away at you later, just walk away."

I didn't tell her that everything Lucas would say to me would eat away at me later. I left Rose with the others and headed toward Lucas, alone, calling his name as I got close. He turned, and when I stopped in front of him, my feet planted firmly, my hands on my hips, he lowered his juice to the ground.

I pointed to the skirt of my dress. "Look what I'm wearing," I said. "A dress." He nodded. "We're on the roof. It's nighttime. All those things that you told me you remembered before, when I barely knew you. You tried to tell me about this memory you had, and I stopped you. But I'm ready now. You don't have to push me away or protect me. I want to know what's happening." I didn't know what else I should say. Or could say. "Lucas. Please."

He put his head in his hands, and I wondered for a second if I'd made a mistake.

But then he looked up and I could see that he didn't have the strength to lie to me again. His face was twisted in pain as he stood. "Come with me," he said, and led me to the back of the bulkhead, our shoes crunching on the pebbly surface. He squinted at the bulkhead's brick wall like there was a sign on it he was trying to read. Finally, he said, "Stand here, facing the wall, okay?"

He slid between me and the bricks, leaning against them, putting his hands on my waist. He checked the view to either side, and then he pulled me toward him. "This is it," he said. "This is what I remembered."

"You *remembered*," I whispered.

"Back in September, I tried to tell you about it. About how I kissed you up here. But you didn't believe me."

"I—" I started.

"You couldn't have believed me. I don't blame you. I didn't even believe me. But still, I know my memory was real." I shook my head slowly, wishing he didn't sound so crazy. "It was our first kiss," he went on.

"But our first kiss was months ago," I protested. "In the park near my house."

"That was *this* time," he said, giving me a moment to absorb his meaning. "I'm talking about a time before."

"You mean—" I couldn't even find the words to explain

what I thought he was trying to say. You think "there was a time—for us—before this one?"

He nodded, and I made a move to step out of his embrace. But he held me tight. "Stay," he said. "Please."

I stayed.

And he began to tell me a story that came out like a confession. I think it was a relief to him to finally say it all out loud. How long had this been eating away at him?

"Like I said, in that time before, tonight was our first kiss," he began. "Things didn't happen as fast for us then. I'd had a crush on you since the day you walked into physics, since you'd smiled at me when I was mowing your neighbor's yard. But I didn't think there was a chance you'd ever like me. You were so smart. You worked so hard in school."

I shivered, and without asking, he shrugged his arms out of his jacket and wrapped it around my shoulders. He pushed the hair off my temples. "I started going to the library, just to be near you. And we'd talk. We got to be friends. I'd tell you these things I'd never told anyone. I told you about my mom and dad. I told you stuff about Tommy and Wendell, stuff I wouldn't generally tell my other friends. You told me about your mom and dad. One time, you got really mad about some current events thing. It blew my mind how much you cared about the stuff I thought of as 'the news,' just endless static.

"You made this big deal about how I shouldn't join the marines, and it was annoying but also kind of nice that you cared. I always felt like you saw the best parts of me. You waited for them to float to the surface, I guess. You trusted that they were there. Even when I was being kind of a dick."

"You were a dick?"

He laughed. I laughed. And then out of nowhere I felt myself tearing up. How could I feel so close to him when what he was telling me ought to be pushing me away?

I swiped at what I knew was my mascara running some more, and he said, "Don't bother." When I kept bothering anyway, he said, "You're cute."

"And you're amazing," I gushed without thinking.

"No, you are," he said. "Back when I didn't know if you liked me," he went on, "back in that other time, you tossed off this thing once. You said you liked how different I was from everyone else you knew. And I held on to that comment. I held on to it tight. It gave me the courage to ask you to the dance, to kiss you up here in the dark."

He was looking straight at me now, and before I could raise the questions that felt like they belonged in books or movies instead of my real life—the crazy details—Lucas kissed me.

I asked myself, *Do I remember this? Has this happened before?* And then it didn't matter if I believed him because I was there on the roof of the gym, with Lucas holding my face in his hands, tears streaming down his cheeks, saying, "I want this to be real. This is what I want to be real."

"Lucas?" All I wanted was for him to know he could trust me. If we could just get there, I thought, I'd worry about the rest later. "Please tell me what's happening to you, how what you're saying is possible."

The orange light shimmering up from the parking lot, the low voices of the kids wrapping around the bulkhead, the wool of Lucas's jacket scratching my bare neck, the awareness my lips still carried of having been kissed hard—these sensations all knit themselves together. Tenuous reaching. Listening for distant bells. I felt for a moment that maybe he didn't have to tell me. Maybe I already knew. Or I almost knew.

Lucas took my right hand in both of his and held it up to his chest. It would have looked melodramatic if he hadn't been so completely serious about it. "Juliet," he said. "I've tried to ignore it, or make it go away, but I can't anymore."

"Make what go away?" I said.

He looked from side to side, then said, "I can't tell you here."

chapter sixteen

When Rosemary saw me leaving with Lucas, she passed her Capri Sun to Dexter and hurried over. "Are you okay?" she said.

"I'll call you later," I said. I think she assumed we were continuing some kind of breakup fight and just trying to find a spot to have it where no one could hear.

But we weren't continuing a breakup fight. We weren't doing anything. We didn't talk or even touch on the way out of the dance, or on the way across the wet parking lot, or in his car, which was cold when we first got inside. He drove, and I didn't ask him where he was going. He was jiggling his hand on the steering wheel, and at one point I leaned over and covered it with mine. "Sorry," he said, and he looked more than sorry. He looked miserable, terrified. I was pretty scared myself.

"What is it?" I said.

He shook his head. "I shouldn't be driving when I tell you this."

I think it was then that I realized he didn't know where he was going. "Pull over," I said, pointing to a church on the right. I don't know how I managed to sound so calm. I felt like someone had twisted my insides like so much spaghetti. "That parking lot. Pull over there."

The church's empty lot faced the woods, and our headlights were shining into a desolate patch of trees and brush littered with garbage—it was a good place to stash a body, I remember thinking.

Lucas turned to face me. He opened his mouth and then closed it before starting. "I thought I could tell you, but I just can't," he said. "It's too nuts. You're going to think I'm crazier than you already do." He paused, then laughed.

I started to reach out to him but stopped myself. He looked so wound up I was worried something would spring loose and go flying if I so much as grazed the back of his hand. "Lucas," I said firmly, as if I needed to wake him up.

He fumbled around for a tape and fed it into the stereo. "I need noise," he said. "Something against this." He tapped his temple.

Then he pressed PLAY.

The song that came on was one I'd never heard before, but it was beautiful. I've tried to find it but have never been able to track it down. A piano. A woman singing about the ocean, about longing, about a lighthouse, about things that used to be and are now gone.

"My mom used to sing this when I was a kid," Lucas said. "She had it on a record, and I made a tape of it the other day." He was biting his lip.

"Lucas," I said. "You can tell me what you think is happening."

"If I do," he warned, momentarily lowering his face into outstretched fingers, "you're going to want to get out of this car, walk back to your safe little house and your mom, go off to become a lawyer or whatever, go to some fancy college. You'll wish I really had broken up with you earlier."

"Lucas," I confessed. "I love you."

That was something we hadn't said to each other before, but I just blurted it out. I wanted him to know. He looked up at me.

"I—" he started. "You *love* me?"

"We don't have to talk about it." I was hoping to sound casual in spite of the fact that I was writhing in embarrassment. Why had I introduced the word "love"? "Sorry," I said. "Forget it. Just tell me your dream."

"Juliet—" He smiled. "I can't believe you just said that."

"It's okay if you don't feel it too," I said, a lie.

"You think I *don't* love you?"

Instead of answering him, I looked down at my hands. I was still wearing Lucas's jacket, and I was pinching the cuffs between my palms and my fingers.

"Juliet, don't you see?" he said. "It's been me, all along, loving you. I tried to hold back, to slow this down. That's why I haven't said the words. But I have thought them. I think them all the time. Frankly, they're not big enough. Because I don't just love you. I . . . I *really* love you."

I ventured a direct look at him now and was rewarded with a flood of warmth that traveled straight from my chest through the rest of my body.

"Jules, every time I glance up and see you—when you come into a room—I love everything about you. Just during this conversation, I'm loving you. I'm *thinking* about how much I love you. I love the sound of your voice, the things you say, the way your eyes move, that thing you do with your mouth when you're annoyed. I love your hands. I even love the way you wreck your own jokes by laughing before you get to the punch lines. I love you, okay? If I didn't love you so much, I'm not sure any of this would be happening."

My face was burning. My eyes were tearing up. "Okay," I said.

"Okay," he said right back, and then, not letting go of my eyes with his own: "Can I tell you now?" I nodded. I felt safe with him again. At least, for now.

He was a soldier in that war, he began, in the city with the flat roofs, the one he'd dreamed about, the one where the buildings were the color of sand.

I told myself he was describing a dream, but he talked about it as if it were real. As if he were remembering something that had happened to him just the other day.

He told me that it was hot and dry in a way he'd never quite experienced, and he was sweating under his body armor. "We were heading into an apartment building," he went on. "We were looking for someone, a guy in hiding. It looked like the neighborhood was deserted, but we knew there were snipers. We knew there were people inside the buildings too. They hid when they saw soldiers."

"It sounds like a movie," I said, because I had to say something. I had to remind myself that it couldn't be real.

But I immediately wished I'd left it alone. Lucas broke away from me, moving his gaze out toward the headlights shining on the scary woods, and said, "Juliet, I can read Arabic."

I honestly thought I'd heard him wrong. And at the same time, I felt my insides clench, as if they were being squeezed by an invisible hand.

"In the dream, there were signs on the stores and stuff. You know those swirly lines with the dots and stuff? That's what Arabic looks like."

"I know what it looks like."

"I didn't realize I could read the signs until last week. I woke up from the dream and found myself thinking about this blue-painted storefront. And I knew it was a bakery. I knew what the letters said."

"You've had this dream more than once?"

He laughed bitterly. "I've been having it over and over again. All fall. And it's killing me. I can't describe what's so terrifying about it, but I wake up with my heart beating so hard it's like I've got an animal trapped in there or something. My whole body is soaked in sweat."

"You can read Arabic." By stating this simply, I was giving him a chance to hear how ridiculous it sounded and take it back.

"I can speak it a little too. Want to hear some?"

"No," I said, pressing my fingers against the tops of my cheekbones, where I felt a sudden pressure.

"'Hello' is *as-salāmu 'alaykum*," Lucas told me. "*Shukran* is 'thank you.' I think the one I knew the best was *Lā ataka-lam 'arabi*. It means 'I don't speak Arabic.'"

I didn't say anything. I wanted to put my fingers in my ears, but I didn't. If I admitted the outrageous ideas coming out of Lucas's mouth scared me, I'd be admitting there was even a chance that they could be real. There wasn't one.

"And the other day," he went on, "in math, I caught myself worrying that the body armor I was wearing might be defective, and I was like *Wha*—? *Where did* that *come from?* But then I realized I knew where. There would be this rumor that some government contractor no one wanted to piss off had cut corners. It drove us crazy."

"But that wasn't in the dream." I was thinking that if I could find holes in his story, I could make him stop believing before he made me begin.

"That's what I'm trying to tell you. I'm not always dreaming."

"So you're adding stuff to the dream," I said. "It's *changing*?"

"Juliet," Lucas said. "I don't think it *is* a dream."

He gave me a few seconds to take in what he meant, but as they ticked by, I realized I was going to need more than seconds. A minute? A year? A lobotomy?

"This is what you're afraid is going to make me get out of the car and walk home?"

Lucas nodded.

And here's the thing: it didn't make me want to get out of the car and walk home. It scared me so much I couldn't think of going anywhere. The windshield had steamed up, and it occurred to me we wouldn't be able to see if anyone was coming toward us. I locked my door.

Lucas took my hand. His palm was damp.

"Every time I wake up, I remember more." His voice was husky, the words tumbling out faster and faster, like a runaway car heading downhill. "The memories come out in flashes. I can remember a Thanksgiving when I ate turkey out of a can, but I can't remember why, or where I was. I remember the day I enlisted, but I don't remember basic training."

"How do you even know there was a basic training to remember?"

Lucas shrugged, embarrassed. "I just do." Then: "You know Sanjay Shah?"

"The freshman?" I asked, even though there was only one Sanjay in our school. I knew him because he'd signed up for newspaper so he could write a column on hip-hop, and resigned after Robin Sipe had explained that 1) freshmen covered student council meetings and JV sports, and 2) no one in our school listened to hip-hop. "I know him a little."

"Well, I don't know him at all, but two weeks ago I was hanging out in the library, thanks to you, and I ran into him by the magazines. I realized I knew his name. I knew that he has a little sister. I knew what his mom looks like. And I knew that his house is going to burn down."

"His house burns down?" I repeated dumbly.

"To the ground. This year sometime. I remember the family loses everything."

Here's what I was thinking: *Not true. Not possible.* I was thinking that this was the sign that Lucas had to be wrong. No one could tell whose house was going to burn down and when.

"I've even approached him, like, three times to tell him. But every time I get close, I'm like, *What the heck am I doing? He's not going to believe me. No one would believe me.*" He looked at me, suddenly pleading, hopeless. "You *love* me and you don't believe me."

Believe him? How could I when I didn't even understand what he was trying to tell me?

"Do you remember anything else? About that fire?"

"I remember that it happens when it's cold out. I remember looking at the house afterward. It was completely destroyed. I remember staring at the charred boiler. The cement slab where the garage was. How parts of their car melted onto the driveway, so you could see this bubble of colored plastic where the brake lights used to be."

These details didn't sound like things you could just make up. "Can you remember anything else like that? What about something from the news? Something that's specific to a particular time?"

He smiled sheepishly. "You know I'm not the biggest current events guy, not like you. But I did remember this thing about Newt Gingrich."

"The Contract with America guy?"

"I guess so. The other day when you were reading the paper in the library, I remembered something that happens years from now. I must have been on a train or a bus or something and someone had left a copy of the *New York Times* behind. I picked it up and there was an article about what Gingrich was up to, and I swear I remember thinking, *Juliet isn't going to like this.*"

"You remember thinking about *me* in the future?" I said. "What else do you remember about me?" I wasn't any closer to believing him, but I was getting curious. A story doesn't have to be true for you to want to find out what happens. "What *happens* to me?"

He suddenly clammed up. "I don't really know," he said, frowning.

"You don't know?" I squinted at him, not letting him off the hook. "Or you just don't want to tell me?" I was seized by panic. "Lucas, does something bad happen to me?" He looked pained. "To my mom?"

"No!" he said. "You're fine." But I guess he could see that his answer wasn't satisfactory, and he took pity on me. "If you have to know, we break up."

"Oh." And it wasn't like I thought we were getting married or anything. It was just that this news that there was a very clear expiration date on our relationship—even if I didn't credit the source—made me feel funny. And shy. "When?" I asked.

"When you go to college."

"Why?"

"Are you sure you want to hear this?"

I wasn't sure, but I shrugged.

"Okay." He took a deep breath. "I don't know exactly when, but I remember writing you an email."

"An email?" I said. "Like, on a computer?" My dad had email at the hospital. I'd listen as his modem dialed in once a day when he checked it. And I think my mom's museum had it too, an account the administrative offices shared so they could communicate with museums in Europe when the fax was down.

"Computers get really different," Lucas explained. "But yeah, an email breakup wasn't cool. I remember thinking that we should break up in person but being too pissed off at you to care."

I said nothing. I *didn't* want to hear about Lucas being pissed off. About Lucas not caring. I reminded myself . . . this wasn't real. This couldn't be.

"Something else I remember," Lucas went on. "I stopped by the MEPS the other day and I had this flash. You know those little offices in the back? I remembered that the one I went through when I enlisted was the second one, and then I remembered that my dad was in a chair out in the front, where you can still hear all the mall music and smell the Cinnabon. And I remember that my mom didn't come. I remember that she was upset with my dad, that she made him move out. That they separate and eventually get a divorce."

"Lucas," I said. Couldn't he see that he was mourning a loss that existed only in his head? "It isn't possible for you to *remember* things that haven't happened yet. This can't be true."

"Christmas!" he said, plowing forward. "You're going to give me a watch with my initials and the number seventeen"—his jersey number—"engraved on the back."

And I guess it just goes to show how desperate I was not to believe him that the fact that I had just ordered that watch at the jeweler's the week before—and there was no way Lucas could have been aware of that—did nothing to convince me.

"I'm wearing that watch in the desert dream," he went on, tapping his wrist with two fingers as if he could feel the phantom watch there still. "I must have kept it." He smiled ruefully. "It sure took a lickin'."

I swallowed. "Lucas, I don't believe this. I can't."

He raised his eyebrows. "Jules, I've told you. I don't believe it either," he said. "I mostly sit around listing the zillion ways it can't be true. But whether or not you or I want to believe it, it's happening. It's real."

My mind was whirling, looking for some way to convince him. "Maybe I was right before," I said. "Maybe this is just a psychological thing. Have you thought about that? It could be fear. It could just be that you're afraid to join the marines, so you're having anxiety dreams."

Lucas gave me the withering look he reserved for our more heated conversations about the marines. "I didn't hate being a soldier, Juliet."

I rubbed a circle in the steamed-up window so I could see out.

Lucas leaned across me to crank the window down an inch. Practical as the gesture was, his body felt good on mine, heavy and reassuring. He was *here*. That was a fact. No matter what he thought or said or imagined, we were in the car now. I was sixteen years old. He was seventeen. Those facts were incontrovertible.

"The first memory, the memory of kissing you on the roof—it came to me that day in physics. When you looked at me, I remembered kissing you. It wasn't like I was just thinking about doing it, or wanting to—I swear to you, Juliet, I knew I'd *already* done it. I knew I'd kissed you up on that roof in the dark, leaning against the bulkhead. I knew you were wearing a dress and that it was cloudy. The memory kind of knocked me out for a second, it was so strong.

"I told you you were wearing a dress. I could have told you you were wearing my jacket on top of it, about the wall we were leaning up against. I could have told you what those bricks felt like against my palms. I could have told you that it had just stopped raining. I could have told you I had a vodka shot in a Capri Sun. I think I've been carrying that memory—you—in here." He thumped his chest. "For years and years."

That was when I opened the car door. I stood up in the cold, damp night air. The woods were still there, the headlights shining on the brambles and the mess of crooked, fallen trees. I felt myself breathing heavily. I remember hugging myself, my back up against the car. I so wanted not to believe Lucas. I felt like a fool. I had told him I loved him, and now I didn't know who he was.

He got out too and came around to my side of the car, offering himself. He could have pulled me toward him and

I would have gone, but he let me decide. He was looking down, and his face—what I could see of it, the tip of his chin, the line where his forehead met his hair—was ghostly white.

I moved as close to him as I could without touching him. "Juliet," he said. "I think I've come back here. From somewhere far away. I don't know how. But I do know why. I've come back here for you."

chapter seventeen

My mom always says that she fell in love with my dad's intensity, but in the end, it's what drove them apart. As I've gotten older, she's explained more. If he was frustrated at work, he couldn't speak to her, she told me. At home, he'd be stone silent in the evening, eating like a robot, then marching upstairs and lying on the bed until his brain had worked out a new theory or potential solution. Otherwise, he wouldn't move or speak until morning.

He hasn't changed. When I visit him every summer, he doesn't stop working. My choices are to hang out in his house, surfing cable and reading magazines, or to join him at the hospital, putting on a white coat and following him on rounds, where I'm introduced as a student—probably not in line with hospital regulations, but doctors like my dad tend to do whatever they want. Mostly the residents, nurses, interns, students, orderlies, and even the patients go about their business without seeming to notice me, but some ask me questions like I'm an adult. When I tell them I'm planning to be a lawyer one day, they make jokes about how I can sue my dad. The hospital is pretty cool, actually, once you get past the whole everyone-here-has-cancer aspect of his job.

But there's only so much hospital observation I can take, and one morning a couple of years ago, I set my alarm for three-forty-five and waited for my dad in the little rock garden he has instead of a lawn because he doesn't want to take care of anything. When he came outside and saw me shivering in the chilly darkness in my shorts and high-tops, he figured out pretty quickly what I had in mind. Without speaking, we ran together, my dad slowing his pace to match mine. I remember there were still stars in the sky. We ran on the beach and through the streets of his little town, and though my dad is not the kind of guy who will admit he likes company, that afternoon he came home from work with a pair of real running shoes in my size.

Now when I run, I channel my dad, his way of thinking. My thoughts organize themselves into a rhythm that actually helps me to keep running. And the morning after the Fall Ball, a little rational analysis was definitely called for. I pulled my hair back into a ponytail, threw on a light fleece and leggings, and headed out while my mom was still pushing buttons on the coffeemaker.

But my thoughts kept stopping me. I'd remember something Lucas had said the night before, or the way I felt when he was talking, and it was like someone had just tied sandbags to my ankles. I actually walked part of my route, feeling stiff and short of breath.

Back home, my mom told me that both Lucas and Rosemary had called. I didn't call either one back. I made myself a peanut butter and jelly sandwich, hopped on my bike, and took off.

When I'm in the library, I feel the way I imagine Lucas does in the MEPS—like the physical space holds the secrets of my future. The books tell me what has happened in the world, what might happen to me, what I can become.

I love our town library in particular. I love the way it smells of clean carpet and furniture polish and the dust-meets-chemical odor the microfiche readers emit. I love the librarians' low voices, the muted thumping of the wood chairs against the tables, the water fountain gurgling politely just inside the door.

That morning, I headed straight for the card catalog, where I identified Library of Congress subjects that led me to other cards in other drawers and eventually to a new computer system that used keyword terms to find articles in the *New York Times* and the *Washington Post* as well as books. I searched "war + Iraq + snipers." I searched "head injury + hallucinations" and learned that the proper term for what Lucas thought was happening was "delusion." I saw medical terms I'd learned from my dad combined with concepts like "recovered memory," things I'd read about in the news.

When I prep for debate, I take all the research points I've organized on index cards and arrange them in patterns, grouping them around facts, assertions, logical conclusions, and links. I make them into a web, a well-thumbed dictionary, a map where lines of inferences lead me from fact to fact to fact.

I did that now, only without index cards, the points of evidence organizing themselves in my brain alone. They were too complex to write down. There were too many lines. I knew they all led somewhere, but I wasn't yet sure where.

I looked up stuff I've heard physicists on *Nova* try to describe—about the way the universe bends backward and things happen to space and time. I paged through magazines the librarians pulled from archived boxes in the back. I gathered research points on ghosts and memory and time travel. I Xeroxed stuff. I underlined. I jotted down facts in a notebook. I read. And read and read and read. I left my research only when I was so starving I had to go outside to wolf down my sandwich.

It was already dark, and when I checked my watch, I saw that it was after four in the afternoon. I shivered, hugging myself in my too-light jacket. Snow had started to fall. This wasn't the first of the season, and the leaves had been off the trees already for weeks, but this time, it felt like winter.

When I got home, my mom informed me that Lucas had called again. I didn't call him. Instead, I got back on my bike. I wore my ski goggles under my helmet and a scarf. I looked like the Red Baron, and I found myself laughing out loud at this idea as I rode.

I needed Rosemary, I'd decided. I would tell her everything. Finally. She was my best friend. I should trust *her*, not Lucas. I should be honest with her.

And I would be honest. I would explain how Lucas could

read Arabic. About his crying in his sleep. I would tell her how he remembered the dress before he saw the dress. I'd tell her how he said his parents were going to separate. About the watch. About the fire at Sanjay Shah's house. I would tell her about the dreams. The buildings with flat roofs in a city the color of sand. The war. Everything I'd learned in the library. I would tell her how Lucas struggled not to tell me. How he tried to run. How I hadn't let him go.

She would read over my notes. She would give me an A-plus for research. She would know what they meant. She always knew; she was always sure. She would decide whether Lucas was crazy. And then she would tell me how to save him.

Rosemary lived at the top of what everyone called Mansion Mountain in a white house with columns. The rooms in the front had high ceilings, dark rugs, white couches, heavy drapes at the windows. These rooms were for guests and Rosemary's rich grandparents, the ones who spent their winters in Aruba.

In the back of the house, it was all tennis and dogs. Tangled leashes and worn collars, chewed-up tennis shoes, tennis balls rolling around under cabinets, dogs rolling under chairs, sleeping with tennis balls grasped gently in their mouths. Tennis balls crowned the mail pile, held up a broken table leg, mixed with the apples and oranges in the fruit bowl, and even, bizarrely, took pride of place in the door of the fridge where the ketchup and salad dressings are supposed to go.

The tennis court itself—of course the Fields have

one—was in the yard behind the pool and the flower beds, and when I got there, Rose had just finished playing a game with her dad, who was now taking on her little brother under the lights. On weekends, he would do that, play one kid after another. The snow meant nothing. The Fields played tennis all year round—in the winter, Dr. Field put a plow attachment on the riding lawn mower and cleared the court. Rosemary and her siblings got enlisted to follow behind, pushing off the remaining puddles with a broom.

I met up with Rosemary under the pergola next to the court. She wiped her neck and face with a gym towel and shrugged into a warm-up jacket.

"We need to talk," I said, all business.

"No kidding," she said. "I've been calling you all day." She poured us each a hot cider from a samovar on the same table where ice water was served in the summer, then gestured to a pair of chaise longues. I sat, my legs wrapped in a wool blanket with a Wimbledon logo, and watched Rosemary's little brother, Patrick, failing to hold his serve. Being at Rosemary's house—being with Rosemary period—was like stepping into another world.

"So?" she said.

And in spite of the fact that I'd been rehearsing this conversation in my mind for the last hour, I found I didn't know what to say. I looked down into the steaming mug between my hands, watching the tiny bubbles trapped in the foam burst one by one.

"Juliet?" Rose prodded.

Flushed from tennis, she sat sideways on the chaise with

her legs spread apart, her elbows resting on her knees, the towel still in her hands. There was snow falling behind her, caught in the lights shining down on the court, and as I looked at her—registered her athletic sureness, the solidity of her world—I realized she was going to think I was crazy.

"So what happened last night? Did you and Lucas break up?"

"No," I said, but had we? With Rosemary asking so directly, I wasn't sure of even this basic fact. Last night, I hadn't told him whether I believed him. He'd stood away from me outside his car in the church parking lot, and when he could have pulled me toward him, he hadn't. He'd waited for me to make a move. He'd left the decision up to me. And I hadn't made one.

But maybe this was me making one now: "He's mad at me about the marines." For a second, I was so surprised at the lie that had come out of my mouth that I just sat there, letting the words settle. Then I continued. "I keep trying to get him to understand that he's throwing his life away, and he told me I had to stop or we would have to break up."

Did Rose know I was lying? She looked at me straight and even, shaking her head. "Don't let him blackmail you," she said. "You get to have opinions."

She knew I was lying. I'm sure of it. But I think she also knew that there are times to confront your friends and times to give them some room. She changed the subject. "Did I tell you?" she said. "Dex is a huge dork. Listen to this. Last night, we got to the supposed party at Nunchuck's and nothing was going on. Dex had gotten bad information. We ended up at 7-Eleven for Slurpees at one in the morning. He bought me a Snickers bar and then he ate it."

"That's kind of . . . sweet?"

"Yep," Rosemary answered, meaning no.

And then Rosemary lay back on the chaise, looked out at the lights shining down on the court, and held her hands out in front of her as if she was asking the universe a question.

"It looks like fun, what you and Lucas have. I guess I just wanted that too."

I stared. Rosemary and I have never been the kind of friends who become clones, who go for that let's-be-twinsies double-dating thing. She was talking about something deeper.

"Okay," I said. "But Dex?"

"Like I said, it looks like fun," she went on. "But me, with Dex? It wasn't fun. Big surprise, right? You have to feel it for real."

"At least Dex isn't a stalker like Jason," I tried.

"Actually, I should tell you . . . ," Rosemary said, her voice trailing off. "I talked to him this morning."

"Who? Jason?"

"I don't know what came over me. He always calls on Sundays because I once told him that I don't go to church with my parents. I knew it was him and I picked up the phone anyway."

"Rosemary!"

She pulled her long, straight ponytail over her shoulder and began to inspect her hair for split ends. "I was bored!

You abandoned me to high-school-boy hell. And Jason's not *that* bad. The necklace was romantic."

"You've got to be kidding me," I said, and she dropped her ponytail. "Rosemary, he's crazy."

"I know, I know. It was a mistake. Jules, he was so *gross*," she went on. "Soooo desperate. And you know what I noticed? All he does is tell me how much he misses me, but when I open my mouth to say something, he doesn't even listen. He just starts in on how much pain *he's* in. Him, him, him."

She laughed. And then her sigh, which was sad, opened a window. A window for me to speak through. Or maybe jump out of.

"I told Lucas I loved him last night," I said as fast as I could. And wished immediately I'd spoken even faster. I wished I'd said it so fast that I could get credit for telling her without having her actually be able to understand. "I told him I loved him, and I meant it. Which I thought would be scary, but wasn't. What *is* scary is that I realized last night that I couldn't handle it if we broke up. If something happened. If I lost him."

I was expecting her to be horrified. But instead, all she said was "I've never felt that way."

"Then maybe you're lucky," I said. "Because I feel like I've somehow lost control. I have no power over whether or not I'm happy."

Rosemary sat up again and lifted her cider to her lips. Blowing on its hot surface, she said without looking at me, "I hear you."

"You do?"

"I'm sort of jealous." She raised her eyebrows in a gesture that acknowledged the persistent irony of life. "But at the same time, I can see what you've gotten yourself into, and it's not good, Jules. I've been worried about this for a while. You should break up with him."

"Break *up* with him?" I honestly was wondering if I'd misheard her.

"Isn't that why you came over? To get me to tell you that?"

"No!"

"Come on."

"Breaking up with him wasn't even remotely on my radar."

"But, Juliet," she said. "How can you not break up with him?"

I didn't say anything then. I was trying not to get mad at Rosemary, but here's the thing: I *was* getting mad at Rosemary. I'd thought she could save Lucas, not get rid of him.

And what if she was right?

I thought about the pages and pages of notes I'd taken that day. I'd been so thorough, keeping my handwriting legible and even, my bullet points logically ordered into headings, quotes, subpoints. I'd kept careful track of the sources I was citing. I'd felt all day that I was making sense of what was happening. But maybe I was just using all that paper and ink to avoid the cold, hard truth: Lucas was crazy. And I was crazy too for not walking away as soon as I knew.

Rosemary put her mug back down on the bricks. She

was staring at me like she'd just figured something out and wished she hadn't.

"What?" I asked.

"It's nothing."

"Come on."

"Okay," she said, and sighed. "I'll tell you because it's plain as day to me and has been for some time. This guy is going to break your heart."

My mom was already in her bathrobe, drinking sherry and eating a bowl of vanilla ice cream when I came in the back door. As it always did after I'd been at Rose's, my own house felt small.

My mom looked positively lost inside her fleecy white robe. And for the first time in maybe my whole life, I thought to ask: *What in the world had happened to my mom after my dad left? How had she let her world get so predictable and safe? Didn't she want . . . well . . . more?*

There must have been something in the way I was looking at her that she could read, because she squinted at me hard and then she said, as if she were joking, and also as if she were picking up a conversation where we had left off, "It would be fine with me, you know, if you just never grew up at all. No one here needs you to move on."

chapter eighteen

I was grabbing books out of my locker after homeroom Monday when I heard two kids talking as they passed me on their way to first period. "—a freshman?"

"Yeah. He goes here."

"That kid whose house burned down?"

Robin Sipe was a few steps behind them. "Hey!" I called to her. "What's going on?"

"You didn't hear?" She was talking fast, the way she does when she's nervous before a test or working on a story for the paper. "That little freshman who wanted to write a hip-hop column," she said. "Sanjay Shah. Juliet—his house. Last night, it burned down. In two hours, the fire was *that* hot. Everything they own is gone. They're lucky they got out alive."

"Sanjay Shah's house burned down." With each word, I was trying to grab hold of something, to gain some control over what I was hearing.

"Didn't you notice the smell this morning?" Robin continued. "He lives right near here. Go out on the football field—you can still smell the smoke. That's my lead. I'll write the story. We can move some stuff around to make space for it on the front page."

I shook my head. I felt myself falling back against my locker, then scooting down into a squat, right there in the hall, my back pressed up against the cool metal. The bell for first period rang. "Hey," Robin asked. "Are you okay?"

I wasn't, but I nodded.

Sanjay. I barely knew him, but suddenly, he'd become hyperreal to me. What would it feel like to be standing in the street in front of your burning house, shivering in pajamas, knowing that life as you knew it is over?

What would it be like to be Lucas, stumbling over memories of a future no one else could see?

And then it was no longer Sanjay Shah in my imagination, shivering in his pajamas. It was Lucas locked out in the cold.

Lucas wasn't in physics. He wasn't at lunch. After school, Mr. Mildred asked me to stay late to go through some back issues of *Foreign Affairs*, but when he saw the look of abject panic on my face, he took his question back without making me come up with an excuse.

Rosemary gave me a ride home, and I sat for a minute in the car before I got out.

"You know, Jules," she said, staring ahead and trying to sound neutral, like she was preparing a general observation on the nature of life. "Guys can be dicks. You can't stop that. But what you *can* do"—she paused here for dramatic effect—"is not make yourself vulnerable to their dickishness. Don't open yourself up to the pain."

There might have been a time pre-Lucas when her comment would've made sense to me. Or a time when it would've made me mad. Even the day before, I probably could have summoned the energy to respond with sarcasm, saying something along the lines of "Maybe you should give that advice to Dex."

But in the mood I was in now, I just nodded, thinking that she was probably right but it was too late for me. I was beyond help. I was already in too deep.

Once inside, I proceeded through my afternoon as if on autopilot. I brought my usual snack—Wheat Thins and a Diet Coke—upstairs. I sat on my usual spot on the floor, my back against the bed, my books spread out around me. I opened my notebook. I was supposed to be writing a paper on *The Scarlet Letter,* but I couldn't think of a single word past "In Nathaniel Hawthorne's *The Scarlet Letter,* images of New England as a wilderness . . ." *What?* I wondered. *Images abound? Images tell the story? Images give us the impression that the place is still wild?* I didn't know. I didn't care.

When the doorbell rang, I ran downstairs so fast one of my feet nearly slipped off a step. Breathless, I yanked open the door. It slammed into the wall. I think something broke. Like, the wall. Then there Lucas was. He looked exhausted. Pale. Was he sick? His eyes were red and his lips looked strangely swollen.

He leaned forward like he was trying to home in on a distant radio signal, then put a foot up onto the threshold but didn't put his weight on it. "Come in," I said, and took a step back to give him room to enter. There was a stiffness to his gait as he swung his body inside.

"Did you hurt yourself?"

"Sore from practice."

"You're lying."

"Okay," he conceded.

"You skipped school."

"My head hurts. It's been hurting all day."

"Sanjay?" I said.

"I know." Lucas leaned against the wall right under the stairs, as if he didn't have the strength to make it into the kitchen.

"Lucas—" I started, but he cut me off.

"If you want me to take it all back, I can try," he said. "I don't know if I can pull it off, but I could maybe keep the weirdness away from you." His hands were pushed into the front pockets of his jeans, his arms akimbo. "And if you want to just break up with me, that's okay. I'll make it easy on you. I was thinking I should just disappear. Leave town."

He finished this speech and looked down at the fake brick linoleum that my mom always hated and was waiting to get the money to replace.

"I don't want you to go away," I said. I reached a hand out to hold his. "I—"

He wasn't to blame for Sanjay, I wanted to tell him, but

just then I heard the distinctive churn of my mother's car turning into the driveway. We didn't have time. "Will you stay?" I said. "For dinner?"

"I don't know," Lucas said. "I don't know if that's a good idea."

"Is it your headache?"

"It's not that," he said. "It's— Juliet, do you *want* me to stay? Aren't you too freaked out? Don't you think I'm nuts?"

The engine of my mom's car was off now. I could hear her shoes clicking on the path from the driveway. Now she was opening the back door, its rubber weather strip sucking on the floor. "I want you to stay."

He was still looking at me as my mom said, "Hello, Lucas!" She had a tendency to speak loudly to him, as if he were deaf. "Are you staying for dinner?"

"Can he?" I asked.

Did my mom see the look of relief on Lucas's face when I asked that question? Did she notice our trembling hands as we helped her chop peppers and onions for a stir-fry? That we laughed a little too hard at jokes and were shy with each other in a way we hadn't been in a long time?

If she did, she didn't say a word.

After dinner, Lucas went home, and I managed to finish that sentence about *The Scarlet Letter*. Then I wrote another one, and another, until the paper was complete, typed, proofread, stapled, ready to go. I copied some debate notes onto index cards, perfecting my super-neat, tiny writing— part of winning was being able to read your own quotes on the fly. I brushed my teeth. I used my mom's nighttime face cream. I cut my fingernails and laid my clothes for the next day out on a chair.

Then, pulling back the covers, I found a letter under my pillow. Lucas's chicken scratch filled only the first few lines of the notebook paper he'd written on.

> *Dear Juliet,*
>
> *I guess the thing about all this, what I was trying to tell you the other night, is that I am not the same guy I was before. I am me, but there's more. Seeing the future, seeing my future, I'm learning a lot. I won't do things the same way again. I love you.*
>
> *If some guy shows up and treats you the way I treated you before, I'm going to break his jaw.*
>
> *But . . . no pressure.*
>
> *And to set the record straight, by the time I wrote that breakup letter, you were long gone. You had a good life. You had all the things you want. You didn't need me.*
>
> *Love,*
> *Lucas*

Okay.

I wept.

Heavy, hiccuping, graceless tears.

I buried my face in my pillow and nearly suffocated myself with sobs. Rosemary was right. My heart was going to be broken. But I didn't care. I wanted it this way.

chapter nineteen

Junior year. Winter term. This was the time for me to be studying as hard as I could. Like Robin Sipe, I should have been furiously editing my newspaper columns, making copies for college portfolios. I should have been mining the Sanjay Shah food and clothing drive for personal essay material. I should have been living and breathing debate. Already there had been a tournament at a high school in Boston, and during December I traveled with the team to Exeter, Providence, and White Plains.

But none of those things held my attention. What did? Lucas. Hockey. Boys beating the living crap out of each other in the guise of an organized winter sport. That was all my brain could absorb.

I fell in love with hockey's can't-look-away energy. Every game is like a train wreck in slow motion. Except it's not in slow motion. It's fast. And it's brutal. Hockey players strap what are essentially knives to their feet. They carry sticks. They hit the puck so hard it becomes a bullet—it's a lethal weapon. If not for the helmets, someone on the team would end up dead before the end of every game. Often when there was a break in play, I realized I'd been holding my breath.

But when you're on the ice, Lucas told me, you can't afford to feel fear. Keeping your head in the game means not leaving yourself open to attack, not needing your teammates to rescue you—though they always will. Team is everything. It's us versus them, and whatever you have done to the other guys—even if it involves blood—you don't stick around to clean up the mess. Stopping, thinking—these make you a target. A liability to the team. Speed—not rules—is what keeps the players from getting killed. Just slip away as quickly as you rushed in.

In hockey, you are looking not at what you are doing but at the puck. Where it can go, how it can get there, who can get open to receive it. You're always seeking out this tiny black disk, and then there it is, darting off someone's skate or appearing at the end of a stick. When I started watching games, it looked like the sticks attracted the puck, like they were magnetic and the puck made of metal. It was only after I'd been watching awhile that I could see it was the other way around. I began to understand the pushing and hitting as the backdrop for the real game, which was—and Rosemary laughed her head off when I told her this—like chess. Strategic positioning. Thinking three, five, fifteen steps ahead of where you were. Speed chess.

Or maybe I just saw the game that way because I was always watching Lucas. He believed in passing, which was unusual for a high school player. I thought maybe I was the only one who noticed, but then I heard Coach O'Reilly commenting on it in a huddle, telling the others to look to Dunready setting himself up for the pass, "thinking," Coach O'Reilly said, "like I tell you, two steps ahead of the other guy." The coach called Lucas's playing "real mature."

But the way Lucas played was more than mature. It was beautiful. Lucas was graceful and sharp; he was fast and he was subtle; he crouched, he swung himself forward, he flew, he stopped on a dime. Just seeing his name on the jersey—and his number, 17—was enough to send shivers down my spine.

Meanwhile, in the month of December, I could have filled a book with the transcripts of conversations I wasn't having. My mom wasn't bringing up the subject of Lucas and I wasn't either. Rose wasn't mentioning Jason and I didn't ask her about Dex. Even when I found them outside the gym doors at the top of the parking lot, their heads bowed over the shared headphones on Dex's Walkman, I said nothing. Even when Dex got drunk and asked me point-blank if he had a chance with Rosemary, I shrugged and walked away. Lucas wasn't talking either. He didn't once mention his memories or his dreams. I think he could tell I wasn't ready.

Here's what we *were* talking about: Lucas spent hours explaining hockey rules, hockey moves, hockey tradition. Rosemary's mom adopted yet another dog, and Rosemary started carrying a lint roller everywhere, using it obsessively and pulling off another masking-tape layer when she saw so much as a single hair on her clothes. Dex got accepted early decision to Boston College, and Rosemary forced him to tell her his SAT scores. Banner news: Dex was actually smart. My mom was put in charge of the annual Christmas tree display at the museum, and I worked the coat check at the opening party. Val got buried under a company merger and we didn't see her for weeks.

By Christmas, this strange state of talking yet not talking and discussing without asking had started to feel normal. When Rosemary left for Aruba for Christmas break with her family, we said goodbye and exchanged gifts (winter-solstice pedicures, our tradition), pretending the silences weren't becoming larger than the conversations, that I wasn't itching all the time to ask her how she could be so cruel to Dex and she wasn't thinking I had given over too much of myself to Lucas.

Dex's siblings and their children arrived in town, and Lucas and I brought Tommy and Wendell over to his house to play touch football with Dex's nieces and nephews. (One of the nephews *was* the football. Lucas held the giggling two-year-old up in the air and Dex shouted, "No spiking!")

Then it was the night before I was leaving to go skiing with my mom and Val for winter break. Lucas's family was trimming their tree, so I went over to join them.

"My dad isn't going to be here," Lucas said when I got to the door—the side door by this time, since I was no longer a guest.

"Is he working?"

"He moved out." Lucas tucked his chin into his chest as he gave his answer. I could see he didn't want to talk about 1) the separation, or 2) the fact that another of his predictions had come true.

"Are you okay?" I tried. He rolled his eyes. He shrugged.

His mom seemed fine, at least. In fact, she was almost giddy. She had her hair up in a scrunchie. She'd brought home sushi. "Isn't this what you eat with your mom?" she asked, and then, not waiting for my answer: "Lucas told me." Tommy and Wendell weren't talking about the separation, but from the way they scowled at their plates and refused to accept Mrs. Dunready's assertions that the crab wasn't raw, I could see that they were mad.

Without asking, Lucas poured out two bowls of Lucky Charms and put them down on the table for the boys.

"Next time, we'll try tempura," Mrs. Dunready murmured, turning up the volume when Bing Crosby's "White Christmas" came on the radio and pulling out a box of decorations for the tree. I loved seeing their ornaments: pictures of Lucas as a little boy, pinecones decorated with glitter, colored glass balls that felt brighter than the ones we used at home.

Lucas pulled one US Marine Corps ornament after another out of the box and hung them prominently on the tree. "Must you?" Mrs. Dunready sighed, but she didn't object any further.

Before I left, I gave Lucas the watch. I didn't say, "You already know what this is." And when he said, "I promise I will wear this all my life," he didn't make it sound like he already knew he would. He broke our code of silence only once, when he buckled the watch to his wrist, held it away to show it off, and said, "It looks so *new*."

His present to me was a locket with pictures we'd taken at the photo booth at an arcade we went to with Dex and Rose. In one side, we were sticking our tongues out. In the other side, he was kissing me on the cheek. Engraved on the back was ALWAYS: 17.

Skiing was something that for the most part I did alone, as my mom had never wanted to learn and Valerie, after teaching me, had given it up in favor of shopping and hitting the spa with my mom. So over Christmas break, I spent time alone with my thoughts, missing Lucas, wondering if he was all right.

Huddled on the chairlift just after a snowstorm, I wondered if it had snowed back home. I wondered if the landscaper who gave Lucas work in the summer had called him to help clear and plow—Lucas had said he might. I imagined Lucas shoveling, stripping down to a flannel shirt and snow pants, making short work of the drifts.

But was Lucas also—at some point in the future—leading a squad of marines into a death trap, snipers hiding in doorways or behind the laundry strung up on rooftops?

Breakfast in the lodge: Valerie's dark, spiky hair, her red-framed glasses catching the light from the fire already roaring, my mom cozy in fur-trimmed boots, her hair blow-dried, makeup in place. A toasted bagel with jam. Dark coffee for my mom. Raisin bran for Val. Both of them talking crow's-feet and belly fat and laughing in a way I remembered from when I was little. All of it should have been comforting, but it wasn't. I felt claustrophobic. I wanted to go home.

Questions about college. There was a choice to be made. There was no wrong answer. Big, small; city, country. Not too close. Not too far. Liberal arts gives you the freedom to make up your mind about a career later. It teaches you to think.

But I didn't want to think. Especially about college. I just wanted to ski. I wanted to escape my mom's and Val's prying gazes and penetrating questions. They could see I wasn't the same; they didn't know why, but they knew better than to ask. Even if I'd tried to explain, they wouldn't have understood. They didn't know what I knew. They hadn't heard Lucas crying in his sleep. They had made safe choices. I was the one out in the cold, seeing the future through Lucas's eyes.

On the last afternoon of skiing, I experienced vertigo for the first time in my life. I was standing at the top of the mountain, poised for the final run of the day, and suddenly, all I could think about was falling. In fact, I felt like I was already falling, my insides dropping out as if I were on a roller coaster. I couldn't feel my feet. I couldn't remember how to move my legs. My skis felt about as useful as a pair of cinder blocks. I couldn't look down.

I was not in a good place to stop moving. It was cold, there was a strong wind, and the icy snow was stinging my cheeks. I let it, squinting at the blue in the ice, the shadows stretching over the trail as snow blew across it in sheets. The sun was sinking lower in the sky.

Lucas, where are you? I thought. I wanted him with me. He knew what it was like to feel your heart pounding in your chest and not understand why. I understood his dream now in a way I hadn't before. I saw it the way he did, bathed in the cold light of anxiety.

In my fear-addled state, the images from the dream gripped me with a new intensity. It was so visceral it was as if an older Lucas, a terrifyingly real, heavier Lucas, had stepped back in time and taken hold of me. By the throat.

The rooftops, the laundry, knowing about Sanjay's fire— I understood why it terrified him so much. And I understood that I believed him. The memories were real.

As if I could outrace them, I finally pushed myself forward over the crest of the hill. I skied in a way I had never skied before. I skied like I was being chased by demons. I crouched into a tuck, turning my skis as little as possible, leaning as far forward as I dared. My breath came quickly. Blood pounded in my ears. I could hear the edges of my skis scraping against ice. I knew if I didn't slow myself down, I would ski into a tree or lose my balance and fall. But I didn't slow down; I raced faster and faster, clinging to the hope that the hill would end soon.

That night, I had a hard time getting warm. Even when I was tucked safe into the lodge, drinking cocoa with my mom and Valerie and watching sappy movies on pay-per-view— a last-night-of-the-trip tradition dating back to when I was nine—my toes were like ice.

"Look at her," Valerie said to my mom when they reached a pause in their conversation and glanced over at me. She was half teasing in the way she always did, and I smiled, clenching my jaw to hide my chattering teeth. "She's growing up. She's nearly an adult."

"Yes," my mom said, and then she giggled, which is something she does only when Valerie is around. Also, they were drinking champagne. "My baby!" she called out, embarrassing me, clearly enjoying it. I gave her the eye roll she was looking for, but I wasn't really there.

I called Lucas later from the hallway, dragging the phone out of the room so I could have some privacy.

"There's something I need to know," I said.

"Okay."

"Your dream," I said, letting it sink in that I was breaking a month of silence on the subject. "Every time you have that dream, you see more. Your head hurts more. You remember more. So what's going to happen when you get to the end of the dream? What happens when your remembering is . . . complete?"

Lucas said nothing for a minute. "I don't know," he finally admitted. Then he sighed. "But I have an idea."

chapter twenty

The day after the holiday break, there was a huge snowstorm and school was canceled. For the first time in my life, upon hearing that particular radio announcement, my heart sank.

I hadn't seen Lucas in four days because of the ski trip, and now it looked like I wasn't going to see him that day either. I wasn't going to see anyone, as a colleague with four-wheel drive had given my mom a ride to work.

I lay in bed with my knees pulled up to my chest, feeling the return of the fear from the mountaintop. In physics, Mr. Hannihan told us the earth is spinning at a rate of a thousand miles per hour. "Imagine an amusement park ride moving that fast," he'd said. "Isn't it crazy that we don't feel a thing?" It was gravity, he explained. There are rules that govern bodies in motion, bodies in space.

But maybe those rules didn't always apply. A thousand miles per hour is awfully fast—how are any of us supposed to hold on?

The phone rang. Lucas: "I'm coming over."

"What?" I said. It was a good ten miles from my house to his, and his car was not okay in the snow.

"I've got cross-country skis."

He hung up fast, and then there he was, about an hour and a half later, standing on the snow-covered porch of my house, his cheeks burning red to match his red fleece vest, the sleeves of his chunky wool sweater rolled up to show off bare arms above black gloves, his cargo pants hanging low on his hips. He was sweating, his hair was tousled, he was breathing hard, and his eyes were bright when I stepped out into the sunshine to greet him. I breathed in his smell, the muskiness, the sweetness on his breath, the damp wool of his sweater, and I could barely stand to breathe out. I wanted every molecule to stay with me forever.

I think Lucas was feeling the same thing. He has large hands and strong arms, and without saying anything, he used the full force of them to press me against him. I looked up into his face and he leaned down to kiss me. His skin was rough and his breathing ragged.

Struggling with the releases on his ski boots, Lucas moved through the front door, still kissing me. I had my back up against the wall, and Lucas was pushing up against me, kissing me harder now. All I wanted was to kiss him back. I felt my breath catching. I wasn't thinking about anything but getting closer to him. He had his hands under my sweatshirt, on the naked skin of my back, and I wanted to strip off his vest and his sweater, to feel what his chest would be like on mine.

Stumbling, holding each other, we moved upstairs.

I wish that I could say I'd planned it, that we'd talked about it, that I'd taken the requisite trip to Planned Parenthood my mom made me swear to years before. I'd always imagined that my first time would be premeditated, that I would be deliberate about it and not rush into something I would regret later. We used a condom and everything, but still, I didn't decide. I just let it happen.

And the moment after, with the sun streaming around the closed shades, the softness of the bedsheets, the quiet of the house, everything was settled. The fear was gone.

I opened my eyes to find Lucas watching me. Part of me wanted to hide from him. I didn't want to wreck the moment by saying the wrong thing, by making a statement that would move us away from the place we were now. But once I locked eyes with him, I couldn't look away, and I didn't want to.

We lay in my bed under the covers, the windows bright with reflected snow, my stuffed animals pushed to the side, the blue quilt and the white-painted bed frame just as they had always been. It was perfectly quiet, the way it can only be when it has snowed, with cars off the roads and the blanket of white an acoustic cushion. My cheek was resting on Lucas's bare shoulder, his arm wrapped snugly around the small of my waist. He was looking at me, straight into my eyes. We were smiling at each other. I think. I barely knew what I was doing with my face, only that I felt happy in a way that went so deep I was sure just then I would feel happy forever.

I said, "Do you remember if we ever felt like this? Before?"

I spoke my question as quietly as I could while still allowing Lucas to hear. I wasn't sure he was going to know what I meant, but I couldn't stand to be more specific. I leaned my nose into the soft skin just below his shoulder and breathed.

"It wasn't like this," he said. "It was never, ever like this."

chapter twenty-one

"So what *was* it like, that time?"

We were still lying in my bed, but now we were eating pancakes from a shared plate. We'd made them together while our feet froze on the linoleum kitchen floor, and then we'd raced back upstairs.

Lucas speared a hugely syrup-saturated bite with his fork, held it in front of his eyes like he was inspecting it, and said, "What do you think? Could I get more syrup on here?" I giggled and sank deeper into the pillows. And then, as if the entire course of our relationship had not been dominated by unanswered questions, he began to talk.

He talked as we finished the pancakes. He talked as we set the plate down on the floor. He talked as the light changed in the windows, as we ran downstairs for cups of tea, apples and peanut butter, tuna sandwiches, Oreos, toast. I asked questions and Lucas answered them. He talked and he talked and he talked some more.

What remains with me from our conversation is images and short bursts of story. Lucas could only remember the parts that had stuck with him for some reason, those memories that are like souvenirs you pull out to look at time and again.

As he shared one memory after another, I began to realize something. Maybe it should have been obvious, but I hadn't thought of it before.

I realized that what he remembered was not guaranteed to happen the same way again.

Most things, Lucas said, were the same. The way he felt when he was around me: a lifting in his chest, a happy shortness of breath. But other parts of that "time before" had been different. And it wasn't just that our first kiss had taken place months earlier. Or that this time we had his terrifying secret between us. Lucas himself was different. He was more careful, more appreciative of what we had.

And I was different too. Or at least, Lucas said I was. The concept was beyond my comprehension—I mean, Lucas's extra memories were changing him. Fine. But how could *I* be different when I couldn't remember anything but the time we were living in now? "Please," I found myself saying over and over. "I think all of this would be a little easier to understand if you stuck to specifics."

"Okay," Lucas said. "I'll try." He said he remembered my bedroom, my house. He remembered sharing an apple bite for bite with me on a sunny afternoon in his car. He remembered a fight we had over his not coming to watch a debate tournament. He remembered the way I smelled. ("That's a good thing," he clarified after I gave him a look.)

He remembered the way my hair felt in his hands, how protective Rosemary had been.

"She's not protective now," I said.

"Last time, she didn't like the way I treated you. This time, she's afraid you're in too deep. She's afraid she's losing you. She's afraid you're going to get hurt."

Lucas remembered that I got him to study a lot more. "My GPA went up a whole point," he said.

I shrugged. "This time, mine has gone down."

He told me the way I look when I study hadn't changed. "You go radio silent, as if everything and everyone around you has ceased to exist. I remember watching you, thinking how I could never do that. I got jealous, the idea that you could be so absorbed by something that wasn't me. But I don't think of it that way now. Now I just see how amazing you are. What makes you you."

I hung on every word. I felt safe and lazy and loved.

He remembered me crying once, he said. We were fighting again in the front seat of his car, but he didn't remember what we were fighting about. "It was the kind of fight where you kept saying the same things over and over. What seemed obvious to you made no sense at all to me." He told me my hair was wild, my face was blotchy. He remembered thinking at the time that maybe I was right, but something kept him from admitting it.

"You were harder to move," he said.

"Move?" I said. "Like, pick up and carry?"

"Yeah, I didn't tell you? You used to be a bodybuilder. You weighed two fifty in your socks."

I stared.

"Kidding!" He kissed me on the forehead. "You were harder to move, like, mentally," he explained. "You didn't trust me. Or anyone, really. It was hard to get you to change your mind."

"It was hard?" I repeated lamely. I felt like he was describing my dad. Ugh.

"Impossible, actually." He lay back on the pillows, looking up at the ceiling, an Oreo raised like a pointer he was using to illustrate a talk. "Which is weird. You should be just the same. But you're more open than you used to be—"

I cut him off. I was mad at him now, and at myself. "Maybe Rosemary is right. Maybe I shouldn't be so trusting." I moved away from him. "I think I need a shower," I said.

Lucas took my elbow, drew me back toward him. Lifting my chin, he peered into my face. "You're mad," he said. "I'm sorry. I didn't mean to hurt your feelings. I'm explaining this all wrong." I gave him a skeptical look. "Juliet, you're exactly the same person. I'm just seeing different parts of you this time around." He broke the Oreo in half, spilling crumbs he didn't seem to notice, then said, "Here, open your mouth, eat this." I did.

"See?" he said. "That other time you wouldn't have accepted the Oreo. You would have thought I was playing a trick on you. Now you trust me."

I wasn't convinced, but I wasn't feeling like pulling away from him again either. He popped the other half of the Oreo in his mouth and then kissed me. "Whatever happened that time around doesn't matter. What matters is *this* time. What matters is that you're the girl. I get to be with you again, the way it should have always been. You're the one I never got out of my head. Serious. Stubborn. Driven. Smart." He laughed. "What can I say? You're you." He kissed me a second time. "I can't believe how lucky I am." He pushed my hair back from my forehead. I think there were Oreo crumbs on his fingertips, but I didn't care.

My hurt feelings had melted away. I nestled back into the pillows. As long as Lucas was with me, everything was going to be okay.

"You're the girl," he repeated with a contented sigh, and I felt a growing warmth in my chest. I felt like the luckiest person alive, like the earth was revolving on its axis at a thousand miles an hour, but the axis was me.

Still, there was something I needed to know. "So what's going to happen?" I said. This was the same question I'd asked on the phone from the ski resort and he hadn't answered.

Lucas swallowed. He looked away. "I don't know," he said at last. "I have a bunch of ideas, but I think we have to wait until I get to the end of the dream to find out if any of them will work."

chapter twenty-two

"Guess who was in Aruba?" Rosemary and I were sitting on a curb outside the 7-Eleven a few blocks from school, sharing a hot chocolate. Our school had a rule—you had to play at least one sport or participate in something called an "extracurricular physical education elective." And this— drinking hot chocolate at 7-Eleven—was our version of the physical education elective called Winter Jogging. As long as you checked in with the coach, Mr. Agassi, who sat outside the locker room grading math homework, you could "jog" on the honor system—that is, go wherever you wanted to. Which for us meant 7-Eleven.

"No way," I said. "Jason?"

"He was surfing. Everyone on the beach was watching him, and then he came up to me, and I don't know. It was a moment."

"*Stalker* Jason?"

"I did *totally* tell him it was over."

Sometimes Rosemary's logic was beyond me. "You *told* him?" I said. "I thought the plan was to not actually talk to him at all. And where does Dex fit in here?" I don't know why I'd made it my life's mission to stick up for Dex. Maybe because I could see how much Rosemary was hurting him.

"Dex?" Like she didn't know who I meant.

"You're always acting like you like him. And you do. I know you do. At least a little. Admit it."

"Of course I *like* Dex. And . . . I like toast. I just don't love toast. And I don't want to *always* eat toast."

Just then, two guys in suits came out of the 7-Eleven. Even though Rose was in a watch cap and jogging clothes and sitting on the curb like a street waif, they both turned to stare. One of them could have even been thirty. Rose shook her head. "Losers," she muttered.

"Yeah," I agreed, and thought, for probably the hundred millionth time, that I had no idea what it was like to be her.

"So what happened with Jason?" I said, sighing, ready for the story.

And she told me how she'd snuck out of the cabana after her parents thought she was asleep. How Jason was waiting for her at the tiki bar on the edge of the beach. How there was live music. How everyone was in their twenties.

Jason kissed her. He wanted to see her again but she'd said no. She wanted to leave the magic moment between them just as it was, frozen in time, etched into polished stone.

Rosemary's and my jogging route back to school took

us by the charred remains of Sanjay Shah's house, and we stopped to look. Rosemary put a hand on my shoulder for balance and lifted her foot to stretch her quad.

"Dex gave Sanjay his old bicycle," she said. "He fixed it up, put a new chain on it, new tires. He used his landscaping money."

"Poor guy," I said.

"He's not suffering!" said Rosemary in a tone of exasperation. "God, Juliet, you act like Dex is some kind of victim, like being my friend is some kind of mental torture."

"I meant Sanjay."

"Oh."

Tuesday. It was my mom's take-a-donor-to-dinner night. Lucas and I were up in my room. And by the time we heard her steps approaching the door, it was too late. My mom was home early. She knocked.

How I wanted at that moment to be dressed, to have my hair not tangled and falling out of a ponytail, for Lucas's shirt to be tucked into his pants, his pants back—well—on. How I wanted to be able to say "Come in!" breezily and carry on the charade that we were very busy up here doing our homework.

Because when I said "Give me a minute," I felt that something more solid than just a closed door came to stand between my mom and me. I heard the embarrassment in her voice as she said "Oh." Then, as understanding dawned: "Oh!" Then: "I only wanted to let you know I'm home. But I don't need to! No need!" I don't know if I was imagining it or not, but I think at one point she might have said "Oh, boy!" I am sure, however, that she was upset. And that she fled.

That weekend, dinner with Mom at a restaurant downtown: halfway through the meal, she took a sip of wine, pursed her lips, opened her mouth to speak, paused, then finally said, "I'm worried about you."

I could feel my eyebrows shoot up to my forehead, heat come into my face.

"I don't want to make you mad, and I trust you," she said. "But I worry. I worry you are losing yourself."

I held my breath.

"Lucas is a wonderful kid," she went on. "But . . ." She reached across the table and took my hand. "But you are a wonderful kid too. You—Juliet, you."

"Is this because of the other day?" I asked. It came out sounding more defensive than I meant it to.

My mom shrugged. She took another sip of wine. "It's that . . ." She waved her hand in the air. "All those hockey games. Juliet, you were never even remotely interested in hockey before, and now . . . But it's not just hockey. It's that you seem so . . . obsessed with him. Like all your priorities have changed. You're so far away."

"No," I said. "I'm right here."

"What I want to tell you, Juliet, is—I just want you to remember that you have your whole life ahead of you."

"But I don't," I said. I could hear how hard and cold my voice had become. "My life is right now."

She stared. I never talked to her this way. I could see

growing hurt in her eyes. But I felt like I had to keep going. It would be more merciful to be clear.

"I'm not you," I went on. "I don't want to always be careful. When I look at the way you live, I want to go out and rob a bank or something."

"I was just saying—"

"After Dad left," I said, cutting her off, "you gave up. Talk about letting a man dictate your whole life. The way you are—you and Val—it's like you both signed on for early retirement. Are you jealous or something that I actually have a life?"

"Juliet—" my mom started, but I held up a hand.

"Don't bother," I said. "I don't want to hear it. And don't try to turn me into you."

Her eyes opened wide in surprise. She lifted her arm, and for a fraction of a second I thought she was going to strike the table like a judge ordering silence in a courtroom. But she only signaled the waiter. "We'll take the check."

She didn't speak in the car. She was angry, I could see that. When we got back home, she told me she was going for a walk.

I was camped out in my room when I heard her come in an hour later. Then I heard Val's car arriving, and then Val's flat-footed step in the hall. She knocked. I braced for a lecture, even though that wasn't Val's style. But Val just said, "Oh, you're still here? Your mother was starting to wonder."

I shrugged. The sight of Val's spiky hair and honest eyes made me suddenly wish I could take back everything I'd said, go downstairs with her and my mom, make our traditional Saturday-night sundaes, pretend I was younger.

"Want some ice cream?" Val said.

And I did. I really, really wanted ice cream. I wanted to stay up with them and watch *Saturday Night Live*. I wanted to be the self I was before Lucas, before his secrets, before everything had gotten so complicated. Or at least, I sort of wanted that. I didn't want it enough to give Lucas up.

So I just shrugged.

"You won't believe me when I say this," Val said as she turned to go. "But I know what you're going through. We've all been there."

It was taking all my concentration to keep from crying. So I didn't explain how wrong she was. I just sat there, trying to transform my face into a perfect blank. Val closed the door.

chapter twenty-three

Lucas's headaches continued to get worse, and apparently the only thing that helped besides double-dosing himself with ibuprofen was drinking.

So my memory of that winter consists of a string of parties. We went wherever the hockey team was getting together, because the hockey team was Lucas's ticket to alcohol. The hockey team did tequila shots in strange kitchens. The hockey team drank out of a funnel. They shook up beer cans to the point of explosion, punctured them with ballpoint pens, popped open the tops, and nearly drowned themselves with the spray. I watched the hockey team throw up in rhododendron bushes. I watched them pick fights with each other. I saw Nunchuck snap a pool cue in half and use the sharp ends to slit the upholstery on a chair.

I don't know if I could have survived if Dex and Rosemary weren't always there. They helped me drag Lucas away.

One time, Lucas, Rosemary, and I were sitting on

landscaping boulders outside a house where a party was raging. Dex was batting a tennis ball against the garage doors. He was showing off for Rose, who studiously ignored him. She was draped across the boulder next to the one Lucas and I shared, wrapped in a puffy jacket, her legs stiff in jeans and boots, as if they belonged to a mannequin. She looked into the distance, seemingly focused on the low clouds in the sky.

"Why donchu give the guy a break," Lucas said to Rose, slurring his words. "Look how hard he's working to impress you? Why not shpread a little love?"

Rose gave Lucas a look that he was too drunk to understand. Gesturing toward him with her thumb, she said to me, "You're not letting Prince Charming here drive you home, are you?"

Dex stepped away from his handball game to back Rosemary up. "Yeah," he said, standing just behind her. "Back off, Dunready." And then, as if the idea just occurred to him, he wound up and threw the tennis ball straight at Lucas, hitting him in the shoulder.

"Oh, you did *not*," said Lucas, and he fished the ball out from under a bush and chased Dex off the driveway into the woods behind the house and then back onto the driveway. Without moving from her rock, Rosemary put a leg out for Dex to trip over as he passed. Sure enough, Dex stumbled, then took a few boxer's steps in Rosemary's direction.

"You want a piece of me too, do you?" he said, shaking the long hair out of his eyes, leaning over her like he wanted her to stand up and fight.

"Don't be ridiculous," Rose said. "I want to play hand-ball. You up for a game?"

And he was. Like one of Rosemary's mom's dogs, he sat up and barked when she called his name.

Lucas was not so easily trained. Winded from his sprint, he went to sit down next to me but missed, landing in the bushes instead.

"I feel like someone cracked my skull open with a rock," he said from the ground. "I don't think I can move." And he couldn't. In his helpless, drunken flailing, his jacket sleeve had caught on a branch. I would have laughed except I could see that he was scared.

I unhooked his jacket and got him to his feet. "It's okay," I said, bringing him to me. He was trembling. He held on to me like he wasn't able to stand on his own. "You're safe here," I said. "You're safe with me."

He took my hand and squeezed so hard that I had to pull it away. I rested it on his cheek. I forced him to look at me. "Where are you?" I said. "Come back here. Come back to me."

His eyes refocused, his breathing slowed. He shuddered. "You fell in the bushes next to Tim Marconi's garage," I went on. "You're drunk but you're okay. It's high school. You know that, right? You're still seventeen."

He nodded and staggered back to the rock. We sat down.

"Is it—is it the dream?" I asked. He'd told me he'd some-times get stuck inside images from the dream even when he was awake.

He nodded again, and I held him there, kissing his

cheeks, holding his face in my hands. Even drunk and frightened, he was beautiful. I loved feeling the shape of his bones beneath his skin.

"What makes it so terrifying?" I ventured. "That it seems so real?"

Lucas shook his head. He rubbed my thigh with his palm, as if I were the one who needed steadying. "It's not knowing who or what we were looking for," he said, whispering. "Why we were there. No one explained it to us. We were just bodies." He laughed, and I watched him without understanding the joke. "Our job—a soldier's job—is to take up space and not die. But even so, that building— I remember wondering how they could send us in there. It was a death trap. I could guarantee you that everyone who lived on that alley was hiding inside, some armed with IEDs they'd made in their kitchens out of tea tins and roofing nails." He pushed his hand through his hair. He was shaking again.

"Lucas," I said. "I'm looking at you. It's 1994. You're seventeen. Don't you see? You don't need to be scared right now."

But it was like he couldn't hear me. "There were stairs, Jules." He nearly choked on the words. I saw sweat along the line of his forehead, even though it was winter and we were sitting outside. "Switchbacks. Endless switchbacks."

I pictured the fire stairs at my dentist's office complex. Every time I took them, I felt like I was in a chase scene from a movie, my footfalls echoing on the concrete steps, my fingers scraping on the iron railing where rust had eaten through the paint.

"Do you know what it's like to lead a squad up eight flights of stairs?" Lucas went on. "You're looking at sixteen opportunities for someone to jump you. Sixteen chances not to get a straight shot. We were rats in a maze. Blindfolded rats. Rats waiting to die."

I held his hand. I stroked his face. "You're here now," I said.

"You believe me, right?" he asked.

"I do," I told him. And I wasn't just saying that. I believed that what he was telling me was real.

Over and over, I reminded Lucas that his vision didn't have to be his future. Sometimes he found this comforting. Sometimes he would let me talk him down from the nightmare. Other times he took it as a sign that I didn't believe what he was saying.

"George Bush, okay?" Lucas burst out once. We were supposedly doing homework in the breakfast nook in my kitchen, but we'd gotten on the subject of Lucas's dream.

"What?"

"He's the next president."

"George Bush already was president."

"No, not him. His son. George W. I just remembered. No one will think he has a chance, but then he'll win. Or sort of win. There's this huge freak-out over whether he actually got elected legally, and for a month after the election no one knows if he's president or not."

I stared. I swallowed hard.

"You know how that guy tried to blow up the World Trade Center in New York last year but everyone was fine?"

171

I nodded.

"He comes back. Or someone just like him. It's horrible. All these people—office workers, maintenance guys, people who work in the restaurant on the top floor—they all die."

As he let this point sink in, he lifted his arm to scratch the back of his neck, his loose-fitting gray T-shirt pulling away from his arm. I loved the way his muscle curved in at the elbow, the way his skin was soft and smooth just there. How could someone so beautiful be the source of such terrible news? Couldn't he be wrong? Couldn't that not be true?

"Lucas," I said. "Please stop."

He did.

But the dream, the memories, the headaches kept coming. One unusually warm day in February, Lucas took me back up to the gym roof and we stood at the parapet again, watching the kids streaming toward the parking lot, the locker rooms, jobs, buses, after-school activities.

The skin on Lucas's face was drawn tight over his cheekbones. There were dark circles under his eyes. His mom had noticed his headaches; she'd confided in me that she thought they came from stress—the stress of his approaching enlistment, of his parents' impending divorce. She didn't know about his dreams. She didn't know he was afraid to fall asleep at night, that he was waking up thinking he was in danger and could not forget what he had seen.

"We started to go up the stairs," he told me up on the gym roof that day. "Inside the apartment building. I remember a baby crying and a teakettle whistling, but like I said, everyone was hiding, so it looked deserted. When we looked in the few doors that were standing open, the apartments appeared to be empty, as if all the people who lived there had cleared out suddenly. But we knew they were still there, that the beds, the curtains, the closets, whatever, were crowded with them. You could smell them."

Lucas put his hands on the edge of the parapet and pushed on it, as if he had the power to move concrete. "I think I felt it before I heard it," he said. "The plaster was ripping itself out of the wall next to me."

"Ripping itself?" I could feel his pain, the fear, as if I'd been there beside him.

"That's what I thought, until I realized it was bullets striking just inches above my head. I ducked and they stopped. I don't remember signaling to the guys behind me, but I do remember looking down the stairs and seeing them all crouching. There were windows at the landings, and I'd been right in front of one."

I wanted to cover my ears. I didn't want to hear any more. But Lucas needed to tell me. I could see that. He needed me to leech the pain away. "Did you? Did you get shot?"

"No. I was okay." He put my hand on his heart. "But this thing was going crazy." I could feel his heart beating now, strong.

"What if you don't join the marines?" I said. "You can get a job that keeps you outdoors. You can become a hockey coach or a wilderness ranger. You can be a farmer."

"My uncle Ray's a farmer," Lucas said. He was back to smirking—I was always glad to see any sign that he was his old self, even if that sign was his dismissing my idea. "My dad told me Uncle Ray makes, like, ten thousand dollars a year."

"Why aren't you taking this seriously?" I said, pretending to be annoyed, pushing his shoulder, hoping he'd push back. But also? I *was* annoyed. Why couldn't he decide not to enlist?

Lucas wrapped his arms around me, buried his head in my neck. "I'm not *not* taking it seriously," he said. "It's just that taking it seriously hurts."

"It hurts?" I said. "I know your head hurts, but you're saying you can feel . . . an idea?"

He broke away, sat down on the pebbly surface of the rooftop. "I don't know how this works, okay? I don't know the rules, if there even are any. All I know is it hurts. Thinking about change hurts a lot."

"But just imagine it," I said. I bent down, forcing him to look me in the eye. "Imagine us married. Imagine—I don't know—kids. A minivan. Whatever."

"I think about it constantly," he said. "All I think about is how much I want to be with you."

"You do?"

"And all I get for my efforts is pain."

"So it really hurts right now?" I said.

"Yeah," Lucas said, grimacing as if to show me. "It hurts a ton."

At a party, Lucas, Rosemary, and I ended up in a hot tub with this senior girl who was drinking vodka out of a Gatorade bottle she'd been carrying around all night. Rosemary

gestured to the senior girl in her bathing suit, the Gatorade, Nunchuck passed out on the patio furniture—it was
like we'd stepped onto the set of *Risky Business*. "This," she
whispered, "is ridiculous." I agreed, but I liked the ridic-
ulousness. I liked that it was something Rosemary and I
could both see without spelling it out. I liked that we were
laughing together. I liked the feel of Lucas's leg next to mine
in the warm water, his hand on my knee.

He slung his arm around my shoulders and gave me a
sloppy wet kiss. "I want you to know," he announced to
Rose and to me in the tone of a drunk, "I'm going to fix
this. I'm going to make this stop." Rose had no idea what he
was talking about, of course, but I did, and when Lucas and
I were in Dex's backseat, headed home, I whispered, "So . . .
you're not going to enlist?"

He pulled away. "No," he said. "I have another idea. I
can't tell you. I have to work it out more in my head. And
I can't promise anything. The whole thing will be a giant
experiment."

And I let it go. Later, I wished I'd forced him to tell
me more.

chapter twenty-four

At the end of February, Rosemary and I were in the 7-Eleven parking lot with hot cocoa on the brain when Rosemary put a hand on my arm. "Stop," she said. "We can't go in there."

"We can't?"

"I just saw Jason."

I could feel my eyes widening. If you can scream and whisper at the same time, that's what I did. "Here?"

Rosemary nodded.

"What is he doing here?"

"I have no idea." *You should be able to guess, though,* I thought. Ever since Aruba, he'd been calling a lot.

"Are you sure it was him?"

"Maybe?" Rosemary said.

We decided that since Jason had never met me, I'd go into the store and try to figure out if it was him. Rosemary said I could tell by looking at his left wrist. He wore a braided leather bracelet—she said he never took it off.

This 7-Eleven was pretty big. There was a circular counter in the center for the cashiers. Off to the left was the to-go food—with counters for coffee and tea, the Slurpee machines, shelves of sandwiches, yogurt, and drinks. On the right there were aisles of chips, magazines, pantyhose, replacement windshield wipers, and gallon jugs of washer fluid.

I felt like a spy as I noted a dark head of hair in the mayonnaise, cereal, and dish soap aisle.

But the man reading the ingredients on a box of Honey Nut Cheerios was way old. He was wearing a suit with the tie loosened. He could have been forty. Or sixty. It was hard to tell.

"Can I help you?" he said when he caught me staring.

"Um . . ." I turned in embarrassment. But then I spotted another dark head of hair, clear across the store by the coffee. Trying not to appear to be hurrying, I made my way over to the doughnut case and pretended to study the options, every now and then sneaking a look at the guy busy reading the tea bags and then putting them back.

That had to be him. He looked rich and young. He had thick, dark eyebrows and conservatively cut brown hair shot through with streaks of blond. A strong jaw. Broad, square shoulders. Everything he was wearing looked like it had just been washed and ironed.

And the tea drinking confirmed it. I mean, a guy our age drinking tea is weird, right? And so was Jason. That had to be him.

But when he reached with his left hand for a cup from the dispenser, the cuff of his shirt pulled away from his wrist: no bracelet.

Rosemary had said left wrist, hadn't she? I turned from the doughnut case, walked past the checkout and through the double doors, and rounded the corner of the building, calling out "Which wrist did you say?" before I realized that Rosemary was not alone. Standing close to her—way too close—was yet another male figure with dark brown hair. Compared to the cute guy inside, this new version of what it took my brain a full minute to understand was the real Jason was a mess.

He looked to have a few days' growth of beard, and he was wearing a thin gray sweatshirt that hung off his shoulders like it hadn't been washed recently. His dark hair was shaggy in the back and long over his ears. But because he was leaning against the open door of his car, one elbow cocked, the loose fabric of his sleeve had slid down and exposed his wrist. His left wrist. Where I could see a braided leather bracelet, plain as day.

"Are you Juliet?" he asked, and smiled in a way that was a little sad and a little scary at the same time. There was something about his eyes that made me wonder how long it had been since he'd slept.

Rosemary looked at me and shook her head slightly to let me know that I shouldn't answer his question, presumably because she had this under control. "What are you doing here, Jason?" she said, her jaw tight, her arms folded over her chest.

Jason blinked hard, but he didn't shift his gaze. He was still looking at me like he was hoping he could read something in my surprise, get access to information that Rosemary wasn't giving up.

"Well?" Rosemary said, stepping between us. Finally, Jason met her gaze.

"I just want to talk to you," he said. "You aren't answering my letters, and I can't get through to you on the phone. Did Aruba mean nothing to you? How can you not want to see me again? I thought maybe if I drove to your house—"

"My *house*?" Rosemary said. "You mean the one where my parents live? My dad will call the cops on you."

"You could introduce me," Jason said. "I mean, I'm not a bad guy. He might like me."

"Jason, you aren't my boyfriend." I could hear the frustration starting to crack through Rosemary's calm. "I'm not going to introduce you to my parents. I'm not going to talk to you on the phone. It's over."

"No," Jason said. "In Aruba, see—"

"I do see," Rosemary said. "I see that you're acting crazy. You have to stop calling."

Her words were harsh, but maybe they were what he needed, because suddenly, Jason was standing up straighter. He tucked his chin like he was literally swallowing her words. "I guess I should go," he said.

Rosemary nodded. She didn't relax her jaw. She uncrossed her arms only to put her hands on her hips. As she did, her half-zipped hoodie shifted slightly. At her neck I could see the glint of a gold chain. She was wearing Jason's necklace.

I saw Jason notice it only a half second after I did. This was bad.

"You *want* me to go?" he said, smirking now. "It's what you *really* want?" Later, Rosemary swore she hadn't heard any kind of smirk in Jason's tone. After all, she pointed out, he probably saw only the chain. Without the diamond, how could he be sure?

But he knew. I'd seen it in his eyes.

"I do want you to go," Rosemary said. "It's what I really want." So Jason got into his car and with a roar of the engine backed out of the parking lot and zoomed off down the road. Rosemary and I jogged back to school.

I didn't tell her how scary I thought this whole situation was getting, because I didn't want to open the door to that kind of conversation. I didn't want to hear how afraid she was for me. But later that night, I found myself teasing out an understanding of what exactly had gone down. I was worrying. Like my mom must have been worrying about me.

Here's what else worried me: something about Jason's gaunt face, his desperate attempt to hold on to Rosemary, reminded me of Lucas.

In the locker room after jogging, Rosemary had thrown her running shoes into her locker in frustration, saying, "Why can't he see that it's never going to happen? Why do people insist on forcing the impossible?"

I could have answered her, but I didn't. I could have explained that until she fell in love she would never know that people in love almost always try to force the impossible. They cannot imagine letting go of what they have. Or what they *wish* they had.

Like Jason, like Lucas, like me, like Dex—none of us could imagine changing the way we felt. And yet Lucas had told me that for him and me, that's exactly what would happen. We would separate. He would enlist. I would go to law school and have a good life.

It seemed impossible. I couldn't accept that that version of the future could be real.

chapter twenty-five

As I write about my time with Lucas, I find I remember so much more than I thought I would. Somehow, one memory leads to another. They don't exist in a vacuum but rather overlap with one another, each image, smell, or sound that I recall just another link in a very, very long chain. I pull and pull and never seem to get to the end of it.

Some of the memories I can tell are important, but others surface for no apparent reason. Dex opening his locker, only to have a pile of books cascade down on top of him. He jumped back, caught a history text in one hand. Why would I remember that?

Rose spraying me with a can of Reddi-wip outside the hockey locker room after a big win, any disagreements between us about Dex and Lucas fading in the excitement of the victory.

Val dragging a coffee table she'd refinished through the

front door of the house in her Shaw Festival T-shirt, spewing swearwords appropriate to a sailor.

Lucas throwing an arm over his mother's shoulder after Tommy announced at the dinner table that he didn't want anything for his birthday except his dad to come back home.

Are the memories we recall governed by the feelings attached to them? Is that why they stay with us? Or do we remember only what we remind ourselves of over and again as the years go by? How is it possible that some memories you'd like to hold on to slip away and others—mundane and sad alike, the memories you'd just as soon forget—stay, bubbling to the surface of your brain for no reason at all?

I remember Rosemary's dad quizzing us on the state capitals over her mother's cornflake chicken, horrified that we were less than two years away from college and didn't know them all.

I remember my mom, who hates games, acquiescing to penny poker with Val and me, shaking her head in annoyance when she forgot the difference between a straight and a flush, giving me her "What have you gotten me into?" look when I threw down four kings.

A Sunday-afternoon phone call with my dad, the click of one metal ball hitting another in the toy he kept on his desk as he told me about a new protocol for fluid absorption.

Lucas waiting by my locker at the end of a school day.

Lucas tying his skates.

Lucas sneaking up on Tommy and Wendell in a snowball fight.

· · ·

My memories of Lucas surprise me in dreams. They come back to me as if I just experienced them yesterday. I remember what he smelled like, how his skin felt when I touched his cheek, how I could shiver with pleasure just hearing his voice on the phone. I can see him fresh in my mind's eye, the way he looked coming off the ice after hockey, his hair matted to his head, his cheeks red, one glove tucked under his arm as he worked the other one free with his teeth.

During a debate tournament where I was losing a round, up on an auditorium stage, in front of a crowd: one of the middle school helpers slipped a note onto my desk. I recognized Lucas's chicken scratch right away.

Chin up.

How had he sent that note? The hockey team was in a tournament too. Lucas wasn't here.

Except he was. All the way in the back, against the wall next to the auditorium doors. His hair was still wet. He must have rushed here between games. He lifted a hand and gave me a thumbs-up before rolling back out the door.

Early in March, Lucas and I were buying ice cream in the mini-mart of a gas station. There was a woman in front of us with a loaf of bread, two cans of tuna, and a bag of Doritos. A little girl in baggy pants and a matching tunic I later learned to call a *salwar kameez* was tugging on her skirt. "Hey," we heard from behind, and turned toward the granola bar and mixed nuts section. There was Sanjay Shah. His "Hey" was for Lucas, as if Lucas was someone he would have said hi to passing in the halls.

I did a quick calculation. The woman in front of us must be Sanjay's mom, the little girl his sister. I knew Sanjay's family was living in our town's one hotel, which you reached through the parking lot behind the gas station. So the tuna fish and bread—was that dinner?

Sanjay took a step closer to Lucas, and Lucas's arm tightened around my waist. "You're the guy," Sanjay said to him. "You're the one who brought back my dog."

By now Sanjay's mom was looking at us too. Even his sister was standing up straighter, as if eager to hear how the stranger her brother was speaking to would respond.

"I don't know what you're talking about," Lucas responded, his voice deadpan, uncharacteristically unfriendly.

"No," Sanjay said. "It was you." He took another step closer. "The terrier, remember? Brown with black ears? The night of the fire, you came down to the fire station with him. I saw you leave him with the guy washing the truck. Where did you find him?"

Lucas sighed. "He ran down to the river. Something happened to his paw, so he couldn't walk."

"He had glass in it," Sanjay said. "The vet fixed it. He said if you hadn't found him, he probably would have been too weak to find his way up the hill."

"Yeah," said Lucas. "That's what I was guessing."

"But how did you know to look?" Sanjay said. His black eyes were flashing, his Adam's apple sticking out like a challenge. He had the beginnings of a mustache on his lip.

Lucas shrugged. "I was down there anyway."

"And you just guessed he was ours?"

Lucas stepped around Sanjay's mother and pushed the quart of ice cream over to the cashier, who picked it up without looking at it. Like Sanjay's mom and sister and me, the clerk was listening to the two boys.

"I figured," Lucas said. "I'd heard about the fire, so I put two and two together."

"Do you have a police scanner?" Sanjay asked. "You found the dog before the fire had even been put out. Also, you could have taken him to the police station or the shelter, but you knew to come to the station. How did you know he was ours?"

Sanjay put his hands in his pockets, determinedly waiting for an answer, but Lucas just stood there without even shrugging. "Okay," Sanjay said when it was clear he wouldn't get a response. He looked down at his feet, then back up. "Thanks. He really could have died."

"Yup," Lucas said. "I know."

Another Lucas memory: We were at the pond in the woods behind his house. Tommy and Wendell were scraping up a fine mist of ice dust behind them as they skated quickly back and forth, their skate blades clacking on the frozen surface. Even though they were playing by moonlight, they went at it furiously, their sticks tangling, their narrow hips checking each other, as if they were one person tripping over his own feet.

When Lucas skated out to meet them, their game became two against one. They tried to shoot against him while he guarded the net. Then he was the monkey in monkey in the middle.

I stayed to the outer edge of the cleared ice—I hadn't been on skates in years, and I was slowly figuring out how to get my balance. But then suddenly, Lucas was behind me. He skated into me as if he were going to knock me over, but he caught me, his hands wrapped around my waist, the two of us moving forward as one. At breakneck speed.

We skated in circles around the cleared area of the ice, twisting into figure eights, Lucas holding my hands and skating backward, then coming back to join me, pushing the pace. I was pretty much screaming the whole time, but afterward I felt completely different about my balance. We could hold hands then and skate and I didn't feel like I was in danger of falling. In the bitter cold, we skated into clouds of our own breath. Beautiful.

"Look up," Lucas said, and there was the full moon and stars and stars and stars. They traveled so deep back into the soft blackness it felt like they were falling on us.

"I feel so small," I said.

Lucas nodded.

"And dizzy," I said.

He nodded again.

And this, now, I remember thinking, this was a moment, a peak moment, like the peak day of foliage I'm always waiting for in the fall. It was a peak of happiness, but "happiness" isn't even the right word. What I felt was a connection, like a tunnel running between our minds had been opened and could never be closed.

"Maybe I won't sign up," Lucas said.

"For . . . for the marines?" I asked. "You'd do that?"

"Maybe being back here, being allowed to return, even with the headaches, maybe this is my chance."

I didn't dare say anything. Lucas wrapped his arms around me tighter.

And then he did this thing. Like we were figure skaters, he grabbed me around the waist and lifted me into the air. I trusted him so completely it didn't make me lose my balance. I landed easily, and when he did it again, I lifted my arms above my head, feeling all the power of the night sky, the fire inside the faraway stars, the sheer momentum and force of my feelings for Lucas giving me the strength to hold the pose. As I landed, Lucas wrapped his arms around me and I breathed into his jacket. All I wanted was to stay like that, holding on to him in the night air.

I was sure we would have more moments like that. That they would go on forever.

I was wrong.

chapter twenty-six

It wasn't a week later that something happened with Lucas's helmet during a game. Skating hard, he faked in anticipation of a pass and collided with a player he hadn't seen coming. The force of the impact sent Lucas flying across the ice, and as if it had been shot from a cannon, his head seemed to separate from his body and skid across the ice, stopping only when it slammed into the boards.

But no, that hadn't happened, I quickly came to understand. The helmet had slid. Lucas's head was still attached to his shoulders, the side of his face pressed to the ice where he'd fallen.

Nevertheless, something was wrong. Lucas wasn't moving. And there was blood.

The rink went silent. I could hear nothing but my own heartbeat pounding in my ears. The pool of blood was growing. Then the coach was there. The trainer too.

When I saw Lucas move, I felt an enormous wave of gratitude pass through my body. He wasn't dead.

A beautiful thought.

He wasn't even unconscious. The trainer was checking him, and he was responding, lifting parts of his body. I saw that he was talking. Then he started to sit up. As he skated off the ice with the trainer on one side and Coach O'Reilly on the other, I pushed my way out of the stands and through the hallway into the locker room.

I found Lucas perched on the examination table in the trainer's room, still wearing his pads, pants, and socks, his face stained with blood, his shoulders slumped like he had lost the ability to lift them. "Are you okay?" I asked from the doorway. The trainer was holding a piece of gauze to Lucas's temple. He pulled it away, and I got a brief glimpse of the gash at his hairline. His face was pale, and his hair was matted to his forehead, which was slick with sweat.

"Lucas?" I said. The trainer stepped away and I approached the exam table. Lucas blinked at me kind of funny, and for a second, everything I'd learned about head injuries the day I ensconced myself in the library came back to me. Were his pupils dilated? Different sizes? Did he know the day of the week? The year?

He sure was blinking a lot.

Then his face opened up into a smile. A Lucas smile— the smile of a boy who says "Hell, no" when asked if he's planning to go to college. He beckoned me in.

"Okay, that was terrifying," I said.

The trainer was reaching into the supply cabinet,

directing Lucas to hold the gauze to his head. "That little tumble?" Lucas said.

"Do you have a concussion or anything?"

"You with your concussions."

"Quick: what year is it?"

"Umm . . . ," Lucas said, like he had to think about it, like it was all a joke. "Elvis is still alive. . . ."

I looked down at the concrete floor and breathed. Deeper than I'd meant to.

"Are *you* okay?" Lucas asked, lifting my chin. I laughed.

And Lucas winked.

Lucas's mom took him to the doctor that night, but he was back in school the next day. He looked different, and it wasn't just the bandage at his hairline where two stiches had gone in. He seemed . . . looser. Happier. He kept laughing for no reason. I turned around in physics to catch him stretching luxuriously, as if he were waking from a deep sleep, not recovering from a head wound.

His good mood lasted into the next few days. I chalked it up to his having survived the fall. To his feeling lucky to be alive. And to all the attention he was getting from his hockey friends, who were calling him Head Fake and going out of their way to high-five him in the halls.

Lucas did not seem even remotely curious about what had happened to his helmet, why the chin strap had broken, how it had managed to fly off his head. But Coach O'Reilly was. He phoned the equipment supplier, and by lunchtime, they'd called back and asked him to send them the helmet. Lucas was getting a free replacement. In fact, the entire team was getting replacement helmets, complete with four-color team logos and new jerseys thrown in for good measure.

A few days later, when Lucas and I were checking his practice schedule on the bulletin board outside Coach O'Reilly's office, Coach called Lucas in to talk about the helmet some more. I waited, listening to every word through the door, which they had forgotten to close.

Apparently the helmet manufacturer claimed the chin strap on Lucas's helmet had been at least partially damaged before the game began. Maybe Lucas hadn't been putting guards on his skates before stowing them in his bag with the rest of his gear? The blades were sharp enough to cut into the strap.

"You've been using your guards, haven't you?" Coach asked. "You don't need me to tell you that."

Lucas mumbled something I didn't catch.

"We can't have helmets flying off kids' heads," Coach continued. "I need to know whether to go after these guys."

"Yeah," said Lucas with a laugh. "That's what my mom's been saying." And by laughing, he got Coach to laugh too.

It wasn't until later that I realized he hadn't answered Coach's question.

After debate practice, I met Lucas at his car, where he was listening to music. Metal. I could hear how loud it was even before I opened the door. "Doesn't that hurt?" I shouted, touching my temple because I wasn't sure he could hear me over the bass. Lately, because of his headaches, he hadn't been listening to music in the car at all.

Lucas smiled the no-holds-barred grin that earned him free samples at candy counters and ice cream stands. "Not today!" he shouted. He was still smiling when he slammed the car into gear. He drove fast, taking curves at a speed that the week before would have made him wince in pain. Something wasn't right.

I figured out what it was as Rosemary and I were coming back from our jog the next afternoon and I saw someone slap the side of the soda machine when it wasn't giving back their change. I stopped dead in my tracks.

"*Lucas* cut the strap," I said out loud. "He cut it on purpose."

"What?" said Rose. She's pretty hard to surprise, but here she was, staring like I'd just sprouted a second head. "Lucas did what?"

"Nothing," I said.

"No," she answered. "It's not nothing. You said Lucas cut his helmet strap."

"I didn't say 'helmet.'"

Rosemary put her hands on her hips. "We both know what you meant."

I wanted to tell her she had no idea, but I just nodded and shrugged like she'd caught me, then pretended to come clean, sticking mostly to parts of the story she already knew. I'd hated lying to Rosemary all year, but right then I was so worried about Lucas I didn't care.

I told her I was guessing that Lucas thought hitting his head hard might make the chronic headaches stop. I didn't tell her where the headaches were coming from, how painful they were, or what was at stake in getting them to go away. "I think he figured it would be like the radio in his car," I explained. "The one you have to hit from time to time to get it to find the station."

"But you think he cut the strap *on purpose*? You think he *wanted* to hit his head?"

"It was just a thought," I said. "I'm probably wrong."

"I hope so," she said. "He could have died."

I attempted a reassuring smile, even as a wave of fear washed over me.

Had this been Lucas's plan, the one he'd announced to me in the hot tub? Had the plan been to rejigger his brain? Or die trying?

After school, Rosemary dropped me at home, where I picked up the phone to call Lucas and then hung it up, remembering that there was a hockey team dinner that night. I thought of leaving a message, but the questions I wanted to ask him—"Did you intentionally try to get yourself hit in the head?" "Did you realize you could have died?"—weren't message material.

To keep from going crazy with worry, I forced myself to study. I memorized five objectives the federal government was trying to achieve during Reconstruction. I read all the way through to the third act of *Hamlet*. It was then that the phone rang. Lucas would be calling, I knew—I had pulled the phone with the long cord into my room, and as I reached for it, I remember thinking it was later than I'd expected.

But it wasn't Lucas. It was Dex.

"Did anyone tell you yet?" he said. "Lucas passed out. He was breathing and everything, but they couldn't wake him up."

"What?" *How can Dex be so wrong?* I was thinking. "Lucas didn't ever lose consciousness," I insisted. "I saw him just after he fell. He was fine."

"I'm not talking about his fall on the ice," Dex explained. "This was at the dinner tonight. Something happened. He just passed out."

I understood the danger Lucas was in in a way I can't quite explain. I don't know what I thought it was. I only knew it was bad.

I was on the stairs almost before I finished listening to Dexter tell me about the ambulance, about how Dex went with Coach O'Reilly to the hospital, about Lucas's mom's being tracked down in the ward where she worked.

"Mom!" I called, running. But the living room was empty. I raced back up the stairs and found my mom in her room, already in bed, her white ruffled nightgown buttoned up to her chin, a novel in her hand, her tortoiseshell glasses sliding down her nose. "Lucas is in the hospital and you have to drive me down there to see him right away!" I said. I was shouting. I was speaking so fast she had to ask me three times to repeat myself. And then she tried to argue that it wasn't a good idea for me to go down to see him, that this was a time for his family to be alone with him, that she would take me first thing in the morning.

"You're wasting time!" I finally interrupted. I told her that if she didn't take me, I was going to walk. And so she pulled out the black sweatpants that make her ankles look like an old lady's and told me to pack up my history notes, as if I might be able to study, and we got into the car, not even waiting a few minutes with the engine running in the cold before putting it into drive.

chapter twenty-seven

My town is not big enough for a real hospital. We have emergency medical care, which is where you go if you have a fever and your doctor's office is closed. For a bona fide hospital, you drive about ten miles to the city.

My mom and I parked in a pay lot across the street from a neon sign that read EMERGENCY. At the entrance, wide doors yawned open as ambulances unloaded.

We followed an arrow around a corner. A woman in scrubs and a cardigan sweater checked the computer for Lucas's name. "He's here," she said. She gestured to some chairs. "You can wait over there. I can't let you in unless you're family?" The way she said it, as if it were a question, not a statement, encouraged us, I believed, to lie.

But before I could announce that I was Lucas's cousin, my mom cut me off at the pass. "We're just friends," she said, and for one split second, I had the thought that she was talking about herself and me, as if my hysterical insistence on driving downtown in the middle of the night had finally proven to her that we could not be related.

The receptionist promised to tell a nurse we were there—she said Lucas would get the message. We sat down next to an old man with a walker and his health aide, who was holding a crocheted afghan. A woman brought a baby in whose cough sounded like a barking dog. "Croup," my mom said. "You had that when you were one."

After about twenty minutes, Mrs. Dunready came through the double doors, spoke to the woman at the desk, and then walked over to us. She didn't say hello or smile, and I didn't know if that was a sign of how serious the situation was or just the way she was at work. "He'd like to see you if you want to go in," she said to me.

I stood, waiting a second for her to lead the way.

"You go ahead," she said. "I'll wait. There's no space for more than a single visitor."

My mom gave me a significant look. "Don't stay long," she said.

I tried to walk purposefully toward the double doors Mrs. Dunready had come through, but as I approached them, I found myself wondering if my mom hadn't been right after all. Maybe I wasn't old enough to be walking into an emergency room, to be visiting my own boyfriend here, to be connected to anything as grown up and real as a serious injury. I'd never even had a broken bone. I hadn't had my tonsils out. I didn't belong here, and neither did Lucas. Maybe if I'd stayed home, all this would have gone away.

Then I caught a glimpse of him on the bed. His arm was in a blood-pressure cuff, and a device I knew from my dad was called a nasal cannula brought oxygen into his nose. The bed didn't have blankets, just a white sheet pulled tight over the mattress. I found it reassuring that Lucas wasn't under the sheet. I also found it reassuring that he was wearing the khaki pants and shirt he'd worn that day at school.

He looked like himself—his blond and blonder hair, his sharp blue eyes, the red patches in his cheeks. His skin was pale, but he was still Lucas. Living, breathing Lucas.

Seeing me, he pulled down the cannula, and in that gesture of "Screw this," I saw echoes of Lucas pulling off a baseball cap or his shirt when we were playing pickup basketball, or ripping a page off a legal pad when he was trying to write a paper and it wasn't going well.

"Hey," he said, and I felt tears come into my eyes at the sound of his voice because it was so . . . him. So not sick or in danger of any kind.

I sniffed and he gave me a questioning look, then saw that I'd started to cry and said, "Hey, it's okay. I'm going to be fine."

"You don't look fine," I spat out, crying harder now, though what I'd meant to do was to stop crying, to get control of myself somehow. "Sorry," I said, sniffing again. "But when Dex said you'd passed out, I thought . . . I don't know what I thought."

"Did you think I was dead?" Lucas said it like a joke. He course-corrected on seeing my reaction.

"Maybe?" I admitted. "With your fall, and then

what Coach O'Reilly said about your helmet, and your headaches— Lucas?" I didn't want to say any more. I tried to pull myself together. "What happened?"

Lucas shrugged. "One second I was out on the deck with Coach—he was grilling burgers and dogs and stuff outside, and we were helping him carry the platters in. And maybe it was the temperature change—it was freezing outside— but when I came in . . . I guess I don't even really remember coming in."

"Do the doctors have any idea what's going on?"

Lucas put a hand up to his temple. "They're going to do a CAT scan."

"You're having a CAT scan?" That sounded serious.

"When doctors don't know what else to do, they order CAT scans," he said in an attempt to comfort me. "My mom says it happens all the time. And she's a nurse, remember?"

Thinking about his mom, I remembered what mine had said about keeping the visit short.

"Lucas," I said. He looked at me, his brow furrowed. "I have to ask you something." He nodded. "Your hockey helmet. When the strap broke. Did you—" This was turning out to be hard for me to say out loud. "Did you cut it?"

"Come here," he said. I took a step closer to him and he took my hand. "I thought . . ."

"I know what you thought," I said. "You thought it would be like your car radio, right?"

He tapped his temple. "Smarty-pants." Then he shook his head. "I was going to tell you—I was waiting to be sure—but yes, I cut the strap."

I gasped. It was one thing to suspect it, another to hear it confirmed.

"Well, not cut, exactly," Lucas went on. "I just nicked it. That took the results out of my hands, you know what I mean? I didn't have to jump off a bridge or drive my car into a wall—it was up to fate." He looked down, suddenly sheepish. "Or luck or whatever. You probably think I was stupid. Though it *did* work."

"Define 'work,'" I said. "I assume you're talking about *before* you ended up in the hospital?"

Lucas looked up at me, shrugged, smiled. I could feel his grin tugging at something inside me. And in spite of my fear for him, I was amazed at that tug, the way we were connected. I knelt by the side of his bed, laid my face against his shoulder.

"It *did* work," he began. "After I cracked my head on the ice, I felt amazing. I had the best two nights of sleep I've had all year. No dreams. And the headaches? Gone."

"The memories?"

"Also gone. Or at least, I wasn't stumbling onto new ones. I thought the whole thing was over."

"And then tonight?" I prompted. I couldn't look at him.

"When I passed out at the dinner, the dream came back. Hard. Like it had stored up energy during the two days I'd managed to dam the flow."

"It was the same dream?"

"Yeah, but there was something new this time. There was a part where I woke up. Or I thought I was waking up. I heard people calling my name, and when I opened my eyes,

I saw doctors. I think my mom was there. It was a hospital. But not this one. The doctors were asking me questions. Did I know where I was, that kind of thing. But I couldn't get my mouth to move. And then suddenly, I felt this pain that was so intense I can't even describe it to you. It was like someone had set fire to my skin."

I cringed, as if I could feel the pain too.

"And somehow—I don't know how I did this—I willed myself to go back to sleep, to go back into the dream. The pain slowed and I woke up and I was lying on Nunchuck's kitchen floor with all these paramedics asking me what day it was and the name of my town and could I spell my own name."

I sat up and held his cheeks in my hands. "Don't think about it anymore," I said. "Just remember, you're here. You're with me."

"I'm sorry, Jules," he said. I took his hand in mine and held it to my face, wetting it with my tears.

"You can fight this," I said. "I know you can."

"I can't fight something I can't see and don't understand."

Lucas was right. This thing was like a giant fog, a monster we didn't know if we were trying to grab by the head or by the tail, or if maybe we had the scale all wrong.

Back in reception, I didn't care if Mrs. Dunready and my mom could see that my eyes were red and I was sniffling. My mom asked me if I was ready to go home, and I nodded.

In the car, she said, "Maureen Dunready thinks this is serious. She thinks there might be some kind of tumor."

"Like brain cancer?"

"She said it's an outside possibility. But she's worried. Lucas told her he's been having headaches for a while. And he's seemed not quite himself. Apparently changes in personality can be an indication of internal bleeding. The symptoms of a brain tumor can be all over the map, depending upon what part of the brain is affected."

"Does she think he's going to be okay?"

My mom sighed. "He's in the hospital," she said. "He's got great doctors. I'm sure they'll get to the bottom of it in no time." But she was worried. I could tell because for the first time ever, we were talking about Lucas without her letting me know with a look or a sigh or a word that she wished he weren't around.

The next morning, Rosemary picked me up, and instead of turning left, toward school, she turned right and took me to a stop where I could catch the city bus. We waited for it in the car with the heater on.

"Juliet, is there anything, you know, going on with Lucas?" Rosemary asked, and I looked at her. My longing to go back to the time when she and I still trusted each other, when things between us had last been okay, was so strong.

I wanted to tell her everything. I had always wanted to, if only to put the confusion and responsibility into someone else's hands. But I knew I couldn't. Rosemary wouldn't have believed me. She's too practical, too much like me. Or at least, how I used to be.

I shook my head. An hour later, I was sitting in a chair

at the side of Lucas's bed. He'd been moved into intensive care.

Maybe it was the fact that he was in the ICU or that he was wearing a hospital gown. Or maybe it was that he hadn't shaved and the stubble on his face made his skin look gray. Or maybe it was that his skin *was* gray. He looked worse.

Mrs. Dunready didn't look too good either. I don't think she'd slept much, or brushed her hair. Mr. Dunready had come. He was sitting in the corner, in a chair that was too small for him, red-faced and uncomfortable, his eyes shifting from Lucas on the bed to the curtained opening that was the door, as if hoping for an excuse to walk right through it. When Mrs. Dunready stepped out for a break, Mr. Dunready waited just long enough for her to be gone before he announced, "I guess I'll go too," and disappeared.

Lucas took my hand. There was a window near his bed. I could see a parking garage across the street, the back of a brick hotel, the tower of the museum where my mom worked, the low purplish mountains on the other side of the river.

"This doesn't feel real anymore," he said. "You feel real to me, but the rest of it—the hospital, the fact that my dad came home to take care of my brothers, this window—" He must have seen me looking at it, so I turned back to face him. "They feel like a dream. I feel dizzy all the time."

He pinched his skin on the back of his hand, and it held the crease when he took his fingers away. "That's called tenting," he explained. "It's because I'm dehydrated. None of the doctors can figure out why."

I smoothed the tented skin down. My hand looked impossibly pink next to his.

"I had a thought," I said. "If hitting your head on the ice put some kind of cap on the dreams, there might be some other physical intervention that can get at the problem. More subtle than breaking your skull open on the ice. Maybe the doctors can actually help you."

Lucas rubbed his temple. "I'm dreaming so much more now," he said. "I think I'm going to get to the end. I—"

"Lucas, please!" I didn't want to listen. But I could see that he was in pain. If talking helped, I had to let him. "Okay," I said, to let him know he could go on.

"It was a bomb," he announced. "A homemade bomb. Nothing special. It was in the kitchen. The fourth apartment we checked. Inside a radio." He'd spoken in bursts, and I couldn't tell if he was short of breath because he was weak or because he was afraid of what he was saying. "This kid was holding the radio. He was young. Maybe eleven?" Lucas closed his eyes. "I can see him. Fat cheeks. Skinny arms. Blue eyes—weird for Iraq. He peed himself. That was how I knew the radio was a bomb. Juliet, they blow up their kids. Little kids." Lucas let out a dry laugh. "The radio was on too. Playing music. I don't know what the song was, but I can hear it." He rubbed his hairline near the bandage he still wore from hurting his head on the ice. "It's the song I hear every time I dream."

"What happened next?" I asked.

"That's it. I see the kid. The radio. I get that it's a bomb. I think, *So this is how I'm going to die.* And I wake up."

Just then, a nurse in puppy-emblazoned scrubs and red clogs wheeled in a pole with a hook on top. Lucas nodded a greeting in her direction, and she cheerfully asked him questions as she checked the label on the bag, attached it to a piece of tubing, flicked the tubing with one finger, then hooked its other end to a port that emerged from a bandage taped to his elbow. I couldn't take it in—the cheery nurse, her scrubs and clogs. What Lucas had just told me.

"Like my IV?" he said.

I shook my head. I was trying not to cry.

"It's just fluids and antibiotics. It's the same stuff you take if you have strep throat."

"You have strep throat?"

"I wish," he said. "I have this fever no one understands because there's no source of infection."

"Oh, don't you worry, honey," said the nurse. "These docs know what they're doing. No one's *that* much of a mystery."

Lucas smiled, but as soon as the nurse was gone, his smile faded.

"The pain I told you about yesterday," Lucas said. "The burning. I felt it again. When I was asleep. I'm guessing it's how I'm dying. In the future."

"Lucas . . . ," I said. He looked up at me hopefully, like I was going to be able to help him, like I could make the pain go away.

But then Mrs. Dunready returned from her walk. "Oh, Juliet," she said, as if she were just seeing me for the first time. "Shouldn't you be in school?"

"Free period," I mumbled. I picked up my backpack from the chair where I'd tossed it down. "But I guess I should get back."

I was headed for the bus stop outside the hospital when I spotted Rosemary's car parked behind the taxi line. She had her left elbow balanced on the car door, her head propped in her hand. She didn't look busy or thoughtful or otherwise occupied with an agenda. She was just . . . there. And even now, when I think of what the word "friend" means, I remember Rosemary waiting for me that day. Her knowing to come, even when I hadn't asked. Even when things between us were strained.

"Aren't you going to get in trouble, skipping school?" I asked once I was buckled into the passenger seat.

She smiled ruefully, that I-know-that-you-know-that-I-know smile that makes it possible to like someone as beautiful as she is. "Aren't you?" she said.

Somehow, I got through the rest of the day. I remember sitting with Rosemary at lunch, my tray filled with food I couldn't imagine eating. I remember standing at my locker, trying to recall which class was next and not being able to.

After school, I went back to the hospital. Dexter came too, and we sat side by side at the foot of Lucas's bed, watching him sleep. For the most part, he slept peacefully, but once, he started thrashing. I put my hand on his leg and shook him, hoping Mrs. Dunready wouldn't see. It was enough of a disturbance that Lucas half woke, then resettled.

Mr. Dunready brought Tommy and Wendell to see Lucas after school, before taking them to a friend's for the night.

I was pretty sure something had happened between him and Mrs. Dunready during the course of the day. I didn't know what it was, but they seemed more relaxed with each other. And as he left, Mr. Dunready put a hand on Mrs. Dunready's shoulder and said, "Maureen, try to rest." He looked at Lucas long and hard. "I'm coming back," he said. And then, as if afraid that his statement would be taken to mean more than it should: "After I drop the boys."

Once they were gone, Lucas's mom fell asleep in a chair, dressed in the same clothes she'd been wearing the night before. Her sweatshirt had a dribble of coffee down the front, but she didn't seem to know.

When the team of doctors came through, Dex blocked them at the curtained doorway. "Give her a minute, please," he said. "She's just waking up."

I was impressed with him. I knew from my experience on rounds with my dad that doctors wait for no one, but Dex was so calm and confident he was able to hold them at bay.

In the conference that followed, the doctors wondered out loud why Lucas was sleeping so much and instructed the nurses to wake him every twenty minutes. They kept coming back to questions about his fever and why, even with antibiotics, they couldn't lower it to the level they wanted to see.

"He presented with loss of consciousness, post–

nonconcussive head injury. So where is this fever coming from? Why is he showing signs of dehydration?"

I saw Mrs. Dunready's back straighten at the words "risk of sepsis" and "strokelike activity," but she nodded and asked questions that made it clear she was a nurse as well as a mom.

Next the doctors woke Lucas, asking him the year, to spell his name, how many fingers they were holding up. You could tell he had to really think about the answers. But once the doctors were gone, he put out a hand for Dex to high-five, hockey-team-style.

Lucas's mom never left the room again, so I didn't get to talk to Lucas alone. Instead, I listened to Dex tell him stupid stuff about what was going on at school. Dex's deliberately casual reporting seemed to calm Lucas, so I tried to match his tone. I think I said something like "I'm going to need your advice on what to do when you cut class on the day of a test." Dex told him that the guys on the team were putting together a highlight reel from everyone's parents' game videos for Lucas to watch if he got bored and missed hockey too much.

Lucas slurred his words when he said, "That's awesome." Dexter looked at me a little puzzled, a little amused, as if we were at a party and someone was drunk.

At dinnertime, Dex offered me a ride home. Saying goodbye to Lucas, I held his hand. He said, "Jules, can you bend down?" I did. He said, "Closer," and I bent down so far my face was inches from his and my hair was falling down around us. He turned his head into my hair and he inhaled, like he was smelling flowers. I looked at him as if to say, "Okay, that's weird," but the desperation in his eyes was too serious for me to make any kind of joke.

"That's real, right?" he whispered. "You're still real?" I nodded. Then he said, "This is why I came back. For this. I remember this."

Out in the hallway, with the elevator door open, I stopped. I could not move.

"Juliet?" Dexter said. "You coming?"

"No," I said, turning back toward the room. "You go."

I called my mom. I told her I was staying late. Could she pick me up at ten? She didn't like it—I could hear that in her voice—but she agreed.

chapter twenty-eight

The next morning, back at the hospital, I learned that Lucas had weakened overnight. His mom was in the cafeteria when I arrived, but his dad was sitting in the chair in the corner, his hands on his knees, staring at Lucas's face. Once, when I left to go to the bathroom and came back, I saw him standing at the bed, his hand on Lucas's shoulder. He moved as soon as he saw I was there.

Mrs. Dunready pulled a chair up next to Mr. Dunready's. They sat together without looking at each other, without talking. Lucas slept on, and eventually Mrs. Dunready reached for Mr. Dunready's hand.

"I can't stop thinking," she said, "that there's something more we can do."

"He's a fighter," Mr. Dunready said, his mouth tightening into a grimace. "We know that. The boy will fight."

Later, on my way back from buying a newspaper, I heard

Mrs. Dunready in the hallway, having a muffled argument with Lucas's doctor. She couldn't understand why they didn't know what was happening. She couldn't understand what was taking so long with the MRI results. She reminded him that Lucas had been having headaches for months—she wanted the doctor to reexamine the scans. "The headaches were severe," I heard Mrs. Dunready almost wail. "I know my son. I'm a neurology nurse. I can tell when a person's in pain."

After, when a nurse was taking Lucas's temperature and blood pressure—something they were doing every half hour, it seemed—Mrs. Dunready called me out into the hall.

"You can see how serious this is," she said. I nodded. "So if there's something you know about Lucas, something that for some reason he didn't tell me, this is the time for you to explain it."

I couldn't tell if I was relieved that she was asking or terrified. I do know I instantly felt a little bit sick.

"I'm not stupid," Mrs. Dunready went on. "I've been watching Lucas for the past few months. I thought it was you. I thought it was stress, but now I don't know. Juliet, why is he quieter? Why is he . . . nicer? As a mother, I can see that he's changed." She paused. "Is this about drugs?"

"Drugs?" I couldn't help it. I laughed. "You think Lucas is taking drugs?"

"I don't see what's funny about drugs."

I quickly squashed my laughter. "No," I said. "Drugs

aren't funny." She was still looking at me like she was waiting for something. "Lucas doesn't take drugs." She kept staring. "He drinks beer," I offered.

"I know that," she snapped. "You think I don't know that?"

And it was seeing her frustration that made me realize I couldn't withhold the truth. "There *is* something," I began before I could think better of the impulse. Mrs. Dunready's eyes immediately narrowed. "It's going to sound strange." I think I actually closed my eyes, the way you might when you're ripping off a Band-Aid or waiting for a loud noise. "He thinks the headaches he's been having are coming from memories." I swallowed. "He feels like he's having memories of the future."

"What?" Mrs. Dunready hissed at me. Her face was contorted, as if she'd just noticed that I was a mutant zombie baby killer.

"He thinks he knows what's going to happen to him in the future. That he's lived in the future and come back, almost like a ghost, inhabiting the body of a younger version of himself."

"That's—" Mrs. Dunready sputtered. "That's crazy."

"He remembers being in a war," I said. "After he becomes a marine. He believes that he will fight in a war in Iraq. He thinks he's dying there. Of burns."

She put her head in her hands. "It's a tumor. I knew it was a tumor. How could they miss this?" I was standing in front of her, but she wasn't talking to me anymore. "I *work* with this," she said. "I *know* this. Personality changes.

Headaches. I just thought . . . I thought he was maturing. Ha!" She turned to me now. "I thought it was *you* that had changed him. Or seeing me stand up for myself with his dad. I'd been hoping he'd abandon his great love of the marines. . . . I *welcomed* this change. I said nothing because I didn't want to"—she took a deep, painful-looking breath—"I didn't want to *jinx* anything. Oh, God."

She started to cry. Gingerly, I put a hand on her shoulder, but she was already spinning away. "I have to find a doctor." Her eyes rolled back in panic.

That afternoon, I met Dr. Katz, a neurologist with a specialty in psychiatric disorders who was a friend of Mrs. Dunready's. He was very undoctorly, wearing Ray-Ban sunglasses on Croakies, corduroys, and running shoes. His dark hair was on the long side and so curly it looked unbrushable. He asked all kinds of questions about Lucas's dreams and headaches and what I thought was happening. I could tell that he was trying to decide whether I was lying. And that he was almost more interested in the girlfriend's telling lies than the boyfriend's being crazy.

But he wasn't entirely dismissive. For one moment he even toyed with a theory that considered what I was saying. "It's a fairly elegant proposition," he said, "from a neurological standpoint, the idea that the brain's ability to assemble memory could, with the right energy surge—the kind you'd muster in a life-and-death situation—reach outside of one brain through space and time and into another. That the host brain would manifest medical symptoms the future body was experiencing." But then with a shake of his head, he abandoned the idea as impossible and returned to the only real option he saw: one of us, either Lucas or me, had completely lost our minds.

Scans were reexamined. Tiny pinpricks of irregularity were considered. Surgery was discussed. Mr. Dunready remained in his chair in Lucas's room, silent, still, his eyes fixed on the bed like he was on guard duty and could keep Lucas out of danger through vigilance alone.

The next morning, I didn't even pretend to go to school, and when I got to the hospital, Dex was already there, waiting on a bench in the hall outside the ICU.

"His mom's meeting with a doctor again," Dexter told me, standing. "I'm supposed to stay out here until they're done."

"How is he?"

"He was sleeping when I got here," Dex said. "I think they tried to wake him up for the doctor."

"*Tried* to wake him up?"

Dexter nodded, like he didn't want to say out loud how bad things seemed. Then he put an arm over my shoulder in a very un-Dexter-like gesture and proceeded to give me the most awkward half hug I had ever received. I guess it was a sign of how scared I was that I was grateful for the contact. He'd heard what I'd said the day before about Lucas's memories and dreams, but he didn't mention it. He was being kind.

Mrs. Dunready appeared in the hall, walking with a doctor I hadn't seen before. She was saying, "I've told you, he's been having headaches for weeks. He reported dizziness. He's been delusional. I agree the scans don't show any hemorrhaging or lesions, but something isn't right."

"Mrs. Dunready," the doctor replied. "I know you're a nurse. I know you're in neuro, but you have to trust us. We've looked at the scans three times."

"So what's happening to him?" Mrs. Dunready growled. "You must have a theory, at least?"

"I'll tell you honestly, we don't," the doctor said. "The fever, that abnormal EKG, the lethargy, the pupil dilation—these symptoms together, they say physical trauma. I don't have to tell you we see them in patients who present with multiple lacerations, internal organ damage, puncture wounds, broken bones."

"I know."

"But in the absence of a physical injury or evidence of brain infection, we can't account for the symptoms."

"What about the head trauma? Do you think he's responding to the fall he took on the ice?"

The doctor paused. "Maureen, you're fishing. Head trauma like Lucas experienced could result in some of these symptoms, but not all of them. It's not enough. There's something else going on."

"I want a team meeting," Mrs. Dunready decided. "Katz didn't rule out a tumor. I feel like I'm carrying information between you all."

"Of course," the doctor said. "Great idea. Let's set something up for lunchtime."

As soon as the doctor stepped away, Mrs. Dunready noticed Dex and me. "Oh, you guys." She sighed as though even the sight of us was exhausting. "Go on in." She was still wearing the sweatshirt with the stain. When Mr. Dunready emerged, car keys in hand—I assumed heading out for an errand of some kind—they clasped hands before he continued on to the elevators.

This time, I wasn't prepared for how sick Lucas looked. All the color in his often ruddy face was gone. Someone had shaved him, which should have made him look better, but it just made it clear how sunken his cheeks were. Something had changed about his hair too. Maybe it was the lighting in the room—the window shade was drawn—but it looked as gray as his skin. He couldn't have gone gray overnight, could he?

"Is he sleeping?" I asked. I spoke quietly; I didn't want to wake him.

"Very deeply," Mrs. Dunready explained. "But we should wake him. We're waking him every ten minutes now." She stood by Lucas's shoulder and gently shook him.

Lucas dutifully shifted, then regulated his breathing without fully gaining consciousness. "Lucas," his mom said. "Open your eyes." She lifted a cup with a straw from the table by his bed. "Drink something," she said. She put the tip of the straw into his mouth. "It's apple juice. Your favorite."

Lucas tightened his lips around the straw, which darkened as juice passed through it. He opened his eyes. "Hey, Mom," he said. I wondered if he knew where he was. If he was thinking he was in the other hospital he had described. His hand lifted and closed around her wrist. He looked up into her eyes. He said "Mom" again.

When I heard the way he said that word, so tenderly, I knew he was scared. Mrs. Dunready brushed Lucas's hair off his forehead. "Your friends are here," she said.

Lucas looked over at us, smiled wanly, then closed his eyes. Mrs. Dunready set a timer on her digital watch. "That's about all he's got right now," she said.

"Whoa," said Dexter.

Dexter and I sat in the room all morning, taking turns waking Lucas on a ten-minute schedule, listening to his mom ask every doctor who dropped in for a meeting of the whole team, which eventually was set for three, when Dr. Katz would be available.

My mom and Val showed up at lunchtime. Mom peeked through an opening in the curtain, saying, "Yoo-hoo!" Val followed her with a white shopping bag with handles made of silk ribbon, saying, "Debussy's, anyone?" As if Lucas's mom would know who Val was and the name of the Parisian-style sandwich shop she and my mom had just discovered.

But in the panic-meets-dreariness hospital context, Val's cluelessness and my mom's professional cheer came as a huge relief. At least for me. My mom's freshly dry-cleaned cashmere sweater dress, Val's funky glasses, the unfortunate Hush Puppies Val loves because they're comfortable—this was my real life, my life before Lucas, my life when it was just my mom and Val, who thought everything I did was perfect, who believed nothing for me could ever go wrong.

At least the sandwiches gave us all something to talk about, with Mrs. Dunready debating between hard-boiled egg and ham, and Dex lifting the top of his tomato and mozzarella baguette, saying, "If you stuck this in the oven, you'd be inventing French bread pizza." Mrs. Dunready drank half a bottle of Evian by herself and saved a roast beef and Boursin cheese baguette for Mr. Dunready.

Lucas didn't eat the tuna salad Val had brought for him. Or even the chocolate mousse. He took two sips of broth and went back to sleep.

Dexter went back to school.

My mom and Val went back to their offices.

And suddenly, things got quiet and still.

Mrs. Dunready's head was drooping when a nurse came in and put a hand on her shoulder. "No one's in the lounge, Maureen," the nurse said. "You'll better understand what's going on in the meeting if you're at least a little rested. We'll send someone to you before the doctor comes. You've been up all night."

Mrs. Dunready stood. "You'll wake him?" she said to me.

I nodded. The nurse explained what they'd already told Dexter and me that morning. They had Lucas's vital signs displayed on a monitor at the desk, and a reminder alarm would sound at ten-minute intervals. It was better to have someone he knew waking him, but if I somehow forgot, we'd be covered.

I woke him at 1:13 and again at 1:23. But then, at 1:30, Lucas's eyes opened on their own. I was watching his face, so I saw his eyelids flutter. He said something I couldn't understand.

I leaned in closer. "What?" I said.

"Juice," he said.

I reached for the apple juice, which I'd just refreshed with new ice chips. I held the straw to his lips. He drank.

"It's almost over," he said. I was so focused on the here and now, on the job of waking him every ten minutes, on things like ice chips and the doctors' meeting, that at first I didn't understand what he was talking about.

"The dream," he said. I ducked my head. I knew I needed to be strong for him and listen, but considering everything else going on, I didn't know if I could.

I wondered if I should explain that I'd told his mom about his memories, that he didn't have to lie to her anymore, but before I could speak, he was talking.

"I know what happens when the bomb goes off," he said.

"You saw?" I was trying to sound casual, but my hand was shaking. I could hear the ice sloshing in the paper cup. I put it down.

"I've been dreaming the same thing over and over. First just fragments, shards. The boy. A desk. The ceiling in the stairwell. Then other shards. Then they start to connect. It's like my brain's putting a puzzle together.

"Right before the bomb went off," he went on, "there was a second, probably, between when I saw the boy and when I felt the explosion. That was important, that second. That was when everything became clear."

"What became clear?" My voice was rising in panic.

"The desk I've been dreaming about. I know where it's from now. It was in the room, with the boy, lying on its side.

It must have been used to barricade the door, but then we pushed it aside when we came in. And in that second when I knew the boy was holding a bomb, I dove for it. The desk." He laughed. "As if it could save me.

"Next thing I knew, I was in the stairwell. The desk was too. The explosion pushed us both clear out of the apartment. I felt like I'd been hit by a wave."

I was listening so intently—I was so with him—that I felt the wave of heat and fear almost as a physical sensation.

"But it wasn't just the bomb. What pushed me back—" He looked for my eyes with his. I think he needed to be sure I was really there. And I was. I'd forgot where and even who I was, I was so completely focused on what he was telling me. "Jules," he said. "It was something else."

"What?"

"My feeling," he said. "My *feeling* pushed me. I could see that my life is—was—wrong."

When I didn't nod or show that I was following, he went on. "I'm not talking about my life now, the way I am with you. I'm talking about my life in the future. How I felt was— Juliet, I didn't want to go."

"And that was the feeling that pushed you out of the room? You think a *feeling* did that?"

"You've got to understand how strong it was. It was—it came from every fiber of my being."

Lucas was speaking so softly I had to lean in close to hear him.

"I landed in the hallway. On top of one of my guys—

Halleck. His AK, I think it discharged. I felt it. He probably hit someone. I don't know."

I held my head. Dizzy.

"When you die, you *do* see your life flash before your eyes," Lucas said.

"Okay," I said.

"The flashing—it's where you and I are right now. All this time that we've been together, I've been in Baghdad too, or somewhere, dying. Seeing you, being here—it's been a gift. From . . . the universe."

"You're real, Lucas," I reminded him. "I'm touching you."

"Not really," he said. "But I'll take it. I've loved every touch, being with you, being seventeen again."

"You *are* seventeen," I said. "You're going to *stay* seventeen."

"No," he murmured, growing weaker. "Iraq—what's happening to me there. I think it's almost over."

"But you think you're *dying* in Iraq," I repeated stupidly. I could feel my voice cracking. "And that can't be, because you're here, with me." I shook my head. The tears were flowing down my cheeks. "You're here because of the strap on your helmet," I insisted. "This is a head injury, and the doctors are going to figure it all out."

"No, Juliet," he whispered. "The strap has nothing to do with this. Maybe it sped up what was going to happen anyway. Maybe not. I can't control this. The future, that's what's in control."

I started to argue, but he stopped me. "I'm sure," he said.

"I'm in a dream here with you, and I just need to not wake up." I could see that it was taking all his strength to talk. "I love this dream," he said. "When I think back . . . to the beginning, when I didn't even know . . . what was happening to me . . ." I could see he was getting sleepy again. He might have drifted off as he was talking. "I just got to see you again . . . to smell you . . . to kiss you . . . to stand with you . . . in the snow . . . skating with my little brothers . . ." He stopped. "When I skied to your house." His voice broke. "I would give anything. To keep this. To keep the dream."

"You have to believe me, Lucas. This is real," I said. "I know it's real. I am real."

Lucas blinked slowly.

"What year is it, then?" I said. "In the future, the place you think is real? How can you remember so many things and not remember the date?"

Lucas closed his eyes, as if the light he was looking at had gotten too bright.

"I'm going to hold on," he said. "As long as I can."

I thought about his mom. I thought about calling her. But I didn't know what would happen if I let go of Lucas, even for an instant. He seemed that weak and afraid. I was holding his hand, trying not to squeeze too hard, because when I did, I stopped being able to feel him squeezing me back.

"You will have a good life," he said. "You will forget me."

"I won't forget you," I choked through sobs. "I couldn't. I can't."

"You'd be surprised." He was speaking so softly now I had to strain to understand him.

"No," I said through clenched teeth, surprised at the anger I felt toward him.

He tried to smile. "Write it down if you want." He swallowed with difficulty. "But, Juliet? Before? Can I hold you? Can I . . . just . . . have you?" My anger lifted.

I climbed onto the bed with Lucas. We lay on our sides, facing each other, our heads resting on the same pillow. I looked into his eyes, tracing the way the lines of darker blue mixed into the light. I watched him blink until I stopped being able to see it. The rhythm of our blinking, our heartbeats, became the same. He leaned toward me to kiss me and then we just lay that close, our noses touching, our lips an inch apart, our eyes locked. I don't know for how long.

A feeling of sweetness came over me. Over us, I believe; I am certain Lucas felt it too. "Lucas," I said, feeling so sure of the way he loved me that I could be sure about everything else too. I could step off a cliff and know that he would keep me from falling. He held my hand.

"Lucas," I said. "I will never let go of you."

"You will," he said, sounding just as drugged as I felt, just as unwilling to disturb the still surface of the pond.

"I think you're fighting it," I said. "And I want you to. I want you to fight this."

Lucas made a noise, part groan, part sign. "I want . . . ," he said. "So much." He was fading. When he blinked his eyes, they stayed closed.

"Keep fighting," I repeated.

I said the words half-asleep, feeling as if I were gazing down on the room from above. And looking back, I remember it that way. I see the stark white bed, the shiny steel bed rails, the dark question marks of Lucas's and my bodies curled toward each other, our noses touching, sharing the same air, as if nothing bad were ever going to happen to us.

chapter twenty-nine

I heard my mother's voice. "Juliet!"

I sat up quickly, before I was fully awake. I felt wonderful, like I'd slept for hours, or taken a nap on the beach. The light of the hospital room was blinding, but it didn't bother me. It took me a second to remember where I was and why, and even after I did, the feeling of peace did not dissipate.

How could I feel so amazing? I couldn't have been asleep long. Or at least, Lucas couldn't have, because the nurses would have come in to wake him two minutes after I'd failed to do so.

"Your shoes," my mom said, frowning in disapproval. I looked down. I was wearing black ankle boots that weren't the cleanest, and yet here they were, defiling a hospital bed. My mom doesn't like dirty shoes anywhere—but especially not in a setting that's aiming for sterile.

"Oops," I said.

"The nurses told me the Dunreadys are in some kind

of big meeting with all the doctors and they'll be back any minute," my mom hissed. "Get off the bed."

I slid down. Lucas slept on. It was probably getting close to the time when I should wake him, I thought. My mom brushed the dirt from the bed with the flat of her palm.

"You came back?" I asked.

"I was worried about you," she said. "I left work a little early. I thought I'd check in."

At this, I felt like Mom had snatched off a warm quilt I'd been cozily sleeping under. "A *little* early?" I said. Last time I'd checked the clock, it was 2:23. My mom leaves her office at five. "What time is it now?"

"Three-thirty. Actually, a little after."

"How long did we sleep?" I screeched. My mom just stared at me, afraid of my voice. She didn't understand. It was impossible for her to be right about the time.

"Lucas!" I said, rushing to the side of the bed. "Lucas, wake up!" I shook his shoulder. Gently, because of how weak he was. Then more firmly, because I was panicking. I pressed the button to call a nurse. Then I stepped into the hall. I shouted, "Nurse! Nurse!" because nothing was happening. Lucas wasn't opening his eyes.

No one came for what felt like forever. I remember my mother's voice: "What's going on?" I remember thinking, *How does she not know? She's my* mother. *She's supposed to know everything.*

Then the nurse with the puppies on her scrubs was frowning, running. The room filled. There were questions with no answers. Someone was on a phone, paging doctors, requesting medications, supplies. A nurse I'd never seen before attached a syringe to the port in the tube coming out of Lucas's arm.

"What are you doing to him?" I asked, though I knew I should just let them work. "What is that?"

"A stimulant," the nurse said. She was calm, with her hair brushed neatly into a bun at the base of her neck.

And just as Mrs. Dunready burst into the room trailing Lucas's team of doctors, all at a run, Lucas shot up in bed.

Bolt upright. For an instant, I swear, even his curly hair straightened. He gasped for air like someone had held him underwater nearly to the point of drowning. His eyes were open wide. His fingers—I remember noticing them—were straining, his arms extended like he was grasping for something just out of reach.

He let out this noise. I hate to even think of it. It was part moan, part strangled cry. It was a noise I can only describe as naked. Internal. It was the kind of noise you make when you are rolling a two-hundred-pound rock off your own crushed leg.

"Lucas!" Mrs. Dunready shouted. While Mr. Dunready hung back, gripping the chair rail on the wall behind him, she charged to the bed and grabbed Lucas's hands, moving quickly, in the way of a nurse used to handling patients. "You're here. You're here," she repeated. "Stay with us, baby, stay here." Mr. Dunready was shifting from foot to foot, as if he wanted to run but couldn't look away.

Lucas's straight back relaxed and his eyes found his mom's. Then his dad's. He shook his head as if he'd been swimming and was getting the hair off his face. Then he slumped forward into his mother's strong arms.

"You're here," Mrs. Dunready repeated.

A pair of orderlies rushed into the room with a gurney. And then a nurse with a bucket of towels and shaving cream. I learned later she was tasked with shaving Lucas's head in preparation for emergency surgery. "What, him?" she said. She looked at the nearest nurse, then at Lucas. "I thought this was a Code Seven."

My mom was the one who explained. "He just sat up," she whispered. "Something the other nurse gave him."

Yet another nurse pushed past the orderlies, this one wheeling a cart with what I thought was a cash register on top until I realized it was a machine I'd seen used a million times in that TV show *ER*. A crash cart.

I actually thought for a second that the nurse with the crash cart was just storing it in Lucas's room, that she had used it on another patient and was returning it. That made more sense than what I learned later.

You see, Lucas hadn't been sleeping. He'd been flatlining. Not for long—thirty-five, forty seconds. Not enough time for brain damage, but enough to scare everyone on the floor half to death. Enough for his mom, hearing the coded announcement and knowing what it meant, to believe that Lucas had died.

Mr. Dunready elbowed his way through the crowd to lay a hand on the rail of Lucas's bed. Mrs. Dunready was crying, gasping for air, as if relief was choking her. The nurses had stepped between her and Lucas. They were making Lucas lie down. My mom moved behind them. She put a hand on my arm.

A doctor I didn't recognize was paging through Lucas's

chart, and Dr. Katz was just watching the whole scene unfold with one hand on his chin, like he was waiting, or thinking, or waiting to think.

I learned later that during a shift change at the nurses' station, someone had accidentally turned off the timer on Lucas's monitor, so when he and I were lying on the bed together, he had fallen deeper into sleep than he was supposed to.

Later, Lucas would tell me his mother thought the deep sleep was what saved him, but I knew it wasn't. I went so far as to re-create the timing, repeating every word we'd spoken and pacing out the steps I'd taken. This convinced me that Lucas had slipped away—started to flatline—only after I'd let go of him and climbed down from the bed. His heart had stopped and his breathing had ceased only when I'd gotten up. He must have been holding on because of me, and when I'd let go of him, he had died.

Dr. Katz shone a light in Lucas's eyes, asked him if he knew where he was. "The hospital," Lucas replied easily, all traces of slurred speech gone.

"How long have you been here?"

"I'm not sure. I remember the team dinner. I wasn't feeling well."

"I'm going to palpate your skull. Please let me know if you feel any tenderness or pain." He put his thumbs under Lucas's jaw, pressed the base of his neck with his fingertips. "Anything?" he said.

"Not a thing."

He moved his thumbs to Lucas's temples. "Here?"

"No."

"Who was president the year you were born?"

"Carter."

"Who's president now?"

"Michael Jackson?" No one in the room laughed except Mr. Dunready, who immediately apologized. Lucas rolled his eyes. "It's Clinton."

"What's the last thing you remember?"

For the first time during this series of questions, Lucas paused. He looked over at me. "Juliet," he said, as if he was remembering me from a long time before. "I didn't know you were here." He furrowed his brow. "The last few days . . . I don't remember them all that clearly. It's not that I don't remember being here. It's just . . ."

"Your body was in a state of severe distress." Mrs. Dunready was leaning down from behind, the closest she could get to him in the sea of nurses and residents measuring, checking, updating. She laid a hand on his shoulder.

"What happened to me?" Lucas asked. He looked around the room, which was rapidly clearing out—the orderlies with the gurney and the nurse with the crash cart departing, floor nurses getting called into other rooms, residents and med students checking their pagers, stepping out to use the phone at the nurses' station. Finally, it was just Dr. Katz, the nurse with the puppy scrubs, Lucas's mom and dad, my mom, and me.

"We don't actually know," Dr. Katz said, looking Lucas in the eye in a way that I had to assume was reassuring to him. "There may have been a bleed, or at least some swelling, in your cranium that caused you to be symptomatic. No concussion was observed from your fall on the ice, and though your behavioral response concerned us enough to order scans, we found nothing unusual. Clearly something was going on with you. We just don't know what."

Lucas's gaze strayed to me again. "I fell on the ice?"

I stared.

"Dad?" Lucas said. "You're back?"

If he didn't remember the fall . . . If he didn't remember that his dad had been here for days . . . If he didn't remember me either . . . What *did* he remember?

Then Lucas laughed.

It was a nervous laugh. I'd seen Lucas nervous before, but I'd never seen him laugh in response to that feeling. Usually he'd do the opposite, looking at whatever he was afraid of straight on, willing himself to stay calm, tell the truth, get what he wanted.

I walked to the bed, put a hand on the mattress next to him. I didn't touch him. But I leaned over, close to his face, so that even if everyone else in the room could hear us, there would at least be the illusion of intimacy. "Do you remember that dream you've been having?" I said. "About the war?"

"Dream?" Lucas said.

"It's not unusual to lose memories in a situation like this," Dr. Katz dipped in to explain. "In situations of trauma."

I looked at Lucas. He met my gaze and then quickly looked away. But it was enough for me to pinpoint what was missing: it was in his eyes. Before, they had always flashed and sparkled, suggesting that he knew more than people might assume. Now his eyes were flat, staring, fixed forward in the way of someone who can't see. Younger, less knowing eyes.

"Stop looking at me like that, Jules." He laughed that nervous laugh again.

"You *can* lose a memory," Dr. Katz continued. "No one yet has a precise, or even rough, understanding of how memory works. All we know is that the memories are likely still there, stored in various regions of the brain. What you lose is your ability to reassemble them."

"You don't remember the dream?" I asked Lucas again quietly.

He shrugged. "I guess I kind of remember that I *had* a dream," he said. "Was it intense?"

"That's an understatement."

"She told us you were convinced this dream was real," Mrs. Dunready said. Using "she," as if I weren't in the room. "She said you had delusions about predicting the future."

Lucas looked at me again. "I did?"

"You weren't exactly seeing the future," I said. "It was more like you could remember it."

"Did I think—" he began. His face, gray only moments earlier, was now nearly scarlet with embarrassment. "I thought I had *time-traveled*?"

Mr. Dunready drew his head back and shuddered, like he was recoiling from the sight of something revolting.

"You have no memory of that now?" Mrs. Dunready asked. I half believed she had her fingers crossed behind her back, begging the universe for the return of her firstborn son from the land of crazy. Just as I had mine crossed as I prayed, *Please remember, please, please.*

"No," Lucas said. He looked at me, as if I would tell him if that was the right answer.

And I guess I smiled. Maybe I shrugged.

How do you react when a face you have touched with your hands, your mouth, eyes you have memorized, imagined, stared into, watched watching you—how do you react when it's become the face of a stranger?

"If you don't mind," said Dr. Katz to Lucas, "I'd like to continue my exam."

Lucas nodded as Dr. Katz asked him to bring the fingers on his left hand together with those on his right and follow Dr. Katz's penlight with his eyes again and again and again.

Watching Lucas alive and healthy in that moment did nothing to comfort me. I knew without question that somewhere, at some point in the future, my Lucas was gone.

I backed out of the room, saying goodbye to no one, not even waiting to hear what more Dr. Katz would say. I couldn't stay there, surrounded by everyone's joy, a moment longer.

I'd forgotten about my mom, though. She caught up to me as I was heading for the elevator. "Juliet?" she said.

How much of what I felt inside showed on my face? Could she read what was there?

"You're leaving *now*?" she asked. I opened my mouth to make some excuse—that I was sick, that I suddenly remembered some homework I'd left undone—but I came up with nothing. Like Lucas, I felt myself gulping air, gasping with the effort to breathe. I collapsed into tears.

My mom held me as I sobbed. She's shorter than me, and I stooped to lay my head on her shoulder, the fingers of her delicate hands smoothing my hair as my body shook. I never told her—not even years later—why I was crying. But I believe on some fundamental level she knew.

Maybe she, like Lucas, had been able to see into the future. Maybe that was what she'd been trying to tell me all year, that my heart was going to be broken, and that I could have no idea how bad it would feel. But that she did. She'd known what was coming and she was there for me. I didn't have to be there alone.

I couldn't have imagined I would need that kind of comfort from her. And perhaps pride would have prevented me from accepting it if I had been in a position to hold back.

I wasn't.

The sobs seemed to come from a bottomless well. I felt them stretching my mouth until I thought my lips would crack. My jaw ached. Mom held me tight, her tiny body surprisingly strong, murmuring over and over, "I know, sweetheart, I know."

chapter thirty

It is amazing what you can forget. But it is also amazing what you can remember.

Home from the hospital, I drank a glass of warm milk, changed into my pajamas, got under the covers, and slept. I woke around midnight when Lucas called. He'd been moved to a room with a phone.

"Where did you go?" he said. For a second, hearing his voice, having him get right to the point, I felt my heart leap. How could Lucas not be Lucas? I must have been mistaken. "You didn't say goodbye."

I squeezed the bridge of my nose between my thumb and forefinger, hoping it would keep me from crying.

"Juliet? You there?"

"There were so many people," I said. "The room felt too crowded. I couldn't believe what I'd just seen."

That was when Lucas told me about the shift change,

how the monitor in the nurses' station had accidentally gotten turned off. "The nurses said you were the one who called them in. If you hadn't been there, I would probably be brain-dead or something now."

"Really?"

"Yeah." Lucas snorted. "You saved my life."

Later, I'd go back and take in the momentousness of that, but just then I was focused on a different train of thought.

"Have you remembered anything yet? From before you went to sleep?" He said nothing. "Lying on the bed with me?" I prompted.

"You mean at my house? Last fall?"

A cold bubble of disappointment rose into my throat.

"Do you remember your dream yet?" I asked instead.

"No," Lucas said.

"Iraq?" I pushed him. "The alley? The flat-roofed buildings?"

"Why would I dream about Iraq? Why does this matter, what I dreamed?" I couldn't see him, but I could almost feel him shudder, and it was the shudder that I clung to—my last hope. Maybe there were still traces of the paths his other self had taken? Like Dr. Katz had said, the memories are always there, you just lose your ability to reach them. Maybe after a night's sleep . . .

"You must be wrecked," I said.

"I just want to get out of this hospital. I don't understand why they won't let me go home."

"They will," I reassured him.

And I guess backing off the questions gave him the

space to talk, because after a minute of my telling him about everyone at school calling him Head Fake and other stuff he'd forgotten, he said out of nowhere, "It's terrifying, you know? Waking up to find out you've been sick but you can't remember? And everyone thinks you're crazy."

"You're not crazy."

He was quiet for a moment, and during the pause a nurse came in. I heard him answer her question about headaches and dizziness. When she was gone, he said quietly, almost like he was talking to himself, "Before I woke up, it was black all around. I felt trapped. Kind of like the time I fell through the ice when I was little."

"Oh, God," I said. And suddenly, I just wanted to leave Lucas alone. I didn't want to take him back to the scariest memory of his life, of being trapped in freezing water, the surface he was trying to pull himself onto breaking under his weight like a cracker, the skates that were supposed to be the best thing that ever happened to him pulling him down, and no one he could call for help. I knew now how it had felt for him to die.

"Lucas," I said. "Oh, Lucas." I was crying now.

"It's okay, Jules," he said. "I'm here."

But he wasn't. As much as I wanted to believe him, I knew he didn't understand.

chapter thirty-one

Here's a letter that probably doesn't often pop up in the advice columns of teen magazines:

> *Dear Random Magazine Editor,*
> *There's something I need to tell my boyfriend, but I'm not sure how to bring it up. You see, until a few weeks ago, he was a spirit inhabiting a younger version of his own body. Or not a spirit, exactly. He wasn't dead yet; he was just seriously injured, dying at some point in the future. His younger self was able to access memories from his future self, connecting to his thoughts across time and space until his older body died.*
>
> *Makes perfect sense, right? Okay, maybe it doesn't, but I promise you, it's all true. I'm not writing to ask if you believe it, anyway.*

Before his future spirit disappeared, my boyfriend
knew he was going to join the marines. He was going
to die in a war. A war that hasn't happened yet.
And now that he can't remember this anymore, I'm
tortured by questions. What I want you to tell me
is this: Should I tell him? Should I beg him not to
enlist? How can I make him believe me when I am
so convinced no one in their right mind would that
I'm not even going to mail this letter?
> *Sincerely,*
> *Confused*

Forget mailing it; I never even sat down to write it. Advice letters are just not me. I don't even read the magazines that print them. But I thought about those questions all the time. I thought about writing to someone, asking for help. Who could I turn to? My mom—and raise her suspicions? Since the day she'd held me as I cried in the hospital, I'd noticed her staring at me when she thought I wasn't paying attention. She'd been suggesting I go visit my dad, and when I reminded her that I couldn't exactly miss school during my junior year, the one colleges look at most closely, she, who was always so enthusiastic about my education, would say things like "What? They have schools in California."

And Rosemary? I hadn't told her about Lucas's delusions before he went into the hospital because I hadn't thought she'd believe me. Why would she now?

· · ·

Lucas was discharged from the hospital two days after he'd flatlined and revived. He wasn't allowed to climb stairs or go to school, but even just sitting on the couch, we had fun. I couldn't stop touching him, reaching for his hand, tucking my head into the crook of his elbow. We watched *Beavis and Butt-Head*, *The Simpsons*, a new channel, the Food Network, that featured this young chef named Emeril.

We ate all the microwave popcorn Tommy was supposed to be selling for Boy Scouts.

A photographer from the local paper came to take Lucas's picture.

I taught Lucas how to make the friendship bracelets I taught the little kids how to make at camp, and he made me an anklet.

All the neighbors dropped off casseroles and we ate ourselves sick on lasagna and tuna noodle.

For a week, Mrs. Dunready set her alarm for two-hour intervals during the night and woke Lucas to be sure he didn't drift too deeply into sleep. They were both exhausted. She joked it was like having a newborn again.

His dad moved back in, supposedly so he could get Tommy and Wendell's breakfast (toaster waffles) and, when the casseroles ran out, dinner (more toaster waffles) while Mrs. Dunready slept on Lucas's clock. But Lucas believed that his dad's moving back in meant the separation was off. "It's disgusting," he said, sounding pleased. "I heard them laughing. The other night, my mom said she needed some fresh air and was going to walk around the neighborhood and my dad went with her. They were like a pair of senior citizens or something."

I tried hard to remember what Lucas had said. That his parents got divorced? Or just separated for a little while? The distinction mattered. Was the future not set in stone?

All the doctors except Dr. Katz lost interest in Lucas's case once it was clear he was out of danger. They said he was allowed to go back to school, but I still went home with him to make sure he was okay. Rosemary gave us rides, as Lucas wasn't allowed to drive yet.

Then Dr. Katz said Lucas was okay to be left alone. He was okay to drive a car and to sleep through the night. But still no hockey. That was when I thought he was probably well enough for me to tell him why he had to stay away from the marines.

But I didn't.

I thought about bringing it up after a round of aggressive thumb wrestling on the Dunreadys' couch (Lucas cheats). I thought about it while sitting on a bench in his backyard on a suddenly warm early-spring day, the moisture from the ground soaking through the soles of the old pair of sneakers I was wearing.

I thought about it when Rosemary showed me and Lucas the latest batch of Jason letters she'd had to hide from her parents and said, "I wish he never even existed." I thought about it when Lucas and I were on a bit of a sugar high after buying Tommy and Wendell a package of Oreos and eating most of them ourselves.

I've lost track of all the times I opened my mouth to

explain, or to ask if any of what he'd told me sounded familiar now, or to try to let him know that there was much more to the story than just the parts everyone was talking about. But there was something sharp, something worried, about the way Lucas looked at me. He was guarded, even when we were playing games or watching TV or listing the fifteen CDs we'd bring with us to a desert island or the top ten disaster movies of all time. It was like he sensed that I had something to say and knew he didn't want to hear it. So I kept waiting. And as I did, the shell of his not-knowing grew thicker, felt harder to crack.

I didn't have much time. His eighteenth birthday was coming up. And since he could drive but not play hockey, Lucas began spending more afternoons hanging out at the MEPS in the mall, counting down the days until he could sign up.

We fought.

"How come all the marines they profile in this brochure end up owning their own businesses?" I said while we were eating sundae cups in his car after he taught me to parallel park in preparation for taking my driving exam. "Are they impossible to hire? Do they have problems acclimating to work environments where it's not okay to settle disputes with your fists?"

Lucas rolled his eyes.

"What about the ones who end up in prison because they can't reacclimate to society after being in the military?" I said. "How come there's nothing in here about the ones who turn out to *like* prison because it reminds them of living on a base? Where do they talk about all the chemicals soldiers were exposed to during Desert Storm?"

"Are you jealous?" he teased. "Because you can't serve in combat? Admit it—handling a rifle is your secret fantasy. You're a closet gun nut."

Lucas still had the power to make me laugh. Really hard.

But laughing or fighting, he wouldn't talk about the marines for real, as if by engaging in a sincere conversation—no matter where things went after that—he would be conceding whatever point he believed I was trying to score.

"Look at this," I said one time when Lucas picked me up after a visit to the MEPS and there was a folder of information "for parents" in the backseat of the car. "See this list of frequently asked questions? Every single answer tells you to 'contact a recruiter.' Look here. They tell parents that every man deserves a chance to serve his country. What's your mom think about all this?" I said.

"She thinks it's great," Lucas said, his mouth a straight line after he told this lie that he was halfheartedly trying to pass off as a joke. And then, as close as he ever got to taking me seriously: "She's made her peace with it. It's part of having my dad back home. So you can see, it's good."

It wasn't good. "Is she going to go down to the recruitment office with you and take pictures as you swear the oath of service?" I said. The brochure said there was a room set up for this at the MEPS.

"Somehow," he said, his voice short and clipped, "I don't think she'll find the time."

While we were arguing, we were still often holding on

to each other. Talking about the brochures in the car, Lucas didn't take his hand off my leg, where he'd casually draped it. Another time, sprawled on the porch furniture at Nunchuck's cousin's beach house, I laid out all the ridiculous defense-spending numbers from the federal budget. I was leaning against Lucas's arm and he had one leg wrapped around mine.

In the school newspaper office, I'd look up from my table a dozen times, hoping to see him swaggering into the room. And he often did. He would usually be waiting for me when debate practice was over.

He could still make me shiver just by looking at me. He teased me; he tickled me; he'd come up behind me, push my knees forward with his so I lost my balance, and then reach his arms around in front and catch me just before I fell.

He was still friendly beyond reason. Strangers smiled at him. Waitresses gave him free drinks. Kids in our school, kids on his team—they liked him. I liked him.

And . . . this is important for me to remember. Lucas still loved *me*. He would still run his finger down this little curve just beneath my rib cage and say, "This is my favorite part of your body." I would finish saying something that seemed perfectly innocuous, and he'd say, "I just don't know anyone else like you."

I remember the last hockey game of the season. Lucas was finally allowed back on the ice. Out of loyalty, Coach O'Reilly put Lucas in the starting line. I guess he felt sorry for Lucas. But Lucas's errors were costly. It was like he'd forgotten about passing. Every time he got the puck, he went in for a score, and he wasn't enough of a player for that to work out in the team's favor.

That was new.

On the Saturday night after that game, when he was still under strict orders from the doctor not to drink, to be home by nine, to take it easy, Lucas decided to hang out with the team and drink himself into a stupor.

"Why don't we just rent a movie and go to your house?" I said.

Lucas said, "No way." Later, I'd realize he was frustrated by the way he'd played, by the limits of his mysterious brain condition. But at the time, his anger felt personal.

He said, "We don't *always* have to be together, you know," and I felt as if he'd slapped me in the face. How could someone who said he loved me lash out in that way?

Monday, it was like that conversation had never happened. We held hands in the hallway. He kissed me in the front seat of his car. He came over after school and we did our homework together on the floor of my bedroom, then chopped the onions while my mom cooked dinner.

Before he'd gone to the hospital, he used to hold my face and just look at me, like he was trying to sear an image into his brain. He didn't do that anymore. But he knew me; he knew the best parts of me, the private self that no one else except maybe Rosemary and my mom could see. I could look at him across a room and know that he knew I was me.

And also that he was going to die.

chapter thirty-two

Every year at the beginning of April, my mom goes through closets. It has something to do with spring-cleaning, except she doesn't do spring-cleaning. (We have a service; the rooms are as clean in June as they are in March.)

But she does care about closets. And when it comes to closets, my presence is required. So here we were, on the second Saturday in April, tossing things I'd outgrown into a pile with sweaters that had lost their shape, cotton pants that had shrunk in the wash, shoes that had worn thin in the soles, scarves that had felt right at the craft fair where she and Val had purchased them but looked a little too craft-fair-y once they'd brought them home.

The decisions were exhausting. Eventually my mom unearthed a Toblerone bar and we split it and a Coke, sitting on the front step of the house, where I had waited for Lucas that first time he came to see me.

Because the houses in our neighborhood are small, it has always been a neighborhood of families just starting out. Over the years, we'd given up on knowing anyone's names, noting when they had new babies, or paying much attention when they moved out to the inevitable big house with a more modern kitchen. But that day, as we watched the kids on bikes, their helmets bobbing up and down as if their heads were balloons tied to the bike handles with strings, I thought, *Where did they all come from? What was the point? Weren't they all just going to grow up, fall in love, have their hearts broken, and die fighting in wars?*

Confronted with the same view, Mom must have reached a very different conclusion. "You know," she said, speaking with her mouth full, gesturing to the kids with her chin. "It's a good life these people are making here."

I turned my head to look at her. Her skin was streaked with shoe polish. Her hair was held back in a scarf. "I keep thinking about what you said last winter," she went on. "How I've been too careful. I remember you asking me about fear, about if it wasn't a good thing, exciting and such, to feel afraid. And I said it wasn't. It's certainly not something I want for you. But I can see how you might think, from the way I live, the way we live, that I'm running from it. You said there's not enough experience in my life. Not enough . . . love." She paused, gauging my embarrassment. "I think you don't see a whole lot in the way of passion."

"Oh, God, stop!" I said.

But she didn't stop. Looking away from me, as if she was talking as much for her own benefit as for mine, she went on. "I know you think I've missed out, and maybe I have, but I don't think so." She started to speak faster, like she wanted to get this out before I got so embarrassed I truly shut her down. "I know it's just me and Val and you, but I want you to know I'm happy. Being happy—what it takes to be happy—that changes as you get older. The way you want things changes. You can't understand this now, but you'll see. . . ." She trailed off.

"I'll see what?"

"That at some point, love goes underground. It goes deep, like some sort of river. The kind of river that never surfaces because it doesn't need to. It just flows deeper and colder and—I don't know—eventually makes it into the ocean through some kind of underground tube."

My mom and geology have never been the best of friends.

"I also want you to know that your dad and I— If I'd truly wanted to be married to him, I could have been. He never would have left us—never would have left you—if I hadn't made him go."

"But I thought it was Dad—" I stopped myself because I hadn't just thought it was Dad who left my mom, I thought she had destroyed her own life by frightening him away. I thought she should have known better. I thought he was impossible to be married to—I still think that—but I also thought he'd broken my mother's heart. "He didn't—" I spluttered. "You wanted—"

"It was me." She took a sip of Coke. "I couldn't stay. It wasn't his fault. He was just—human. Everyone is. I guess that sounds trite, but it's true. We're all trying to get everything perfect, but in the end no one can get past the fact that we're all flawed. We don't have any idea what we're doing."

"Okay," I said.

"You know what I mean?" she said. "About the river?"

Strangely, incoherently, I did.

Dex got a haircut. He got the kind of haircut that made me wonder if his mom had been cutting his hair up until then. The kind of haircut that makes you see a person in an entirely new light. Like, suddenly, it was clear that Dex had a very significant jawline. The cheekbones of a Lenape warrior. Shoulders under those sloppy, too-big shirts.

He'd set up a fund-raiser for Lucas's family to help with medical expenses. For fifty dollars you could have five guys from the hockey team come to your house and clean out your gutters or spring-clean your lawn. The fact that he scratched all the appointments into a free calendar his mom had gotten in the mail that had pictures of babies dressed in flower costumes took nothing away from what he was doing. At school, Dex was now important. Teachers would pull him aside to talk lawn care or commend him publicly for the initiative he was showing. Robin Sipe put him in charge of organizing volunteers for prom.

"I think Dex has a new girlfriend," Rosemary teased when the four of us were in Dex's basement one Friday night eating pizza and watching episodes of *Columbo,* which Dex's mom had set the VCR to tape. "Robin *loves* you."

Dex blushed. "Not my type," he said.

"So what is your type?" said Rose, chewing, laughing.

Dex blushed some more. He shrugged. He was about to reply when Lucas cut him off. "Oh, cut the shit," Lucas said, his anger at Rosemary cloaked in deadpan jocularity. "His type is you. Isn't that what you wanted to hear? Will this save us from your pulling it out of him strand by strand?"

"Lucas!" I said.

"No, no, fair enough," said Rose. "I should leave poor Dex alone." She turned to Lucas, her eyes flashing. "Let's turn the spotlight on Lucas, shall we? Lucas, how would you describe *your* type?"

"That's obvious," he said, not missing a beat, though he knew enough to be on guard taking on Rose. He slung an arm over my shoulder and flashed me, then Rose, his huge grin.

Rose didn't grin back. "Well, yeah, but what is it *about* Juliet that gets your heart racing?" she said. "What qualities in her do you predict will show up in the next girlfriend you have, and the one after that, and the one after that?"

"What are you driving at?" I said, trying to slow Rosemary down. She ignored me.

"You're not planning on marrying Juliet or anything, are you?" Rose said. "You're going to eventually break up, right? I mean, let's face it, your lives are going in totally different directions."

"Okay," I said. "That's enough."

But Rose wasn't done. "Do you think you'll always date brunettes, Lucas?" she went on. "I heard guys always end up dating women who turn out to be just like their mothers."

"God help us," said Lucas, shaking his head. "After Juliet breaks up with me, I'm not going to date anyone else ever again. I'll just become some cranky control freak who hand-carves wooden lawn ornaments, then dies alone."

"Yeah," I laughed. "And after Lucas, I'm going to become a nun."

Rosemary rolled her eyes, deciding, I guess, to be done. She turned to Dex. "Disgusting, right?" she said.

Dex smiled helplessly. All he wanted was for her to turn her smoky blue eyes in his direction, to look at her, to feel her attention on him.

But then the phone rang, and it was another call about the hockey team lawn service. And for once, Rosemary was left waiting for Dex instead of the other way around.

That spring, Valerie arranged for me to intern at her law firm, helping with background research for a pro bono case.

I loved it. I loved taking the bus downtown after school, stepping into the wood-paneled hallways of the firm, smelling the fresh flowers on the receptionist's desk, helping myself to one of the free sodas from the kitchen, where the young associates would tell me about the law schools they went to, what they studied in college. I found hours passing when I wasn't thinking about Lucas, or Rosemary and Dex, or all three. It was a relief.

But then, when I exited the building through its heavy glass revolving door, moving from the air-conditioned thrum of the ventilation system into rush hour and the warm spring air, I would think about Lucas, and it was almost as if there were a rope tied snugly around my waist and he were tugging on it. Riding the bus home, I'd close my eyes and see his, remembering the way he looked at me, remembering what it was like to feel myself mirrored in his gaze.

On one of these afternoons, the paralegal supervising my project was out sick, so I went home early enough to try to catch Lucas while he was still at school, lifting weights with the team.

I was cutting it close and had to hurry from the bus. I was speed-walking. Maybe I was frowning. I remember my backpack feeling heavy.

Then I heard a car going fast enough that I looked up, and when I did, I saw that it was Lucas's rusty red heap, stuffed full of hockey guys, their cut arms and rough faces filling the front and back so I couldn't have said how many of them there were besides Lucas, who was driving, and Dexter, riding shotgun. The music was loud, some kind of metal. I remember that Dex was smiling a little too broadly and that Lucas wasn't smiling at all. And then Lucas's eyes met mine. He saw me, I'm sure of it, but he didn't give me any sign. He kept driving, fast, while arms and shoes and wet hair were waving from the windows.

All winter I'd felt like the car was mine. I kept my favorite flavor of gum in the glove compartment. You could see my footprints on the passenger-side windshield when the light struck it in just the right way. But the car didn't belong to me anymore. Maybe it never had.

I stopped walking.

Lucas had seen me. I knew he'd seen me.

He hadn't stopped.

I remembered the other time when I thought he'd picked the hockey guys over me, when I'd been at debate practice and I'd seen him take off with his friends. I remembered his crooked smile when it turned out he was waiting for me in the hallway, the way I'd felt sure I was what he most wanted in the world.

I remembered the night he went drinking with the hockey guys even after I asked him to stay with me.

He'd seen me. He hadn't smiled.

I waited a long time, as if he might turn around and come back to me. He never did.

"I didn't *see* you," Lucas insisted that night when we talked on the phone.

"You looked right at me," I said. "You couldn't have missed me."

"Maybe I was lost in thought," Lucas said. "Does it ever occur to you that sometimes I'm thinking about something besides you?"

I felt myself sputter.

"It wasn't like you'd asked me to pick you up," he went on. "Sometimes it's just time for me to be with the guys, you know what I mean?"

"Yeah," I said, my voice a deflating balloon.

"Don't be like that," Lucas whined, and I knew what I was supposed to do now, what he wanted: what Dex did for Rose. I was supposed to make myself sound cheerful and happy and too busy to care.

"Come on," Lucas groaned. "This is high school. It's supposed to be fun. All that debate stuff you do, burying your head in back issues of *Time* magazine. Is that really good for you?"

"What, I should try lighting tennis balls on fire?"

"You know," Lucas said, "it might not be the worst idea." He was laughing like he was kidding. Then he said "Hey" in that way that belonged just to me. I knew that if we hadn't been on the phone, he would have tickled me or grabbed me or moved me, reminded me that we belonged together, that we knew each other through touch as well as words. But still, something had changed. I didn't want to even say what it was.

"Keep in mind," Rosemary said, "that the way Lucas is acting, being a dick to you, this is totally normal." We were at her house, on the patio, the first time we'd hung out alone since Lucas got released from the hospital. "We're in high school, after all."

My eyes filled with tears, and I didn't know if it was because of Lucas or because of the satisfaction Rosemary was clearly taking in telling me that.

"You can cry," Rosemary said. "But do yourself a favor. Don't cry in front of Lucas anymore. Don't wait around for him at school. Don't act like such a puppy. You are probably freaking him out. Obviously he still likes you. He's just not *obsessed* with you. He's a senior. He's got other things on his mind. Give him some space. And then break up with him. You need to do it to save yourself."

I was staring at her. "But I love him," I said.

"I know you *love* him," she laughed, landing on the word "love" like it was a bug she was crushing with her shoe. "But I also understand something about love you don't, maybe because I'm not *in* love personally: if you let him walk all over you, given the way you feel about him, you will be stuck loving him for life."

I didn't break up with Lucas. I wasn't like Rose. I wasn't even like my old self—careful, in control.

I guess I was the kind of person who, even though I knew better, found myself saying "I need to tell you something" to Lucas when we were sitting at the table in his kitchen, doing homework. He had his books spread out in front of him, but he was actually just doodling the globe and anchor with an eagle on the top that is the marines' emblem. I covered up the drawing with the flat of my hand.

His brow furrowed. He put down his pencil and said, "What?"

I said, "It's just—" And then he looked worried, so I rushed in quickly with "It's not bad."

He still looked worried. "Actually," I said, "it is bad."

"Are you breaking up with me?"

"No," I said. "But after I explain something, you might want to break up with *me*." I picked up the pencil he'd put down and rolled it back and forth between my thumb and fingers.

Now his worried look was replaced by a raised-eyebrows expression of curiosity, hope, intrigue. "It's not funny," I said, and he instantly, dutifully, repressed what had only been the beginning of a smile anyway. "Listen," I said. And I told him everything, from the very beginning. I told him about Friendly's, about kissing in the park after, about the dance, about the dream, about the hospital, about the way the dream ends.

I talked. And I could see that he was only pretending to listen. I could feel my face start to burn in humiliation—I could only imagine how ridiculous this sounded to him—but I continued.

Finally, he took the pencil out of my hands, as if it were a microphone and he wanted to turn the sound of my voice off. It was a gesture of mercy, saving me from myself. But I didn't need saving. It was Lucas I was trying to save. I took the pencil back.

"You told me things," I insisted, my voice growing sharp. "About the future. Things you couldn't possibly have known were going to happen, and then they did."

Out of my backpack, I fished the Post-it on which I'd been collecting a list of Lucas's predictions as I remembered them. "You knew your parents were going to split up," I read. "You knew Sanjay's house was going to burn down. You knew I was going to give you that watch for Christmas."

"That's great, Juliet."

"You told me George W. Bush was going to be the next president."

"Wasn't he already president?"

"Not that one. His son, W." Lucas gave me a blank stare. "He's the governor of Texas."

"Juliet," he said.

"You told me something bad was going to happen in the US. That we were going to go to war. In Iraq. And see—"

"We already had a war in Iraq."

I pulled out an article I'd printed off the *New York Times* microfiche in the library that day after the dance, back when Lucas first told me about all this.

"This is about people in Washington who want us to go back to Iraq. They used to work for George Bush, so if his son gets elected, their opinions will start to matter again. It makes sense. Look." I pointed to the smudged printout. "It's all about oil. These people think they can use Iraq to turn the countries in the Middle East into democracies and then it will be easier for us to use their oil."

Nothing.

"Look." I stowed the printout and opened up the notebook I'd brought with me to the library that day. "I've done research. Here's stuff on head injuries," I said. "Déjà vu." I flipped the page. "The biochemistry of the human brain. Recovered memory. What you told me about could happen. I don't know how, exactly, but the dots are there. Someday some scientist's going to connect them, but for now all I can say is that I swear to you it's real. What you told me is real."

He looked up at me, his eyes sharp and hard. He took the notebook and Xeroxes out of my hand and pushed them to the side as if he were putting a screaming child in time-out. "I get it," he said. "Research. Note taking. Reading. This is what you do best. And you never miss a chance to dump on the military."

I opened my mouth to protest, but Lucas stopped me. "Don't even pretend," he said, "that this isn't completely convenient, your premonition that everything bad happens after I join the marines, which you've been against from the get-go."

"It wasn't a premonition," I said. "And it came from you, not me."

Tommy and Wendell ran into the kitchen just then, making a lot of noise. One of them had something that belonged to the other. There was a chase. When they were gone, Lucas was looking down. "I know myself," he said, his voice guarded and low. "I know who I am. Don't talk to me about this anymore, okay? I don't want to hear it."

He took my hand, looked up at me again, and cracked a smile, and I knew I wasn't going to be able to save him. He wasn't going to believe me.

chapter thirty-three

Early May: Lucas, Dex, and I were driving to minigolf, meeting Rosemary and her little brother, Patrick. And also? We were meeting someone named Coach Pete, although I think I was the only one aware of that.

Coach Pete was not a full-fledged adult like the other coaches of Rosemary's little brother's baseball team. He was just a guy taking a semester off college, living in his parents' garage. And flirting with Rosemary whenever he had the chance. Thursday, at the game Rosemary had dragged me to, he couldn't stop teasing her about our minigolf plans for Friday. At the end of the night, she had tossed over her shoulder, "If you think you've got something to prove, we'll be there at seven." She didn't think he'd come, but I mean . . . duh.

"What about Dex?" I'd said in the car after the game.

"I'm not his babysitter," Rosemary snapped. "He won't even care."

But Dex did care. When we showed up at the course to find Rosemary laughing through a practice putt, Coach Pete wrapping his arms around her from behind to adjust her form, Dex's face went bright red. "Who is *this*?" he growled. At me. As if I had any control over the situation.

"Uh-oh," Lucas mouthed.

"This is Pete," Rosemary said forthrightly. Pete flashed the crisp smile that had turned Rosemary into such a Little League fan in the first place, and Rosemary launched into an explanation of how Pete thought he might want to teach PE.

Dex didn't wait for her to finish. He shouldered his way through our little group, grabbed a club without paying— Lucas took care of that for him—stepped onto the first green, dropped his ball, hit it randomly, and, boom, scored a hole in one, straight through the legs of an obese teddy bear that was frozen in laughter like the Buddha.

He stormed to the next hole, took another shot, got another in the hole on his first try. And on his next turn, same thing.

"What is he, a ringer?" Pete asked Rosemary.

"He's nobody," she said.

"No," Lucas leaned into their conversation to interject. "He, ladies and gentlemen, is the Jack Nicklaus of minigolf."

A couple of girls our age had stopped to watch Dex. One said something to the other behind a hand. Dex was not aware, but I saw Rosemary shoot them a hostile glare. I rolled my eyes at her. I guess I was feeling a little hostile myself. Maybe anger is contagious.

Or maybe "contagious" is the wrong word. Maybe it's

"inspirational." Maybe seeing Dex storming from hole to hole, cutting in front of little children taking too long to set up their shots, made me see my own feelings of frustration for what they were.

Dex was sick of Rosemary playing games with him? Well, I was tired of Lucas playing with me. How could Lucas say he loved me and then drive by as if I weren't even there? How could he not believe me about his dreams? Refuse to even consider my opinion about the marines?

Dex didn't want Rosemary to keep jerking his chain? I too was sick of never knowing where I stood. I'd been tossing back and forth between sadness that the version of Lucas I'd fallen in love with was gone and blind attempts to pretend that he was still here, and he . . . he wasn't tossing at all. He was proceeding with his plan for his life as if it had been written in stone.

But where Dex's anger translated into flawless play, mine was absolutely debilitating from a minigolf perspective. I took so many swings and sent the ball in so many fruitless directions that Lucas started making jokes about it.

Which I seized on as an excuse to let my anger fly.

He said, "I don't want to say I've found your Achilles' heel . . . but I think I've found your Achilles' heel," and I turned on him, threw my club down at his feet, and said, "Don't talk to me."

"What—" he began.

"Don't even look at me." He was staring. "This was your idea."

"Minigolf?" He was smiling as if he thought I was joking.

"All of it," I said. "You brought me up on the gym roof.

You told me you remembered me. You told me you'd come back for me."

The smile was gone now. "Juliet," he said. "I've explained to you—"

"You've explained *nothing*," I hissed, because people were waiting to play and they were staring. "Because you *know* nothing. You're throwing your life away and you're acting like I'm the one who's delusional."

"Come on," he said, holding out a hand for me in a gesture that begged for me to see reason. But I didn't want to see reason. I didn't want any of this. I wanted time to move backward. I wanted the old—new—whatever. I wanted *my* Lucas to come back.

Turning my back on him and his uncomprehending gestures, I stormed ten greens ahead to where Dex was just finishing up the course. "I need to get out of here," I said to him. "And I don't have a ride. Can you drive me?"

"That's the best idea I've heard all night," Dex said. Without so much as glancing at the others, he started walking, leaving me to follow. I did.

I didn't try to talk to Dex in the car. I could see how mad he was, and I didn't want to get in his way. But when he pulled up in front of my house and broke his silence to say "I am done," I said, "Me too."

Dex said, "Every time she looks at me, I think, *Maybe this is* the *time. I'll tell her how I feel now.* But I don't even know what '*the* time' means. She doesn't care about me. She pretends to, but she doesn't. Do you know what I mean?"

I did. "She doesn't deserve you," I said. "She's my best

friend and I love her, but what she's doing to you—it isn't fair."

"I know!" Dex said.

"I haven't said anything out of loyalty, but I'm sick of loyalty."

"Me too. I'm sick of trying so hard."

"I'm sick of Lucas."

"You should be. And I'll tell you something. About the hospital." I was so carried away I barely registered the ping of dread that last word inspired. But I was also relieved—at last someone was talking about it.

"All that stuff you told Lucas's mom," Dex went on. "About his dreams and stuff. You believed it. You believed the things he'd said were real. And I know why." Dex paused. "When you love someone like that, you'll believe anything."

If, two hours before, someone had told me I'd be sitting alone with Dex in his car, nearly crying over something he'd said, I would have said they were crazy. But there we were, sharing secrets. And there I was, choking up. It felt amazing to think that he had seen. That even without knowing all the details, he had understood.

"You're right!" I said. "You *should* believe people. The problem isn't with trusting too much. The problem is the people who take that trust and throw it in your face."

"I am so sick of always feeling like a chump," said Dex.

"You're not a chump."

"Thank you!"

We talked that way for a good half hour. We declared to each other that we were done being someone's sidekick.

Being the person no one listened to. But eventually the anger faded and we were left alone in the car together, feeling the other's sadness. That was when I got out.

I let myself into the house and stood in the front hall. I was thinking. My mom was at a show with Val in New York—they wouldn't be back until the next day—so the house was dark. I threw my keys into the basket on the mail table without turning on the lights. I was thinking about the night Lucas and I went to Friendly's, the night he started telling me what was happening and I thought he was crazy. I was afraid of him then, but I didn't walk away. I already felt connected. I remember thinking that it wasn't fair, that I'd already been hooked on him. But maybe now I wasn't as hooked as I'd once believed.

I decided I would get into my pajamas, curl up on my mom's spot on the couch, and watch television until I was too sleepy to stay awake anymore. But when I turned to look in the direction of the couch—my hand on the light switch in the front hall—I saw something I couldn't believe was real. I saw a person sitting in my mom's spot already. Alone, in the dark, the TV off. When he saw that I'd seen him, he leaned forward so I could see his face.

Lucas? I thought. I guess I was expecting a ghost. But the someone sitting on my mother's couch in the empty house with all the lights turned off was Jason.

chapter thirty-four

The scream came automatically. I felt my hand grasping my throat. I knew I should run for the phone, but instead, since I was still in the entrance hall next to the stairs, I ran halfway up the flight, then crouched down, hiding behind the rails, where I could see through to the hall and the arched opening that led into the living room. I was acting on the kind of impulse that causes you to jump onto the counter when there's a mouse in the kitchen. It was important, I thought, to get as far away from Jason as possible while keeping him in view.

"Where's Rosemary?" Jason said, turning toward me, but staying put on the couch. Hearing his voice, I felt my panic intensify. Before he'd spoken, a small part of my brain could cling to the hope that he was just a shadow, a figment of my imagination. But shadows don't talk.

"She's not with me," I said.

"No," he said, his voice trembling. "She is. I called her house. I pretended to be some kid whose name I got out of the yearbook. Her mom told me she was with you, that Rosemary would be sleeping over here."

I couldn't tell what I was supposed to be paying attention to. Through the banisters I saw a copy of the L.L.Bean catalog lying on the top of our pile of mail. It was there because I needed a new raincoat and my mom had told me to pick one, but I hadn't done it yet. Did that matter? Or was what was really important the fact that Rosemary had told her mother she was sleeping here?

A knot formed in my stomach. My breath came fast. Ideas traveled in circles.

I saw some dust on the stairs. My mom hated that, I knew. I was supposed to have vacuumed before going out to meet my friends, but I hadn't. Rosemary had lied to her mother. I had lied to Jason. I had lied to Rose. Rosemary was with Pete. Rose was lying to Dex. Lucas didn't understand.

Jason was here.

Sitting in my mom's spot in the living room.

And I was alone.

"Rose changed her mind," I said. "She was going to sleep over but she wasn't feeling well, so she went home." To whose home, I didn't say.

"Don't bother," Jason said. "I used to be on the inside of the game, remember? If she's not with you, she's with a guy."

I think I nodded. "Want me to call her?"

I could hear the trembling in my voice, but could he? If I

was calm, would I change his mood? "I could call her," I said again. I felt like whimpering, but I made my voice go steady. "It wouldn't take a sec."

Jason didn't answer me. I swallowed hard. My throat was so tight the swallowing hurt. I made a motion as if to stand.

"Sit down," Jason growled. I sat.

Jason stood. I could see he was holding something that glinted in the streetlamp light coming through the front window. Metal. A knife?

Before I could see for sure, he sat down on the couch again and put whatever he was holding on the coffee table in front of him. In our kitchen, we had one good knife with a wooden handle bolted to a steel blade. It was the knife Lucas and I traded back and forth when we helped my mom make dinner, the only knife we owned that didn't get stuck on the skin of a tomato.

"Do you respect me?" Jason asked.

"Okay," I said. I'd heard his question, but I was having trouble processing it. I was trying to breathe. I was thinking I might throw up. I was wondering if that would make Jason mad or if it might make him feel sorry for me, if he'd let me go into the kitchen to clean up. Or the bathroom. Upstairs. I could sneak into my mom's room on the way, get the cordless phone.

"Do you?"

"What?" I said. Then, remembering: "Yes. I respect you. A lot."

Jason was quiet again, looking out the window as if Rosemary might come up the front walk any minute.

"She just won't listen."

"Okay," I said.

"But she listens to you. You can explain to her. You can get her back for me."

I didn't point out that he was wrong. That Rosemary didn't listen to anyone. Instead, I said, "Sure." I said, "Just let me call her."

"Stop asking me that!" He was really angry now. "I'm not stupid. I know you're probably thinking of ways to get rid of me, just like Rosemary always was. But I don't want to be gotten rid of. I want to be with someone who can appreciate me. She always said you were smart. She said you thought things through carefully. She said you were a good listener." He was calming himself down. I could hear it. "So maybe you can help me."

"Jason—" It should have been easy to explain to him that no one could listen under these circumstances. But then he reached toward the coffee table. And maybe if I'd screamed loud enough a neighbor would have heard. Or maybe, from where I was sitting, I could have beaten Jason in a dead sprint to the front door—it was right there, at the bottom of the steps. I could bust my way through it before he crossed the living room. But I wasn't thinking about those things. I was thinking: *Sharp. Danger.* Lucas had said that in the marines, all you needed to be good at was not dying. I hadn't understood what that meant until now.

"Rosemary likes you," I said. "Deep down."

"I'm sure of it," Jason said. "In Aruba last summer, she was the one who came up to me. I wouldn't have even tried with her, but she called out to me as I dragged my gear up the beach. She asked me what kind of board I was using. She made it sound casual, you know, like she was interested in getting into the sport."

"But she wasn't?"

"No," Jason chuckled, remembering. He was calmer. That had to be good. "She told me later she didn't know anything about surfing. We hiked up to a waterfall, which is where we got together for the first time. And she told me like she thought it was funny. She was lying to me from the beginning."

He'd started to sound angry again, so I tried to steer him back. "But it was fun, when you were in Aruba?"

"It was amazing," Jason said, the bitterness out of his voice. He started to talk about all the things they'd done together. They went scuba diving. They did the waterfall hike. They lay on the beach and looked up at the moon. It wasn't until they got back home that things started to go wrong.

I tried really hard to show Jason I was listening. "Uh-huh," I said over and over. I wouldn't say I got comfortable, but I did relax enough to notice that my fingernails had been pushing into my palms. I opened my fists, willing my hands to lie flat on the step I was sitting on.

"Rosemary," Jason said. "She just makes me feel ... I can't describe it. But do you know what I mean?"

"Of course," I said.

"You have a boyfriend, right?" Jason said. "I've seen you with him."

"Lucas," I said. Just saying his name made me both sad

and hopeful at the same time. Couldn't he save me? "He's about to enlist in the marines." I don't know why I mentioned that, except that I was grasping at reasons for Jason to let me go. Maybe if he thought my marine boyfriend was going to come looking for me . . . Although Lucas wasn't a marine yet. And he wasn't looking. He was probably too busy getting a good night's sleep—he was taking this ridiculous military recruitment test called the ASVAB the next morning, which was supposed to determine whether he'd be better at landing helicopters or filling them up with gas between flights.

"I've thought about doing something like that," Jason said. "I look at those guys and I envy their sense of purpose. It seems like if you're a marine, you know who you are."

"If you're a marine, you're someone who's going to let the government pay you seventeen thousand dollars a year so you can get yourself killed before your twenty-fifth birthday," I said.

"What about honor and country and all that?"

"That's a line." I could feel my brain switching over into debate mode. "If you look at US foreign policy since the end of the Cold War, it's all about oil," I said. It felt good to control the information. "Our foreign policy debacle in Nigeria, the whole mess of the Middle East, our refusal to confront China on reports of human rights abuses. That's oil."

Jason raised a hand. "You sound like the kids in my dorm. They're so caught up in their ideas. They never say hi to me. They don't notice anyone but themselves."

And when he said that, I was suddenly, out of the blue, completely enraged. Maybe it was spillover from thinking about Lucas's becoming a marine. Maybe it was the stupidity of Jason's comment—I mean, okay, he thought his hallmates were selfish because they were more interested in talking about big ideas than in taking care of Jason's fragile ego?

In the lucidity of rage, I decided that the knife was an impulse Jason didn't have the guts to follow through on. I also decided that because the knife came from *my* kitchen, it wouldn't be possible for it to hurt me, as if, instead of a regular kitchen knife, it was an enchanted weapon that could not rise up against its master.

This harebrained logic caused me to do what I did next, which in hindsight I can see was colossally dumb. I said, "You know what, Jason? Why don't you and your pea-sized ego get yourselves out of my house."

He stared.

"You know what Rosemary really said about you?" I went on. "She said you were too sad and pathetic to scare her."

Jason stood up fast. He groaned, looking to the ceiling as if Rosemary were up there, or as if he was angry at heaven.

The fear I'd managed to push away rushed back.

I ran up the last few steps and turned into the upstairs hall. I careened into the first room I got to—my mom's—grabbed the cordless phone off her bedside table, and then practically leapt over her bed into her bathroom, pulling the door closed behind me and locking it.

I'd vaguely heard Jason calling "Wait!" when I'd started to move. I'd heard his footfalls on the stairs. Seconds after I slid the lock into place, the handle turned. I felt him push against the door.

"Hey," he said. "I thought you understood!"

I didn't answer him. I was holding the phone. I'd already dialed. All I needed to do was wait. All I needed was to get through to someone before he had a chance to knock the door down.

I've heard that the difference between a disaster and a near disaster comes down to snap decisions, and the snap decision I'd made just then was a bad one.

You see, I hadn't called 911. I'd called Lucas.

All I can say to explain why I made that choice is that when people think they're in danger of dying, they do strange things. I called Lucas because I felt really scared and alone and I knew he would understand. As if what I needed was understanding.

My memory of that moment is all shaking fingers and the sound of my own breathing in my ears. Lucas's phone rang once, twice. He picked up groggy on ring number three.

And then the line went dead.

"Rosemary said you're smart," Jason said from outside the bathroom. "You didn't think I would just unplug it?"

He was pushing the door now, I assumed with his shoulder. I saw the latch moving. The doorframe was splintering.

I thought about the knife.

I thought about the tiny window in the shower wall. It opened onto a sheer drop of twenty feet. Stone patio below.

Then the rattling on the door stopped. And a second later, I heard Jason say, "What the—"

There was a whack. An "Oomph." Something hit the wall. The door shook. A muffled "Argh." Another whack. Then a thump on the floor like someone had dropped a heavy book bag, and Rosemary's voice: "Juliet, open up."

chapter thirty-five

There was Jason, facedown on the floor, his head on the throw rug next to my mother's bed, his legs splayed so I had to step over them on my way out of the bathroom.

There was Rosemary, standing over him, her tennis racket dangling casually from her right hand like she'd just finished a match.

And there was Dex, kneeling, holding Jason's wrists up behind his back so he couldn't move. Blood was trickling out of Jason's ear. I guess Rosemary had hit him with the full strength of her seventy-mile-an-hour serve.

Jason twisted his neck to try to look up. "Rosemary?" he said. "Are you there?"

"Get down," Dex said to him, his voice fierce but clipped, as if he didn't want to waste his energy on someone as unworthy as Jason. Jason put his head back down. "I've already called 911," Dex said to me. "We just have to watch him for, like, one minute, and then the cops will be here."

"Rose," I said. I think I was whispering. "He had a big knife."

"It wasn't a knife," she said. "It was this." She held up a flashlight. A silver one.

"You thought I had a knife?" Jason's voice was muffled by the rug.

"No one is talking to you," Rosemary said.

"How did you know I was here?" Jason said.

"Because you're a moron," Dex said.

"And because when I called my house to say I'd got to Juliet's all safe and sound, my mother said Brian Wozniak had called looking for me," Rosemary added.

"And you guessed it was me? See, you do think about me."

"I haven't spoken to Brian Wozniak since first grade. I happen to know that he is terrified of me. He would never call."

"Maybe he would," Jason said.

"Well, he didn't say so when I asked him," she went on. "So I drove on over to check things out. And I found Dex in the front yard."

"You've been following me around for days," Dex said. "So when I saw your car parked around the corner from Juliet's, I was like, *Nope, not good.*"

"You're the new boyfriend," Jason said.

Rose and Dex both said, simultaneously, "Shut up."

"I just wanted to talk to you," Jason said, straining to lift his head again to address Rosemary directly.

Dex pulled Jason's arm up a little tighter. "She didn't say you could speak."

Rosemary looked at me over Dex's shoulders and Jason's sprawled body, something about the insanity of the moment cutting through the wall that had risen between us. She looked down at her racket. Then back up at me. "I'm really sorry," she said.

The police arrived. Two big men in uniform took Jason out of the room, and a female cop and a male cop with red hair asked Rosemary, Dex, and me all sorts of questions about who lived here, where our parents were, how we knew Jason, what had happened. Dex's parents were the first to come, and the cops took Dex with them into another room.

Alone with Rose, I started to cry. I just stood there, sobbing, my arms at my sides, the tears streaming down my face, the hiccups following unchecked.

Rosemary took me by the shoulders and held me still. And I finally told her. I told her everything. About Lucas. About the roof, the kiss, the dance, the headaches, the dreams. I honestly don't know if she understood a single word. I was blubbering. I was talking fast. I was shaking. I was going out of order. I was skipping important parts.

But she was nodding. She was looking at me with her calm, even gaze.

"I don't know what to do," I said when I'd reached the end. "I've lost you. I've lost myself. I had a chance to make a call." I was whispering now. "When Jason was here. And do you know what I did? I called Lucas. Not 911."

"Oh, wow," Rosemary said. "That was really dumb."

"Yeah," I said. "It was."

"Look," she said. I'd sat on my mom's bed and Rosemary

bent down so she could look into my eyes. "I'm sorry. This was my fault. This whole year—" She paused, then sat down too. "I wish it had never happened."

"Jason was scary" was all I could say. "He scared me."

"We shouldn't have lied to each other, or hidden things." She set her jaw, letting me know she meant it. I believed her. She wrapped me into a hug until the shaking stopped.

"Where's Pete?" I said, wondering if she'd left him waiting in the car outside.

"Pete is over," she said. She looked around the room. There was blood on the carpet from Jason's ear—a stain about the size of a quarter. She stood her racket up so the bottom of the grip covered the stain. "Now just stand like this," she said, gesturing for me to take the racket from her, to lean on it like it was a cane. "Can you hold this position for, like, ever?" she asked.

And for some reason, we both found that to be totally hilarious. We laughed together so hard we ended up having to sit down on my mom's bedroom floor, waiting for our shared hysteria to die down. It took a very long time.

Rosemary's parents arrived, shaking hands with the female cop. We were all in the living room, and Rosemary and I were drinking juice boxes that the cop had brought with her.

Rosemary was being interviewed by the officer when Lucas burst in. I watched him look around incredulously, taking in the flashing lights of the cop car coming through the windows, the radio static emitted from the walkie-talkie of the officer interviewing Rosemary.

"Juliet?" he said wonderingly when our eyes met.

I could only shake my head.

"What's going on?"

And I explained, watching his face tighten as I told the story. At the end, I thought of a question that had been hovering in the back of my head since he'd arrived: I hadn't called him yet to explain all of this, so what was he doing here?

"You did call me," he said. "About forty-five minutes ago."

"But the line went dead," I said.

"Yeah," he said. "But I guess I knew it was you."

I gave him a questioning look. "No one else ever calls me that late," he added.

Which was true. We both slept with phones pulled into our bedrooms, the cradles next to our pillows in case the other called late.

But still. "You *knew* to come?"

He hung his head, looking embarrassed of all things. And then he admitted that he didn't *know* something was wrong. It was more like he *felt* it. "It made no sense," he explained, shrugging. "But I just didn't feel right."

"Really?" said the cop interviewing Rosemary, who had taken a break from questioning in order to listen to Lucas's story. "That's all it took for you to decide your girlfriend was in danger? Sounds like you could get work as a psychic."

Lucas didn't say anything. But he sat with me while I told the police about seeing Jason at 7-Eleven, about the phone calls, the jewelry.

The whole time they were talking to me, Lucas was jiggling his left leg in a way that reminded me of the Lucas from before—anxious, impatient. Was the part of him I missed the part of him that understood danger? That was afraid?

"Jeez, Juliet," he said when we were alone in the living room, waiting for my mom and Val, the cop filling out paperwork in the kitchen. He ran his hand through his hair. "Think of what could have happened. I can't believe I didn't go kick the crap out of that guy months ago."

"I never thought he'd come here," I said. My teeth were chattering again. An afghan my mom had knit a long time ago lay on the back of the sofa. I wanted it, but somehow the idea of reaching all the way across the couch seemed overwhelming. The cop had told Lucas to look for signs of shock. I couldn't remember what they were.

"Can I—" I couldn't remember the name of the thing I wanted. I pointed. "Can I—" I said again.

Lucas looked behind him. He pointed. "This blanket?"

I nodded vigorously. Nodding seemed to be the only way to make the chattering of my teeth stop. Or maybe it made the chattering worse. I couldn't tell.

Lucas picked up the blanket. He took one look at me and, instead of passing it over, stood, unfolded it, and wrapped it around me like you would wrap a towel around a little kid just out of the bath. He turned me into a blanket burrito.

"I feel like you, that time when you were nine, after you got out of the ice and climbed into bed in your wet underwear."

"Yeah, and you know I got sick after that. It didn't occur to me to take off my underwear."

"You'd know better now," I said. My teeth were chattering so much I had to repeat myself twice to make him understand me, let alone get the joke.

Once he finally did understand, he raised his eyebrows twice, in quick succession, the equivalent of a wink, acknowledging my lame attempt at humor. It was his gesture that made me laugh even through my chattering teeth.

"I know a *lot* better now," he said.

"Ooh, baby, tell me." I bit down and pressed my lips closed. "Tell me more about your nine-year-old underwear."

Lucas laughed, the kind of laugh where the person isn't just being nice to you, or friendly—it wasn't a social laugh. It was the laugh of someone who can't help it, who you have caught off guard with a joke.

And there was something about the fact that I could make him laugh that undid me.

"Jules?" he said. "Juliet?" He was holding my face in his hands. I'd started crying again, and he wiped away my tears with his thumbs. "What's wrong? Why are you crying?" he said. "Are you scared?"

"No," I answered. "I'm crying because it's so perfect."

"Huh?"

I couldn't explain. As with the blanket, I couldn't think of the words for things.

"I don't want it to end."

"It won't," he promised. He pulled my face toward his. He kissed me on the forehead, then on the lips. Then we leaned toward each other, our foreheads touching, the tip of my nose grazing the tip of his. Like the time before, the time Lucas no longer remembered.

"We don't need to let it end," he said, and I tried to believe him. I tried to believe that Lucas was Lucas. That he was mine in just the way I wanted him to be.

"Promise it will never change," I said, and Lucas promised it never would.

But then, of course, it did.

chapter thirty-six

Lucas enlisted in the marines the day after his eighteenth birthday. I'd thought I was prepared for it, but when he stopped by my house on the way home from "processing in," I burst into tears and ran up to my room. I didn't want to look at him.

At school the next day, we snuck out when we both had a free period and went outside, behind the school where we couldn't be seen. Lucas kissed me up against the wall. It was June by now, and as hot as summer. We stood in the shade.

I threaded a finger under the chain he wore his fake dog tags on, and I lifted them out of his shirt and held them in my fist. "These don't make you anything," I said. "They don't tell you who you are."

Lucas uncurled my fingers, let the tags fall back onto his chest. "I'm going to get new ones," he said. "Real ones. So you're right. These are nothing."

"You're going to die," I said. He rolled his eyes.

"I'm sorry," he said without actually sounding sorry. "I'm sorry that I obviously did such a great job of convincing you that my hallucinations—"

"Delusions," I corrected him, thinking I knew more about this than he did. Why didn't he trust me?

"Whatever," he said scornfully. "I'm sorry I convinced you they were real."

"They *are* real. Listen. You're going to walk into an apartment building in Iraq. You're going to see a boy holding a radio that's really a bomb. You'll lock eyes. He'll pee himself. The bomb will go off. And then you will die."

"You have to cut it out, Juliet," he said. "You're going to end up in the nuthouse."

"You heard me, though?" I said. I pulled him as close to me as I could. I wrapped my arms around his waist and held him to me in the shade behind the gym. "You're going to die. You will die of burns."

"We're all going to die," he said.

I squeezed my eyes tight against the tears. "You're going to die sooner."

Lucas was gone by the Fourth of July, training in North Carolina. For six weeks he couldn't even call. He came home at the end of the summer, just after I'd started school, but then only for four days.

I didn't see him again until Thanksgiving. I remember we were at a pizza place waiting for our pie to be cooked and he was telling a long, bragging story filled with military acronyms, and I stood up and pretended I had to go to the bathroom. "If he uses another acronym as if I should know what it means," I said to myself in the mirror, "I am going to scream."

Add to that his comments about the college I'd applied to early decision being "fancy."

My college wasn't fancy. It was small, way out in the middle of Maine, the kind of place where you have to wear long johns and snow boots from November to May. My senior year, I hung a poster of it in my room and pictured myself there even as I took Mr. Mildred's advanced course on Faulkner and won and lost debate rounds and went to parties with Rosemary and waited for Lucas's visits home, during which we fought as much as anything else.

My mom worried I was so excited for college it was going to be a letdown once I got there, but from my first moment on campus, when Mom and I showed up with my three enormous duffel bags, a standing lamp, a Gustav Klimt poster, and a year's supply of toiletries, I loved it. The kids on my hall stayed up until four in the morning talking about everything there was to talk about: music, the existence of God, the inevitable corruption of politics, what the deal was with Mr. T from *The A-Team*, who of all of us was the most likely to become famous.

When Lucas got notified of his first overseas tour, and I explained it to my new friends, they said "Really?" in this half-choking way, trying to hide their surprise and distaste. All my friends were pacifists, like me. I'm sure they were wondering how I could even know someone in the military, let alone be dating him.

Lucas was sent to Saudi Arabia. We said goodbye over

my winter break. I remember crying. I remember tasting the salt of my own tears, they were flowing so freely. Then he was gone.

And just as he'd said, he was the one who finally wrote the breakup email. He sent it from Saudi Arabia. He wrote:

> I guess this shouldn't come as a surprise to you.

He wrote:

> I don't see how we can even consider ourselves to be together when we don't write for weeks at a time.

He wrote:

> I don't know what you're doing at college and I don't think I want to. It feels pretty irrelevant from where I'm sitting.

He wrote:

> I had three days' leave in Dubai, and I did some thinking there.

He wrote:

> We are not in the same world. We are not going in the same direction.

I was a sophomore by then, and my suitemates baked me a cake to celebrate Lucas's departure from my life. They called him GI Joe; they found the idea of him—the picture of him in fatigues with a gun—creepy. They were relieved to have him gone and thought I was too, because that was what I told them. That was what I told myself.

chapter thirty-seven

I studied in Paris my junior year, and while I was there, I saw a short article in the *International Herald Tribune:* Governor George W. Bush of Texas was considering a run for the presidency. I was in the mailroom at the university where I was studying, and as soon as I understood the gist of the article, I stood up, walked straight to the bathroom, and vomited.

Fall of my senior year, with friends, I stayed up to watch the election results in my dorm's lounge. I had a paper due the next morning, so I stepped away from the television as soon as they'd called the election in Gore's favor. I stayed up the rest of the night writing, set my alarm for early in the morning, printed, proofread, and printed my paper again, and walked to class with my head still buried in it, correcting typos, sliding into my seat at the seminar table five minutes after class had begun. It wasn't until the subject came up in discussion that I heard the news: the networks had made a mistake. The election had been too close to call. Gore was not talking. Bush was not talking. I felt like I had swallowed a rock.

The next day I called Lucas. I had to call his mother first to find out how to reach him—he was rarely in the same place for long. I left a message and he called me back.

We talked for about half an hour. He asked about my mother, about Rosemary. He'd just broken up with somebody, he said. She was a biology grad student. He'd met her at Sea World.

"How about that election?" I said at last, testing the waters. I'd told him he had predicted the result. Would he remember?

"Yeah, I try to keep my nose out of all that BS," he replied, not missing a beat. "What a messed-up system."

Three weeks later, with about a hundred other students, I was filing into my college's largest classroom to take the LSAT. I made it through two sections of the test before getting to logical reasoning. "The red shirt is hanging on the clothesline next to the blue shirt, but not next to the yellow . . ."

I drew a diagram. I labeled the diagram. *G* for green, *P* for pink. I looked up at the board to check the time the test ended. And then at my watch.

And in that gesture, I remembered Lucas.

Lucas long ago, counting on his fingers, checking *his* watch, saying, "Two years left of high school, four of college, three at law school," as if he could tell time on his watch in years. He'd accepted that I was destined for law school as easily as he accepted the idea that at some point in the future he was dying.

The sob that came out of me was sudden. A lot of my fellow test takers looked up, but I was able to successfully disguise the noise I'd made as a cough.

Not now, I pleaded with myself.

I looked down at the question. Laundry. Red shirts, green ones, pink. But I couldn't drag my brain back. I couldn't recall the action I was supposed to be taking. I saw letters for each color written down on scratch paper. A grid with six columns neatly laid out.

Slowly, I colored in the squares. I knew time was of the essence, but my breath was coming fast and I thought coloring might help me refocus. I drew a new rectangle of new squares. I colored those in too.

Lucas had joined the marines. Lucas had been right about Bush and Gore. And here I was, taking the LSAT, marching forward just as Lucas had predicted I would.

And okay, I was crying. I assumed that by now, the people around me were aware. I didn't have any tissues and I was sniffling up a storm, so I ripped out a sheet of the test booklet—again, at the tearing sound, heads popped up from exams like gophers coming out of holes. I used the test paper to blow my nose. Then I crumpled it up. I took my answer sheet and crumpled that up too. I stood—*everyone* was looking now—and I inched my way past the people in my row. The proctor looked at me questioningly, but I didn't even bother to lie about not feeling well. I just shook my head at her, tossed my snotted piece of paper and crumpled answer sheet in the trash can, and, clutching my water bottle to my chest, pushed through the double doors to the quad, where I had to squint against the sparkling snow.

I didn't go to law school. I moved to France. I traveled in Africa. Chicago. Seattle. I ended up in New York when Rosemary was living there with her boyfriend. I took a job at a not-for-profit for teen moms, writing policy papers. I made a life for myself. I dated.

I still got the occasional email from Lucas, usually something random. Around the time of my graduation, he'd sent me a letter from Heidelberg letting me know he'd seen someone on a train in Germany who looked like me. He'd sent me a postcard from Kuwait on my twenty-first birthday, when I was in Paris. I'm sure I thought of him when the Twin Towers fell, but that day was a blur—Rosemary's boyfriend was incommunicado for six hours that morning, and I sat with her speed-dialing his phone, fielding calls from his family and hers. And then 2003 came around, and the United States went to war in Iraq. Around that time, Mom ran into Mrs. Dunready in the grocery store and reported that Lucas hadn't gone. He'd been fighting in Afghanistan for the past two years and was about to be sent to the Philippines.

I don't remember making a conscious calculation, but somewhere in the back of my mind, I decided that the future as Lucas had envisioned it was changing. His coming back had altered history. He'd said I would go to law school, and I hadn't. He'd said he'd be fighting in Iraq, and his only deployment had been to Afghanistan.

More time passed. I went to graduate school in public health. I dated a guy who lived in San Francisco and taught me to rock climb. He gave me a subscription to *Outside* magazine. We met for vacations and long weekends in Utah, in Arizona. We went to France. When we were apart, I trained to go rock climbing, and I got as close to having washboard abs as I ever will. But I stopped seeing him when I realized I wouldn't move to San Francisco for him, and he wouldn't move to New York. That essentially we were friends.

My mother retired from museum fund-raising. With Valerie managing the business side, she opened a knitting store, where they sell yarn and beautiful, expensive, wearable art my mom makes from her own hand-dyed wool. I went through a phase where I convinced myself that Rosemary had been right all along, that my mother and Val were an old married couple. But now I'm not so sure. The only thing I can say with certainty is that they have shown me how love can take many forms.

I ran into Lucas's brother Tommy at a holiday party back home a month before my thirtieth birthday. I asked if he was finished with college yet, and he laughed. He was out of college three years and married.

Tommy told me Lucas was fighting in Afghanistan again—after the Philippines he'd been to South Korea, Hawaii, San Diego. He was leading a unit, and if I breathed a sigh of relief that he was not in Iraq, I don't remember doing so. This was after Obama had been elected. Did I make a quick calculation that the Iraq War was ending and it wasn't likely he'd be sent back there before all the US troops pulled out? I don't remember.

I suppose I'd actually managed to forget, as Lucas had promised me I would. Or maybe "forget" is the wrong word. The memories were there, but the paths to reach them had been covered with sand.

chapter thirty-eight

About a year later, I got in to work late. There had been de-lays on the subway—fifty minutes trapped underground—which meant I had pit stains on the silk blouse I was wearing under my suit. I changed into a spare tank top from my workout bag and put the blouse in the trash. I'd have to remember not to take off my suit jacket during the meeting I had later with people from the mayor's office.

This meeting was a huge deal. The mayor's people were finally talking seriously about implementing a plan my agency had been advocating for ten years. It called for a series of education centers for new teen moms—flexible classes, on-site day care, caseworkers, tutoring, an alumnae network. I was really excited about the idea—I'd come up with it. Teen moms need the world to wrap its arms around them and let them know that they have the support to make it through.

With ten minutes before the team from my agency would be leaving, I blotted my temples with a paper towel and opened up my email. My assistant, Tracy, came into my office, noticed the blouse in the trash, and fished it out. "This is redeemable," she said.

I took a sip of my Diet Coke. Tracy raised her eyebrows at that too.

"I realize this is not a perfect nutritional statement," I said in an attempt to head her lecture off at the pass.

And that's the last thing I remember before the phone rang.

Tracy ran to her desk to answer the call, and I listened to her half of the conversation to make sure it didn't have anything to do with the meeting.

And then I kept listening as I registered the surprise in her voice.

Her attempt to put the caller off.

The failure of that attempt as the conversation went on for several minutes. Tracy sat down in her chair and started scribbling intensively on her message pad.

And then I heard her voice, coming to me through both the open door and the intercom. "Juliet, don't go yet."

I was slipping my arms into the sleeves of the jacket. Then Tracy was standing in my office door, her tight curls pushed back by one hand.

"That was a nurse," she said, reading breathlessly from her message pad. "From some kind of military hospital in Germany. Juliet, are you expecting this kind of news?"

This is what I heard: "Military." "Hospital." "News."

This is what I felt: a flash of white wiping out the circuitry of my brain. There was a part of me that had been expecting these words for years, and yet they felt unreal.

"You don't know anyone in the military, do you?" Tracy asked. "Serving in Iraq? Do you know what I'm talking about?"

I'd been standing when she started to talk, but now I was sitting in the desk chair where I had spent so many long days and nights. The one with the broken wheel only I knew how to balance on just right.

I looked at the green-and-white-paneled walls of my office, as if I was seeing them for the first time. I looked down at the skirt of my suit, the brown spectator shoes, the skin on the back of my hands.

Tracy didn't need to tell me the rest. I knew. Lucas. This was the news—Lucas had died.

Leaning forward in my chair, I grabbed at my legs to counter the tugging feeling in my gut. I couldn't form the questions. I couldn't speak. I might have been crying. I know the tears came eventually.

"Juliet?" Tracy said gently.

Time was standing still. Except it wasn't. It was moving backward. And forward. And sideways. It was doing what happens at the edge of the universe, shimmering, stretching.

I was sixteen again. As if a great wind had come up and swept me inside it, I felt Lucas with me. I could smell him, could feel the touch of his hand on mine.

"I thought he was in Afghanistan." I could barely hear my own voice. "We're supposed to be pulling out of Iraq."

Tracy's eyes were wide with concern. "Listen—" she said.

But I couldn't listen. I felt as if I was looking down on myself from the sky above New York City. From that perspective I could see halfway around the world to Lucas too, his body lying still in the hospital bed in Germany, bandages covering blackened skin. In my imagination, it was the same hospital bed where I'd held his hand when I was sixteen, but he looked older now, stockier, the way he'd described himself inside that dream so many years ago. His eyes were closed. He wasn't dreaming anymore. He'd given up the fight. I could see how he had suffered.

Then, somehow, in my vision, I was there with him. I was telling him I loved him, telling him it was okay, that I knew he'd tried, that his body, not his soul, had given out, that I forgave him, that I had never forgotten.

I was myself at thirty-one saying these things, but I was also sixteen. I was myself. I was sixteen. And then the distinction blurred.

For a second, I caught Tracy's eye, and she took a step back, toward the door and the relative safety of the general office. She must have seen what I felt like inside.

"How—" I remember saying. I looked up at the ceiling, down at the carpeted floor, then at Tracy again, still holding her message pad, frightened.

"Listen," she began again. She swallowed hard. "This nurse. She insisted on telling me all this stuff." She looked back down at the pad—I glimpsed her notes scrawled across three different WHILE YOU WERE OUT slips. "I tried to write fast. Do you want to hear this?"

I nodded.

"Okay. I guess this soldier, it was pretty bad. He walked

into a bomb, the nurse said. An IED. Given the force of the explosion, he should have died, but by some miracle he arrived at the field hospital with a pulse. Do you want to just call the nurse back? Who is this guy?"

I couldn't look at Tracy. I couldn't raise my head. Each passing second was more painful than the last. "Just tell me the rest," I whispered. "Please."

"Okay." Tracy consulted her notes. Her hand was shaking. I would have felt sorry for her if I had been allowing myself to feel anything at all. "He lived long enough in the hospital in Iraq that apparently they decided to fly him to Germany. I guess his doctors had no idea how he was holding on. The first time this nurse saw him, she said, he was in a coma, which she said is very common for burn victims, but he'd stabilized. His burns had started to heal."

I sat perfectly still. If I moved—if I blinked—I'd need to make sense of Tracy's words. But if I kept myself from moving, they would fall lightly around me, like snow.

"And yesterday, after months, he regained consciousness. The nurse, she was almost crying when she told me this. She called the family and they're all on the way to Germany now, so when he started to talk, she couldn't reach any of them. But he was talking, I guess, a lot. At first they thought he was hallucinating. None of the nurses understood what he was talking about. They almost sedated him, but he protested so violently they held off."

"What did he want?" I dared to ask.

"You," Tracy answered. "He knew your name. He knew where you worked. He made them look you up online. He dictated a message he wanted them to read to you, word for word. I wrote it down."

She was shuffling her notes again. I didn't move. I didn't breathe. Tracy adjusted her glasses. Agony. "His message is: 'I just woke up from a dream that you were in. I believe you saved my life. If you know what I am talking about, please come. Lucas.'" Tracy checked her notes. "His name is Lucas Dunready. Do you know him?"

Tracy pronounced his last name wrong, but I didn't need her to get it right.

I stood.

I was dizzy.

"Um, Juliet?" Tracy said. "You know what this means?"

And you know how before, I felt like I'd been swept up into the sky, to a place where I could look down on Lucas in the hospital? Well, now I began to fall, the way you sometimes fall just as your body is going to sleep. Down, down, and then you catch yourself, as if the brakes on an elevator have finally grabbed hold. Except the braking part wasn't happening.

Tracy had her hands on my shoulders. She was holding on to me, helping me remain upright.

"Juliet!" she was saying. "Help, someone!"

There were other voices. "She's sweating." "Her skin is gray."

Footsteps, movement, then a straw. Orange juice. Cold. I could almost feel the sugar being absorbed by my blood. It filled me with hopefulness. I sat up straighter. There was a thought I was trying to form. I could feel my arms and legs regaining control of themselves, my back tingling, my eyes opening. I drew a deep breath, almost a gasp, like the one Lucas took after the nurse brought him back to life in the hospital so many years before.

It wasn't just the orange juice that was making my heart start to pound.

Lucas . . . left me a message?

Lucas . . . just woke up?

I felt afraid of these words, as if the second I let them mean something, I would learn they were a mistake.

The words could not be real. What was real didn't matter.

What did matter—I could see this now—was the waters of memory, the rocks that bore the mark of the waves.

Lucas woke up.

I had been in his dream.

That was no dream.

Tracy looked at the clock on my wall. "The meeting?" she said. "Maybe we should call and tell them you're running late."

"Cancel it," I said.

Tracy's eyes opened extra wide.

"Tell them I'm ill." When you have a meeting with the mayor's people, you are not allowed to be ill. But I was already standing, rummaging for my passport. I jammed a pile of folders on my desk into the outbox, hoping someone would go through it eventually. "Tell them I am violently ill. Tell them I am going to the hospital. Yes, that's right. It's not even a lie!"

"Juliet—" Tracy began. She was going to tell me to sit down, I knew, that I wasn't well.

But I couldn't sit. I could never sit again. I was pulling my purse from the closet, rifling on the desk for my phone. I would run. I would change my shoes. I would find an airport. I would use my credit card. I would get on a plane. I still felt dizzy, like my brain no longer trusted the orientation of the floor, like I was standing on a wildly rocking boat. But it didn't matter. I didn't have to feel confident in the ground beneath my feet, because I was about to fly.

epilogue

In the airport I bought a notebook. A pen. I saw my reflection in the bathroom mirror and I bought a hairbrush. I haven't used it. I haven't had the time.

I have been writing and not writing, daydreaming, then writing some more—it's been hours. I've barely registered the whine of the plane engines, the hum of the ventilation system, the soft questions of the German flight attendants. Am I done with my drink? Do I need a blanket? I stare at them as if I don't speak the English they address me in, and they move on.

By the tiny pinprick of light coming from overhead, I have been writing so fast and for so long my hand is sore. But I keep at it. Writing is the only way I can organize my swirling thoughts, the moments I'm remembering and the feelings that remain so strong.

My body believes that it's the middle of the night, but

I am watching the sunrise through the ungenerously small window, so I know it must be morning. There are clouds below me. They are all I can see, though the GPS screen in the seat in front of me lets me know we are somewhere over the North Sea.

I keep cooling my tired hand against the window. My thoughts continue to flow. I'm swigging water from an Evian bottle, and the man next to me is distracted by my movements. I am a mess—and being a mess makes me laugh out loud. Again, the man next to me is not pleased. And yet I smile at him. I graciously offer him a mint.

"You have been busy," he says, shaking his head at the mint, and I nod. I smile. I resist scaring him further by saying something crazy-sounding, like "I understand it all now. I remember it all." But I *do* understand. You see, here's the thing:

Whatever I said to Lucas in the hospital that day, whatever I took from him, and whatever I gave him of myself, whatever happened between us before he slipped away, it gave him the strength to stay. Lucas beat death. He beat time. He beat everything we think we understand about a physical and spiritual divide.

He is here. Because of me. Alive. Whole. And I am going to him. I can't think past that. I can't imagine the rest and I don't need to or want to. I want only to live it, to watch it unfold.

I scan the pages of my notebook, looking back over my scrawl, seeing the places where the pen was pushing down hard and where the ink seemed to flow smoothly. I wonder what I will think of these words when I look back on them later, whether they will twist themselves around, whether I will remember the way I remember right now.

Lucas: I'm going to tell you this story. I will hold your hand. I will look into your eyes the way I did when I was sixteen. I will learn what has become of you. Although I believe I already know. I remember.

Lucas: I remember you.

acknowledgments

I came up with the idea for this book after a weekend with my high school friends during which the intensity of those years came rushing back and time folded in on itself. Thank you to Christine Collins, Kirsten Lundeberg, Kate Snell, Maureen Murphy, Kelly Mulderry, Krystn Forcina, and Karen Febeo for the "mystical" time.

I always love reaching out to friends for research when Wikipedia, Google, and my library skills fail me. Thanks to Kim Woodwell, Ed Mitre, Jacob Kahn, Theresa Kahn, Mark Bertin, Nick Soures, Jeff Lind, Laura Lind, and Rick Kahn for helping me figure out chickens (for another project), hockey, hospitals, and whether email existed in 1994.

Along the way, readers gave me a great deal of encouragement and invaluable advice: Sophie Bell, Rick Kahn, Claudia Gwardyak, Anita Kapadia, Gayle Kirshenbaum, Marcia Lerner, and Jen Nails. Your reactions kept me going and gave me direction.

My agent, George Nicholson, has been unstintingly supportive of this book and me, as has Caitlin McDonald. Melanie Cecka has again proven a wise diagnostician and deft surgeon. I feel extremely lucky to be reunited.

Friends and my extended Bell-Kahn-Gwardyak-Breitbart-Diggory-Entin-Ouk clan have been helping me keep the dream alive, especially all my Kahn-Diggory-Entin-Bell-Ouk nieces and nephews who read and ask for more. Seeing my own children's interest in my books is the thrill of a lifetime. Rick: I might have been able to do this without you, but never as happily.